**Two brand-new stories in every volume...
twice a month!**

Duets Vol. #61

Little wonder veteran Duets author Kristin Gabriel has
received two RITA Awards from the Romance Writers
of America for her fabulous, funny stories. This month
she delivers a delightful duo—the Kane brothers and
their adventures on the path to true love. Enjoy!

Duets Vol. #62

Voted Storyteller of the Year twice by *Romantic
Times*, Silhouette writer Carol Finch always "presents
her fans with rollicking, wild adventures...and fun
from beginning to end." Making her Duets debut this
month is talented newcomer Molly O'Keefe with a
fun story about the matchmaking Cook family—and
what can happen when there are *too many Cooks...!*

Be sure to pick up both Duets volumes today!

"Say hello to the new, improved you."

Dexter stared in the mirror at the image of the perfect man. He could hardly believe *he* was that perfect man.

"Now we just need to teach you how to kiss," Kylie said.

Dexter's jaw tightened. "I assure you I know how to kiss."

Kylie cleared her throat. "Don't take offense. I'm not criticizing you. It's just...you're not what I expected in a gigolo." She grabbed a copy of *How To Jump-Start Your Love Life.* "According to the tutorial, there are three key components to the perfect kiss—proximity, pressure and pizzazz."

"Let me see if I've got this. Proximity—" Dexter took a step closer to her. "Pressure." His lips touched hers gently at first and then with increasing firmness. "Pizzazz." And with a subtle movement she found herself pressed against him, her arms around his neck.

"Kylie, there's one thing you should know...." Dexter lifted his head and gave her a searing look. "I'm a *very* fast learner."

For more, turn to page 9

Operation Beauty

Sam lay on his back with his legs sticking up in the air.

This yoga class was the biggest challenge he'd faced disguised as Philomena Gallagher. He struggled to hold the position, hot in the bulky sweat suit he wore to cover up his fake figure.

"Take a deep breath." The instructor's voice flowed over them.

Sam's wig shifted and the synthetic hair tickled his nose. His gel bra twisted slightly. He wiggled to try to get everything back where it belonged.

"Close your eyes and think of a place that makes you feel special."

Sam turned his gaze to Lauren. The black leotard she wore hugged her body in a way that made sweat break out on his forehead. Her long, slender legs pointed gracefully toward the ceiling. He closed his eyes and imagined those legs wrapped around him.

"It's your turn, Philomena," the instructor called out. "Share your special place with us. I can tell by the expression on your face that it brings you great pleasure."

For more, turn to page 197

HARLEQUIN DUETS

ISBN 0-373-44127-4

Copyright in the collection:
Copyright © 2001 by Harlequin Books S.A.

The publisher acknowledges the copyright holder
of the individual works as follows:

OPERATION BABE-MAGNET
Copyright © 2001 by Kristin Eckhardt

OPERATION BEAUTY
Copyright © 2001 by Kristin Eckhardt

Visit us at www.eHarlequin.com

Printed in U.S.A.

Operation Babe-Magnet

Kristin Gabriel

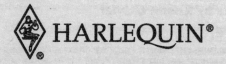

TORONTO • NEW YORK • LONDON
AMSTERDAM • PARIS • SYDNEY • HAMBURG
STOCKHOLM • ATHENS • TOKYO • MILAN • MADRID
PRAGUE • WARSAW • BUDAPEST • AUCKLAND

Dear Reader,

Have you ever had the urge to get a complete makeover? What if you didn't have any choice in the matter? That's what happens to Dexter Kane when Kylie Timberlake gets her hands on him. New clothes. New hairstyle. New look. But does that make him a new man? That's for Dexter to decide, once Kylie transforms him from a gigabyte nerd into a bona fide babe-magnet.

Dexter's brother Sam is forced into a completely different type of makeover—he's supposed to impersonate a woman! Sam's not sure he's up to the job, especially when his sexy new roommate, Lauren McBride, constantly reminds him he's very much a man.

The Kane brothers were so much fun to write. I hope you enjoy their unusual adventures on the road to true love.

Kristin Gabriel

P.S. I love hearing from readers! You can reach me online at www.KristinGabriel.com or write to me at P.O. Box 5162, Grand Island, NE 68801-5162.

Books by Kristin Gabriel

HARLEQUIN DUETS

HARLEQUIN TEMPTATION

For Mary Ann McQuillan—
Thanks for always being just a phone call away.

Prologue

"I WANT YOU TO JUMP OUT OF the plane."

Dexter Kane's ears popped as the small airplane ascended into the sky. So he was certain he'd misunderstood his grandfather's last words. "What did you say?"

Amos Kane smiled at his grandson. "I want you to jump, Dexter."

Dexter glanced at his younger brother, Sam, who was flirting with a woman on his cell phone. An inveterate playboy, nothing could keep Sam away from the ladies, whether he was on the ground or in the air. "Time to hang up now, Sam."

Sam held up two fingers, signaling for just a little more time.

Dexter turned back to their grandfather. "Did you forget to take your medication this morning?"

Amos shook his head. "I haven't taken any of that crap for the last month. Made me tired and cranky. But I can see you're a little confused, so maybe I'd better start from the beginning."

"Good idea." Dexter leaned back in his seat, his hands gripping the armrests. He hated flying. Hated the feeling of being out of control. That was one of the reasons he'd planned out his life so meticulously. After growing up with two parents who spent more time on their yacht in the French Riviera than with their sons, Dexter knew exactly what he wanted to do with his life.

For the last twenty-eight years, he had been willing to do anything and everything to inherit the family business conglomerate that his grandfather had started over forty years ago with the success of a simple board game. Dexter had started proving himself when he was fourteen years old, working as the office janitor at the Kane Corporation. From there he'd moved on to the mail room, then on to being a courier. After college, he'd started at an entry-level position in the accounting department, working nights and weekends before slowly and steadily ascending to management level.

Amos had long ago made it clear that the Kane Corporation would be his grandsons' legacy, since he intended to leave the rest of his estate to charity. He wanted Dexter and Sam to make their way in the world, unlike their father, who had frittered away his trust fund.

Just last week Amos had announced his intentions to retire. Only he hadn't given any indication of who his successor would be. A fact that had made Dexter more nervous with each passing day.

"We're going to play Chameleon," Amos began, referring to the career role-playing board game that had made the Kane Corporation famous.

Sam snapped his cell phone shut and leaned forward. "What did I miss?"

"Grandpa wants us to play Chameleon," Dexter replied, skipping the part about jumping out of the plane.

"Cool." Sam looked around the cabin of the Cessna 206. "So are we playing the original version or millennium version?"

"The real-life version," Amos replied, pulling two small, sealed envelopes out of his coat pocket.

"I'm not sure I understand," Dexter said, although the sinking sensation in the pit of his stomach belied that statement. Chameleon was a board game that allowed players to take on different career roles. The path they chose to follow and the decisions they made along the way led them to either victory or defeat. Dexter and Sam had played it often when they were younger, although a fistfight usually ended the game before a winner was declared. Dexter was a stickler for following the rules, while his younger brother was always looking for a shortcut.

"It's simple." Amos placed the envelopes in the center of the table. "You'll each take on a new job for exactly one month. Each of these envelopes contains a game card listing your new occupation. Whoever can pull it off will win the game. And the company."

"What if we both pull it off?" Dexter asked, though he knew he had an advantage over his brother. Sam had a commitment problem, whether it was with women or with work. He tended to lose interest fast and move on to something new, although, Dexter did have to admit that Sam had stuck it out at the Kane Corporation for longer than usual. No doubt the freedom he experienced heading the creative team of product development had something to do with it.

"In the event of a tie," Amos explained, "I will ask each of your employers for a performance review. Whoever scores the highest will be the winner."

So they not only had to do the job, but do it well. Not a problem, Dexter thought to himself, since he'd been a terminal overachiever since his preschool days.

"Wait a minute, Gramps," Sam said, his brow furrowed. "Dex and I already have jobs at the company. Why do we have to work somewhere else?"

Amos leaned back in his seat. "The purpose of the game is to prove how important the family business is to you. Absence makes the heart grow fonder and all that. You might even enjoy it."

Dexter didn't want to work anywhere else. He'd lived and breathed the business for the last decade. Running the Kane Corporation was a natural for him. He didn't have his brother's charm or his parents' social acumen, a fact made painfully clear to him as he was growing up. After a while, Dexter had quit trying to fit in with the crowd and concentrated on his intellectual skills.

Now he was so close to achieving his dream. And certainly more qualified than Sam to take over the business. Hell, his brother would probably institute a four-day workweek and a casual dress code. It wasn't fair. Sam had always had everything going for him. Looks. Charisma. Women. All Dexter wanted was the company.

But to get it, he had to play a silly game.

Dexter glanced at Sam, all the old feelings bubbling to the surface. They'd been fierce competitors since sharing the same playpen. Dexter had organized their blocks by color while Sam had cajoled their nanny into giving him the extra cookies. They hadn't changed much since then. Dexter thrived on work, while Sam preferred playtime. But they did have one thing in common—they both wanted the family business. And their grandfather was a firm believer in winner takes all.

"The game will end at midnight exactly one month from today," Amos continued. "We'll meet at my office to crown the winner. There are only three rules to follow. First, you cannot tell anyone you're playing the game or your real occupation. Second, you cannot contact each other during the duration of the game." He smiled. "And third, you must follow the directions of any game card you receive along the way. So expect a surprise or two in the next few weeks."

"Well, count me in," Sam said. "It sounds like a blast." He held up his envelope. "Can I open it?"

"The sooner you do, the sooner we can start the game," Amos replied.

Sam ripped the seal and pulled out his game card.

"Well, look at this." He flipped the card around so Dexter could see it.

"Salesman for Midnight Lace?" Dexter read aloud. "You have to sell ladies' lingerie?"

Sam grinned. "Now that's what I call a dream job."

Dexter carefully slit open his envelope, then pulled out his game card. He looked at it, then blinked and read it again. This had to be some kind of joke.

"Well," Sam asked, leaning over to look at the game card, "what's your new place of employment?"

Dexter swallowed. "A male escort agency."

Sam grinned. "You mean my brother is going to become a gigolo?"

Dexter turned to his grandfather, ready to argue for a different occupation. He was the last man qualified for such a job. He wasn't even sure it was legal.

But the parachutes in Amos's hands made the objections die on his lips.

"Here you go, boys. Put these on, then you can hit the ground running."

Sam frowned. "What are those for?"

"To break your fall when you jump out of the plane." Amos handed a parachute to each of them.

Sam glanced up at Dexter, then back to their grandfather, who was affectionately known as Crazy Amos around the office. And for good reason. "Did you forget to take your medication again?"

Amos waved the question away. "We've covered

that topic already. I think jumping out of this plane is the perfect way to start the game.''

Dexter glanced out the window. "Where exactly are we?"

"Just outside of Pittsburgh," Amos replied. "Lots of grassy pastures and flat farmland around so you shouldn't get hurt when you land."

"But how are we supposed to find our way back to the city?" Sam asked.

"That's part of the game." Amos rubbed his hands together. "This way neither one of you has an unfair advantage. You both start from the same point."

One of the co-pilots emerged from the cockpit and helped Dexter and Sam strap on their parachutes, giving them a crash course on skydiving at the same time. As Dexter was strapped into the harness and learning new words like altimeter, free fall and static line, he wondered if this was some kind of nightmare brought on by pulling too many all-nighters at the office.

But the next thing he knew, they were standing near the open door of the airplane. The pilot announced over the intercom that they had reached an altitude of thirteen thousand feet and could jump anytime.

"You go ahead, Dexter," Sam yelled over the roar of the plane. "You're the oldest."

Dexter wanted to argue, but his pride prevented him from backing out now. He took a deep breath, then moved toward the door, his fingers fumbling for the rip cord of the reserve parachute. His life flashed briefly before his eyes, filled mostly with images of him hunching over textbooks in the college library on Saturday night and working long hours at a computer terminal. He hadn't come this far, made this many sacrifices, to give up now.

"Need a push, big brother?" Sam asked with a grin.

Dexter ignored him, his heart pounding in his chest. This was it. The moment that he'd been waiting for and working for his entire life.

All he had to do was take the first step.

He leaned forward, his right hand tightly gripping the top of the door frame. For one brief moment, he panicked, realizing he couldn't recall any memories other than school or work. No special moments. No special woman. But what did it matter now?

Then he jumped.

1

KYLIE TIMBERLAKE HIT the ground hard as an arrow flew over her head and imbedded itself in the towering fir tree behind her. She inhaled the pungent scent of pine needles and heard the menacing growl of the Doberman pinscher chained up on the front porch of the secluded cabin.

"That was just a warning shot," called a gravelly voice from the open window. "You're trespassing on private property. Next time I won't miss."

She lifted her head far enough to make certain the dog was still tethered. "It's me, Mr. Hanover. Kylie Timberlake."

As she lay on the damp ground, she wondered if her family was right. Maybe she was too impulsive. Maybe she wouldn't even be in this predicament if she'd ever paused long enough to consider all the consequences of her actions.

But it was too late for regrets now. She'd based her reputation and her brother's livelihood on a promise to make Harry Hanover a household name. She intended to do just that—with or without his cooperation.

"Warn me next time before you sneak up on me like that," Harry shouted. "I told you I don't like visitors. So you can go on back to Pittsburgh and leave me alone.''

Kylie gritted her teeth. She hadn't spent the last two hours driving up narrow, winding mountain roads just to turn around and go back home again.

She took a deep breath. "You know why I'm here."

"I already told you no on the phone. No way. No how. I'm not doing it."

"But…"

"Goodbye, Mizz Timberlake."

Kylie sighed as she stood up, brushing the damp soil and dead leaves off her camel silk suit. She'd ruined her favorite outfit, her flourishing career as a publicist, and her brother's business all in one fell swoop.

The Doberman growled menacingly at her movement.

"All right, already. I'm leaving." She turned toward the white Honda Accord she'd left parked on the side of the road. She'd almost reached the driver's door when she heard Hanover call out to her.

"Wait just a minute, Mizz Timberlake."

She turned around, his words igniting one last spark of hope inside of her. Then her breath caught in her throat as the Doberman, free of its chain, bounded off the porch and barreled straight toward her.

She backed up against the car as the dog leapt up,

planting its huge, muddy front paws against her chest.

To her relief and surprise, the dog didn't go for her throat. Instead, he tried to asphyxiate her with his fetid doggy breath.

"Take the newspaper clipping," Hanover called, still invisible behind the cabin window. "I stuck it in Eugene's collar."

Eugene? She glanced warily at the slobbering Doberman, then noticed the ragged clipping tucked underneath the thick leather collar.

"Don't worry," Hanover said. "He won't bite."

Now he tells her. Still leery, she carefully reached out and pulled the clipping free. "Nice doggy."

Eugene lapped her chin and lower lip with his wet tongue.

"Thanks a lot," she muttered, wiping her mouth with the back of her hand.

Harry whistled, causing the dog to drop down on all fours and run back to the cabin.

Kylie unfolded the clipping, surprised to see it was some kind of advertisement. Frowning, she turned it over in her hand, then looked toward the cabin. "What is this?"

Hanover emitted a low chuckle from his hiding place. "The answer to all our problems."

THUNDER RUMBLED IN the sky as Dexter stood in front of his potential new place of employment. The storm had followed him from the country into Pittsburgh, soaking him to the skin. If he was the least bit superstitious, he'd take it as a sign that this fiasco could only lead to disaster. But he didn't believe in omens. Or in fate. A lucky charm or a palm reading couldn't replace the value of simple, honest, hard work.

He and Sam had parted ways before they even hit the ground, Dexter landing in a cornfield a couple of miles away from his brother. But he had no doubt Sam had found a ride into Pittsburgh—his brother's lucky streak was legendary.

Dexter, on the other hand, always seemed to do things the hard way. He'd jogged half the distance to Pittsburgh in the rain before a sympathetic trucker had picked him up and hauled him the rest of the way. After a quick stop by his apartment to change into dry clothes, he'd hurried down to the business address listed on his game card.

Dexter winced up at the bright blue neon sign above the front entrance. This was the company his grandfather had specifically chosen for Dexter to prove himself as the right man to steer the Kane Corporation into the new millennium.

Studs-R-Us.

The plate glass windows were plastered with huge posters of men in all types of attire. One wore a tuxedo. Another was bare-chested, wearing only tight denim jeans and a cowboy hat. But at least he looked better than the guy in the Speedo swimsuit.

He shook his head in disgust, wondering if the owner would be open to some basic marketing suggestions. Dexter reached up to straighten his tie as the idea evolved. Perhaps that was the answer. He could work as a business consultant for Studs-R-Us instead of as a male escort. Give them the advantage of his financial acumen and administrative skills. That would both fulfill his grandfather's mandate and keep Dexter from thoroughly humiliating himself.

With a new sense of purpose, he squared his shoulders and walked through the front door. A melodic chime announced his entrance and the receptionist looked up at him with a flash of irritation, as if his arrival put a glitch in her busy schedule. She blew on her fingernails, newly polished a burnt orange to match her teased hair. A tiny portable television sat on her desk, tuned to a talk show featuring pregnant mud wrestlers.

She recapped her fingernail polish. "Did you want something?"

"I'd like to apply for a job."

Her gaze skipped over him. "Here?"

His jaw tightened. "Yes."

She slapped an application in front of him, the words *Are You A Stud?* were emblazoned in bright red ink across the top. "Fill this out, then leave it in the basket."

He looked at the wire basket on the corner of her desk, stuffed full with other job applications. His instincts told him they'd been there awhile. Not willing to leave his fate to a receptionist who had her calendar turned to the wrong month, he took a step closer to the desk. "Look, filling out a job application would be a waste of my time and yours. I have…very unique qualifications that I can bring to Studs-R-Us.''

She raised an orange brow. ''Kinky stuff?''

''Perhaps I should speak to your boss.''

With an aggrieved glance at the television set, the receptionist got up and tapped on the closed door behind her. Then she disappeared inside.

Dexter could hear the voices of two women, but couldn't discern their words. No doubt the receptionist was describing Studs-R-Us's newest applicant. He flinched at the sound of their laughter.

Dexter D. Kane was once again the butt of the joke. He should be used to it by now, considering the numerous taunts he'd endured growing up. The D in his middle name stood for Dependable, following a Kane family tradition of giving each newborn a virtuous name. Both he and Sam had been involved in numerous playground brawls thanks to their unusual middle names.

Strangely enough, the name did seem to fit his personality. Dexter was dependable to a fault, which made him the first person people called when they needed help, whether it was an elderly neighbor with an errand to run or a business associate who wanted him to head a charity drive.

Unfortunately, Dependable wasn't one of the names he'd been called as a youth. A variety of nicknames had stuck while he was growing up. Noodle nerd. Boy Wonder. And his favorite, Frankenbrain. All monikers he probably deserved, since he'd spent more time at the library than the local hang-outs.

He was certainly nothing like his brother, Sam, whose easy charm and boyish good looks had made more than one person ask if they were really related. A perennial favorite with the opposite sex, Sam had won more hearts than he could count. Too often Dexter had sparked the interest of a woman, only to find out later that she was just using him to get closer to Sam.

So several years ago he'd decided to forego the social scene and focus on his talents—accounting and acquisitions. Maybe when he finally reached the pinnacle of success in the business world he'd have time to figure out how one actually talked to an attractive woman without breaking into a cold sweat.

"Mistress Helga will see you now."

He looked up to the see the receptionist back at her desk, a smirk on her young face.

Mistress Helga? Dexter pushed up his glasses, then walked into the office, half expecting to see a gallery of sadistic sex toys. Instead, he entered a light, airy room with a white ceiling fan and a wicker love seat and matching armchairs.

A middle-aged woman sat reading a magazine in one of the chairs, a pair of bifocals propped on her nose. She looked up and smiled at him. "Hello."

"Mistress Helga?"

She laughed, then stood up and held out one hand. "I see my granddaughter is playing games again. My name is Betty. Betty Brubaker."

"Dexter Kane," he said, surprised by the tasteful decor of her office. It was certainly an improvement over the garish display in the entrance. Betty wasn't what he expected either. A slightly plump woman with ash blond hair pulled back into a neat bun. Thick eyebrows dominated her face, but her green eyes gleamed with intelligence.

"It's a pleasure to meet you, Mr. Kane." She sat back down in her chair and motioned for him to do the same. "Now, how can I help you?"

"I'm here to apply for a job. Perhaps as a bookkeeper or even an investment consultant. I have considerable experience in corporate management."

She gave him a maternal smile. "I appreciate the offer, but my son might take offense if I replaced him. He's worked as my business manager and financial advisor for the last five years."

He thought about telling her that the front window display and the attitude of her receptionist were probably driving potential business away. But the numerous family photographs covering the walls and every nook and cranny of her office told him the advice might not be well received. Instead, he took a deep breath and said, "I really need a job."

"I see." She studied him for a moment, then leaned forward in her chair. "Actually, I do have an opening for a male escort. Did you bring any references?"

"No, this is my first time." Heat crept up his neck. "Well, not my first time, of course. I do have some experience." He decided not to elaborate. His romantic encounters had left him physically satisfied, but strangely hollow. Yearning for something more that he couldn't name or even fully understand.

"Tell me, Mrs. Brubaker..."

"Betty," she reminded him.

"Betty." He cleared his throat. "What exactly are the job requirements for this line of work?"

"We are an escort agency, Mr. Kane. Our employees accompany women to a variety of social functions and also serve as companions."

"Both day and...night?"

She arched a brow. "We're here to serve our clients at their convenience. Is that a problem?"

He cleared his throat. "Not at all. I just want to be fully prepared."

"Now that I've answered your question, please answer mine." She leaned forward in her chair. "Why are you really here?"

He blinked. Did she know about the game? Or was this some kind of test to prove to Amos that he intended to follow the rules? "I'm not sure what you mean."

"I mean you don't look or sound like our usual applicant. In the first place, you're wearing a tailored three-piece suit. In the second place, I've never seen a man blush so much since my honeymoon. So either you're a lousy lover who is looking for some free experience or you're a lousy undercover vice cop hoping to make a bust."

"I'm neither." Dexter feared he'd lost the game

before he'd begun. "But I'm afraid I've given you the wrong impression."

"It doesn't matter," she interjected. "Studs-R-Us does not sell sexual favors to its clients. I run a clean operation. There are a lot of lonely women out there, Mr. Kane, and it's my mission to provide them with the company of a respectful, upstanding gentleman. In fact, if I suspect any employee of mine is indulging in a physical relationship with a client, he will be immediately terminated."

Dexter swallowed his sigh of relief. He was a red-blooded American male, but selling his body wasn't exactly the way he'd envisioned obtaining the company of his dreams: He gave her a curt nod. "A sound policy."

"Now, if you're really interested in the job..."

"I am."

She opened the file folder on her desk. "I had a job request earlier today that has presented some problems. Since the majority of escort requests are for evening duty, dances and such, most of my employees work elsewhere during the day."

"I'm available twenty-four hours a day," Dexter assured her.

Betty glanced down at the open folder. "Actually, that's exactly what Miss Timberlake requires. A man at her disposal twenty-four hours a day for approximately four weeks."

"That sounds perfect."

She arched a brow. "Aren't you even interested in hearing about the job?"

He shook his head. "I'm completely flexible."

She looked bemused. "Well, that's good, because she refused to give me many details. Although she did make it clear that confidentiality was of the utmost importance."

"My lips are sealed."

She smiled. "See that you keep it that way. I've not yet met Ms. Timberlake but she sounded quite young on the phone. As I said before, any physical relationship with a client results in instant termination."

"Understood." He took a deep breath. "Does this mean I have the job?"

She stood up and held out her hand. "Congratulations, Mr. Kane. You are now officially a Stud."

2

KYLIE TIMBERLAKE sprinted through the door of Studs-R-Us, her heart pounding in anticipation. She'd almost given up finding a way out of this untenable situation. Now it looked as if her biggest problem was about to be solved.

She stopped short when she saw the man standing in the front office. His short, dark hair was slicked back and he wore a pair of wire-rimmed glasses. He was tall and looked as if his gray pinstripe suit concealed finely honed muscles. Her first impression was that she'd run smack dab into a superhero in disguise. But she didn't need a man who could leap tall buildings in a single bound. She needed a man who had a way with woman. And one who didn't mind a little deception.

"Excuse me," she said, still a little breathless from her sprint. "I'm looking for Mrs. Brubaker."

"She just took the receptionist out to dinner." The man pushed his glasses up on his nose. "I'm filling in until they get back."

"Oh." Disappointment spiraled through her. Had she gotten the time wrong? "Do you have any idea when that will be?"

"No, but perhaps I can help you."

"I'm here for an interview." Kylie bit her lower lip, telling herself not to panic. She still had a little time to sort it all out.

"Are you Miss Timberlake?"

"Yes," she said, giving him a quick smile. Her preoccupation was no reason to be rude. "I'm supposed to be meeting one of the studs here. But I must have mixed up the time."

He glanced at his watch.

"Actually, you're three minutes late."

"You mean he already left?"

"No." The man shifted on his feet. "I'm...the stud."

She blinked. "You?"

"Yes." He arched a dark brow. "Is that a problem?"

"No. Not at all." Her cheeks burned. She'd imagined spending the next few weeks with one of the men in the pinups plastered in the front windows. Slick, polished playboys who didn't affect her in the least. Not this superhero in the making. The last man she'd suspect of making his living as a gigolo.

On the other hand, superheroes did rescue damsels in distress. And her distress was on the verge of becoming an all-out disaster. She stepped forward and extended her hand. "Hello, I'm Kylie."

"I'm Dexter." His eyes widened slightly at her firm grip. "Dexter D. Kane."

She wondered what the D stood for, but couldn't afford to waste time by asking him. She wouldn't be referring to him by his middle name anyway. Or his first name, for that matter. "Has Mrs. Brubaker told you anything about me or this job?"

"Only that you require my services for the next four weeks."

To her mortification, she felt another blush creep up her neck. She hadn't enjoyed the services of any man—let alone a gigolo—for too long to remember. Not that she was contemplating a relationship with Dexter. No matter what images his words evoked. "That's true. This is a rather unusual job. And one that requires the utmost secrecy."

He smiled. "You can count on my discretion, Miss Timberlake. My job depends on it. And I'm depending on this job."

She barely comprehended his words, too dazzled by the dimple that flashed on his chin when he smiled. It almost made her forget her mission. But the chime of a wall clock brought reality rushing back. She had about fifty phone calls to make within the next few hours.

"I'll have to give you the condensed version and fill in the details later." She took a deep breath, hoping she could trust him. "Have you read a book called *How To Jump-Start Your Love Life?*"

"No," he said, looking a little confused. "I've never even heard of it."

"It's new on the market, but it has the potential to become a bestseller. I'm the publicist for Handy Press, the small press that published it. It's my responsibility to see that it gets the right amount of media coverage necessary to attract national attention.''

His brows furrowed. ''And?''

''And I've scheduled an array of book signings, radio interviews and even a couple television spots for the author. We'll hit twelve cities in just under four weeks. It's an all out publicity blitz. There's only one small problem.''

''You need an escort?''

''No. I need someone to play the part of the author, Harry Hanover.'' She waited, letting the words sink in. Dexter D. Kane certainly looked intelligent enough to understand all the ramifications.

He folded his arms across his chest. ''You're serious?''

''Absolutely. You see, Harry suffers from agoraphobia,'' she explained, ''which is a fear of social situations. It's impossible for him to appear in public. In fact, his case is so severe that he refuses to leave his home. Unfortunately, I'd already scheduled all the media events before I found that out.''

''So why not just cancel the tour?''

''Because Harry believes there will be negative repercussions on the sale of his book. And frankly, that's a real possibility. Booksellers can make or break a book. And many of them have already started advertising the upcoming book signings. Broken promises don't make the best public relations. Not only could Harry's book suffer if he fails to make his scheduled appearances, but Handy Press could suffer as well.''

"In what way?"

"The company stays afloat by publishing how-to manuals and technical guidebooks. If booksellers retaliate by pulling all the Handy Press books off the shelves, the company could go bankrupt."

He looked thoughtful. "There has to be some other solution."

She shook her head. "Believe me, I've lain awake nights trying to think of a way out of this mess. I know it seems a little extreme, but this is the only answer."

"How will Mr. Hanover feel about another man taking on his identity?"

"It was his idea." She pulled a folded newspaper clipping out of her jeans pocket, smoothing out the wrinkles. It was an advertisement for Studs-R-Us. She handed it to him, their fingers touching. Her skin prickled at the jolt of electricity that shot up her arm. And judging by the way Dexter was staring at her, he'd had the same reaction.

Then he cleared his throat and looked down at the advertisement. "A man for all occasions," he said, reading the company motto. "I'm not sure this covers impersonating an author."

"I know it sounds a little unusual," she replied, glancing at her watch. "But it's really not all that uncommon in the entertainment world. There are ghost writers who write all those celebrity books. Musicians who do voice-overs on albums. Some authors even send in a phony glamour picture for the back of their book. It's all about presentation."

He still looked skeptical. "What happens when people find out I'm not the real Harry Hanover?"

"That won't happen," she assured him. "When the book tour is over, Harry is going to disappear. Handy Press will decline any further interviews on his behalf, earning him a reputation as an eccentric recluse. Which is the truth. The press loves that kind of stuff."

Dexter hated to put a damper on her enthusiasm, but the obstacles to her plan seemed almost insurmountable. "What if someone who knows Harry attends a book signing?"

She smiled. "Not a possibility. Harry's been shut up in his cabin for the last six years. And before that he lived in the Yukon."

Dexter couldn't seem to take his eyes off of her. Kylie Timberlake was the most vibrant woman he'd ever met. Even if her plan was crazy. "Well, what if someone recognizes me?"

Her smile faded. "I can't believe I didn't think of that. Especially when you've probably got legions of women in your past."

His pride prevented him from disabusing her of that ridiculous notion. "I'm sorry I can't help you."

Her face suddenly brightened. "Yes, you can. I think I know a way to make it work. A way to make everyone just wild about Harry."

"I LOOK RIDICULOUS." Dexter stood in the living room of Kylie's apartment, wearing a short fuschia cape protecting his clothes and silver foil wraps in his hair.

"I know, but we're trying to fix that." Amy Kwan, Kylie's roommate, sorted through the clothes hanging on a portable rack.

He never should have let Kylie talk him into this. But something about her made it impossible to say no. Maybe it was her big brown eyes. Or the smile that sparked a warmth deep inside of him. Or the overwhelming urge he had to touch her again.

"You're a tough case, Dexter," Amy said, "but I'm always up for a challenge."

"Amy used to do hair and makeup for the stars of 'The Young and the Restless,'" Kylie informed him, studying the day planner on her lap.

"But I needed a break." Amy selected five outfits and tossed them onto the sofa. "So now I'm doing freelance work. Mostly working on models for fashion shows and photo shoots. But my favorite jobs are makeovers. Enhancing the beauty of soap stars and models is easy. But transforming a loser into a knockout takes real skill."

"Not that you're a loser, Dexter," Kylie hastily assured him.

"Thanks," he said dryly as the timer on the kitchen stove dinged.

"Time to rinse," Amy announced. She led Dexter over to the sink, then began removing the foil wraps.

"Exactly what color will my hair be?" he asked as Amy pushed his head under the faucet.

Amy carefully rinsed his hair. "The same color,

but we're hoping to add some fabulous golden high-lights.''

"What do you mean, hoping?" Dexter asked.

"I'm sure it will be fine," Kylie called from the living room.

"Well, there was that time we ended up with lime green on Carlo." Amy laughed. "Remember that, Kylie?"

"Green?" Dexter repeated, starting to feel a little panicky. He'd only done this to make Kylie happy, to see her smile again. Now the absurdity of it hit him full in the gut.

"It was a temporary color," Kylie assured him. "It only took a month to wash out."

"That makes me feel so much better."

Amy shut off the tap, then towel-dried Dexter's hair. By the time he returned to the living room, his hair was standing straight up in golden brown spikes.

"That's already an improvement," Amy said, admiring her handiwork. "Now for the clothes."

He frowned. "What's wrong with my clothes?"

"Nothing if you're starring in a black-and-white fifties flick. The three-piece suits have got to go." Amy stepped back and surveyed him from head to toe. "Fuschia isn't really your color."

"Well, that's a relief."

Amy tapped her chin. "And I've got to admit, it looks like you've got a great body under all those clothes. Of course, you're a gigolo, so I suppose it's one of the job requirements."

"I think he prefers the term male escort," Kylie said, scribbling something in her planner.

"I prefer to wear my own clothes," he said, as Amy pulled another outfit off the rack.

"You've got to trust me," Amy informed him, holding a pair of skimpy black leather pants up to his waist. "Once we get rid of your old hairstyle, your old clothes and those horrendous glasses, you're going to be every woman's fantasy."

"The glasses?" Kylie looked up. "Don't you think we should keep them? I think they're sexy." Her cheeks grew rosy. "I mean, in a subtle, intellectual sort of way."

Dexter's heart warmed at her words, along with another part of his body. He liked the way her hair hung in a profusion of wild, thick curls around her shoulders. His fingers itched to touch it, to feel the slide of that silk against his skin.

"Look, Ky," Amy replied, as she pushed Dexter into an inflatable chair, then ran a comb through his wet hair. "I know what I'm doing. Women don't like subtle. They like raw sex appeal."

Dexter cleared his throat. "I take it my ability to see doesn't matter when it comes to fashion."

Amy snorted. "Haven't you ever heard of contact lenses?" Then she stepped back and looked into his eyes. "Ooh, we could go with colored lenses. Wouldn't violet be awesome with his coloring?"

"No." Kylie's voice was firm. "Dexter's eyes are perfect just the way they are."

The telephone rang before Amy could argue with

her. Kylie picked up the cordless receiver, then placed her hand over the mouthpiece. "I'm going to take this call in the bedroom. Yell if you need me."

Amy nodded, then reached for the blow-dryer. "Relax, Dexter," she said, flipping on the switch. "This won't hurt a bit."

He closed his eyes, his tension easing as she finger-styled his hair. Despite his initial reaction when Kylie suggested a makeover, he really didn't mind all the changes. They were only temporary, after all. Anyway, the fewer people who recognized him as Dexter Kane, the better. In exactly one month, he'd take over the helm of the Kane Corporation and leave this farce behind him. Fulfilling his dream was all that really mattered. Although the thought of spending the next four weeks with Kylie made him drift into a very different sort of dream....

"Wake up, sleepyhead," Amy said, gently shaking his shoulder.

Dexter started in his chair, opening his eyes to see her wrapping the cord around the blow-dryer. His body still throbbed with the erotic images that had danced in his head and he was thankful he still wore the plastic drape to keep the hair dye from staining his clothes. "Are you finished already?"

"With your hair," Amy replied. "We still need to work on the wardrobe."

"Can I see it?" he asked, as she spritzed him with hairspray.

"Not until we're all done. I want you to experience the full effect."

He looked around the living room. "Where's Kylie?"

"Still on the phone." Amy walked over to the clothes rack, once again perusing the choices. "That girl never stops working."

He leaned back in his chair, forcing himself to relax. "I'm surprised she told you about the Harry Hanover masquerade. I thought it was supposed to be a big secret."

"It is, but Kylie was a little nervous about pulling it off and needed someone to talk to about it. She knows she can trust me."

Dexter wondered if there was anyone in his life he'd trust that much. He loved his brother, but Sam always seemed too laid back to take life's problems seriously. There was always his grandfather, whom he trusted implicitly. But Dexter had always been so determined to prove he could handle any situation that he'd never allowed his grandfather see any of his fears or insecurities. Besides, the key to being an effective business owner was maintaining complete control at all times.

"How do you feel about silk?" Amy asked, pulling out an orange shirt with long puffy sleeves and draping it over the dressmaker's dummy standing in the corner.

"I'll sleep on silk, but I won't wear it."

She frowned. "You know, you could be a little more cooperative. Kylie is paying for all of this and she could use a few breaks."

"She seems fine to me."

"Of course, she's fine. Nothing can bring that girl down. And believe me, she has had plenty of reason to start popping anti-depressants."

"Like what?" he asked, surprised by this revelation. He would have guessed a woman with Kylie's vivacity had lived a life full of sunshine and roses.

"Well, for one thing, she gave up a great job in Hollywood a year ago so she could come home and take care of her brother."

"Was he sick?"

Amy nodded. "Hodgkin's disease. It looks like he'll make a full recovery, but it was scary there for a while. And now that Kylie's nursed her little brother back to health she's determined to do the same for his business. Handy Press has been teetering on the edge of bankruptcy for years. So instead of going back to work for her famous clients, she's staying in Pittsburgh and working for peanuts until Handy Press is in the black."

"Famous clients?" Dexter asked, his curiosity getting the better of him.

"I'm not supposed to name names, but one of her clients was just chosen as People magazine's Sexiest Man of the Year. And he thinks the world of Kylie." She dropped her voice a notch. "Both professionally and personally, if you know what I mean."

He nodded. Dexter didn't have time to read *People* magazine but he'd seen enough pictures of Hollywood hotshots to imagine the type of man who had hired Kylie. The kind of man who dazzled all the women. The kind of man who was the complete opposite of Dexter Dependable Kane.

"Actually, Kylie and I met in Hollywood," Amy continued. "I was doing makeup for a movie of the week and she was on the set to lend moral support to one of her clients. He was her high school sweetheart and she'd followed him to California and helped arrange his big break. He repaid her by breaking her heart. But he kept her on as his publicist."

"He sounds like a real winner."

Amy nodded. "She's better off without him. She's got good, midwestern integrity along with a wild imagination. That's one reason she was such a hit with the glitterati. That, combined with her tendency to take risks."

"Such as?"

"Such as volunteering to be the target when one of her clients performed a knife-throwing exhibition on 'Circus of the Stars.' Fortunately, Kylie only needed twelve stitches when it was over. Then there was the time she wagered a month's salary to get her client a part on a television miniseries."

"What did she wager?"

"That the guy would make it to work on time every day. She lost the bet, but her client was a big hit on the show."

"Did he ever reimburse her?"

Amy smiled. "It doesn't work that way in Hollywood. She'd probably still be there, trying to salvage her heart and her bank account, if her brother hadn't gotten sick. Kylie would do anything for Evan."

At least now he knew why his successful portrayal of Harry Hanover was so important to her. "So that's what this book tour is all about? Saving her brother's business?"

"That's right," Amy replied, studying the clothes on the rack.

He tried to imagine giving up his dream of owning the Kane Corporation. "Sounds like she's throwing away a great career opportunity for a hopeless cause."

"Yeah, you tell her that," Amy said with a laugh. "Tell her not to breathe, too, while you're at it."

He shrugged, then removed the plastic drape. "I just believe a person should have a good career strategy. Otherwise you end up drifting though life without any purpose." *Like his parents.*

Amy squealed. "I found it!" She pulled an outfit off the rack. "Put it on."

He stood up, frowning at the clothes she'd selected. "That's not really me."

"It will be." She snatched his glasses off his face, then pushed him toward the bathroom. "Change in there, then come out and show us the new Dexter Kane."

"Harry Hanover," he reminded her.

"Whatever."

Ten minutes later, Dexter stepped out of the bathroom, then walked down the hallway to the living room.

Amy and Kylie sat chatting on the sofa. They both looked up at the same time.

"Oh, boy," Amy breathed.

Kylie just stared up at him with her mouth open.

Dexter shifted self-consciously on his feet. No doubt he looked ridiculous in this outfit. He'd tried to tell Kylie this makeover wouldn't work.

"Don't move," Amy said, jumping off the sofa and running toward her bedroom.

He looked at Kylie, his heart pounding in his chest. "Well?"

She swallowed. "I don't know what to say."

Her brown eyes looked large and luminous as she stared up at him. He wondered if she ever resented the fact that she'd put her life and career on hold.

Amy ran back into the living room, camera in hand. "Okay, I've got to have a shot of this for my portfolio."

The camera flashed, making Dexter blink. "You mean you *like* this look?"

"Don't you?" Kylie and Amy said in unison.

He shrugged. "The bathroom mirror was too small for me to get a good luck. Besides, you've got my glasses, remember? Everything is a little blurry."

Amy picked up Dexter's glasses off the coffee table and handed them to him. He put them on, then Kylie steered him toward the long wall mirror in the dining room.

"Say hello to the new, improved you," Amy said.

Dexter stared in the mirror. His hair looked completely different. Slightly windblown and carefree, as if he'd just hopped off a motorcycle. The black muscle shirt Amy had picked out was just a tad too small, accentuating the broad build of his shoulders. The snug black denim jeans hung low on his narrow waist and hugged his hips, leaving very little to the imagination.

"It's amazing," Kylie breathed, staring at Dexter in the mirror.

Amy clapped her hands together. "I knew there was an Adonis underneath all that tweed. Congratulations, girl." She turned to high-five Kylie. "Your Harry Hanover is a hunk!"

Kylie took a deep breath. "Are you sure this is the look we want? He seems so...different."

"Exactly," Amy exclaimed. "He's perfect."

Dexter didn't say anything, because he completely agreed. The man in the mirror was perfect.

He was also the spitting image of his brother, Sam.

3

THE NEXT DAY, DEXTER walked into Riley's Bar and Grill, a popular restaurant located in downtown Pittsburgh. He saw Kylie waving at him from a corner booth. As he walked toward her, he noticed several women turning to look at him. It had been like that ever since Amy had worked her magic.

He still wasn't sure if he liked it.

"Where are your glasses?" Kylie asked, as he slid into the booth across from her.

"I stopped by a one-hour optical store at the mall and picked up some contact lenses." He blinked twice. "They take a little getting used to, but at least I can see. What do you think?"

"They're fine, I guess." She opened up her menu as the waitress approached their table. "But I liked your glasses better."

"I'll have the quarter-pound burger with all the extras," he ordered, "and a side of fries." He handed the waitress his menu. She gave him a smile and a saucy wink before turning to Kylie.

Dexter looked down at the green Formica table-top, unaccustomed to such blatant flirting. He could blush burning in his cheeks. It was amazing a simple change of hairstyle and wardrobe could completely alter the way women reacted to him. Especially since he was the same man on the inside that he'd always been.

For the first time he wondered if Kylie was attracted to the new Dexter Kane. She certainly hadn't treated him any differently since his transformation. If anything, she was more businesslike than before.

"I've written up an itinerary," she announced after the waitress walked off with their order. Opening her brown suede briefcase, she pulled out an array of multicolored file folders. "The tour officially starts tomorrow, but I've got a book signing scheduled for this afternoon as a trial run. Hopefully we can work out any kinks before we embark on the real thing."

"This afternoon?" His stomach flip-flopped. "Where?"

"In New Castle. The manager is expecting us at three o'clock, so we should have plenty of time to get there. I'll drive."

Dexter wondered if there was enough time for her to find a new Harry Hanover. He reached up to loosen his tie, then remembered that he wasn't wearing one. So why did he feel like he was choking?

"Then tomorrow we go on the road" she continued, sliding a yellow file folder across the table. "We've got book signings scheduled in Ohio, including the cities of Columbus, Cleveland and Youngstown. Plus a couple of radio and newspaper interviews. Then we'll circle back into Pennsylvania and hit Altoona, Harrisburg, Allentown and Philadelphia. And I'll be setting up more appearances during the tour. I'm hoping you'll be in high demand.''

He opened the folder and looked down at the itinerary. "Looks like we'll keep busy for the next few weeks."

"Definitely." She bent over her briefcase, sorting through more files.

Dexter looked at her, admiring the way her curly brown hair was tamed into a loose French braid, with silky tendrils spilling over her cheeks and forehead. The style accentuated the alluring curve of her neck.

She snapped her briefcase shut, then looked up at him. "I've already made reservations at hotels along the route. They're nothing fancy, but a couple do have pools if you want to pack some swimming trunks."

He nodded, turning his attention to the detailed schedule in front of him. Kylie was definitely thorough. It looked as if she'd accounted for every possible contingency. The businessman in him was impressed.

The other part of him was impressed by the clingy, hot-pink sweater she was wearing. It had a scooped neckline that drew his gaze to her generous breasts.

"Dexter?"

He blinked and looked up. "What?"

"Do you have any questions about the book tour or the itinerary?"

He sat up and cleared his throat, focusing his attention back where it belonged. "Just one. Who's paying for all of this?"

Her gaze dropped to her briefcase. "Handy Press is sponsoring the tour."

"Amy told me that they were pretty strapped financially." He fluttered the schedule in the air. "An excursion like this can't come cheap."

"I'm covering the costs initially," she explained, stirring her soda with a straw. "Then Handy Press will reimburse me when the profits on *How To Jump-Start Your Love Life* start rolling in."

He stared at her. "You're not serious?"

She picked up her soda. "It's a perfectly acceptable business practice. So tell me what the D in your middle name stands for?"

"I think you're trying to change the subject."

"David?" she guessed. "Dennis? Durwood? Dastardly?"

"You're close with that last one," he replied. "The D stands for Dependable."

She smiled. "Now you're the one not being serious."

"It's the truth. I'm Dexter Dependable Kane. Thanks to some zealot in my family tree who thought all the Kanes should be given a virtuous middle name to live up to."

"So are you dependable?"

"Through and through," he replied. "That's why you should listen to my advice about forking out your own money for this book tour. Most businesses give you an expense account. They don't expect you to shell out your own money.''

"This is different," she countered. "I've already volunteered to cover all the expenses." She took a long sip of soda. "Besides, the owner is my brother. I'm sure he'll repay me as soon as he can."

Dexter rubbed one hand over his chin, amazed at her naiveté. "He won't have to pay you a dime if his business declares bankruptcy. You'll just be one in a long line of creditors."

She set her briefcase on the floor. "I'm not sure why we're even having this discussion. If the book is a hit, bankruptcy won't be an issue."

"If," he echoed, leaning forward. "A great big *if*, in my opinion. *If* everyone believes I'm Harry Hanover. *If* the book sells big. *If* I don't blow it."

She smiled. "Don't worry, Dex. I have faith in you."

AN HOUR LATER, THEY climbed into Kylie's car. She unspooled her seat belt and snapped it in place. "Are you ready, Dex?" She switched on the ignition.

He nodded, squinting into the afternoon sun. The glare was giving him a headache. "It's Dexter."

"What?"

"You've called me Dex several times," he shouted over the roar of the engine. "I prefer Dexter."

She shook her head.

"I can't hear you." With a quick glance in the

rearview mirror, she shot out of the parking space. A horn blasted behind them.

"Oops," she said, waving behind her. "Sorry."

Dexter reached out to grip the dashboard. "Maybe I should drive."

She glanced at him, then back at the road, braking suddenly to make a left turn. Another horn sounded. "I need to get the muffler fixed. But the car should quiet down once we hit the highway."

"If we make it to the highway," Dexter muttered to himself. Recklessness seemed to be in her blood, whether it was driving a car or extending credit to an insolvent business. Both could prove dangerous.

The breeze from the open windows fluttered the neckline of her sweater. He looked away, but not before catching a delicious glimpse of her lacy white bra and the luscious curve of her breast.

As he stared out the window, he found himself wondering if she was as unabandoned in bed as she was behind the wheel. Not that he'd ever find out, Dexter sternly reminded himself. The Studs-R-Us no-sex policy put any potential fantasies to rest. He could never put his future at risk for a woman.

Not even a woman as enticing as Kylie.

They turned onto the highway and to Dexter's surprise the car's roar did die down just enough to make normal conversation possible.

"I'm going to call you Harry from now on," Kylie said, edging the car into the passing lane. "That way we won't get confused."

He pointed to the digital clock on the dashboard.

"I don't think we're going to make it to New Castle by three."

"Sure we will."

"Only if you drive ten miles over the speed limit."

"That's the plan, Harry."

Dexter didn't say anything else for the rest of the trip. The woman next to him was obviously delusional. There would be no way they could pull this off. A hundred things could go wrong. Just thinking of all the possibilities was making him dizzy.

Or maybe it was her perfume. A light, airy scent that teased his nostrils. It smelled like summer. In fact, everything about her was bright and fresh and cheerful. She wasn't flashy or even classically beautiful. But there was something about Kylie, a natural warmth that drew you to her.

Not that he intended to draw any closer. For one thing, this whole charade would probably fall apart before the day was out. Then he'd have to find some way to convince Mrs. Brubaker to keep him on staff.

"We're here," she said at last, speeding past the New Castle city limits.

Perspiration broke out on Dexter's forehead. "Has it occurred to you that I haven't even read the book I'm supposed to have written?"

"Don't worry about it, Harry." She slowed the car as they approached a stoplight, then turned to him. "This is a rehearsal more than anything else. We'll be lucky if five customers show up. Just smile and sign your name. Harry Hanover, not Dexter Kane.''

He had a premonition of impending disaster. Pulling off this charade couldn't be as easy as Kylie believed. ''But I don't even know what this Harry Hanover's signature looks like.''

''It doesn't matter,'' she assured him, turning the corner, then pulling into the parking lot of a store called The Book Attic. The lot was packed with cars, but she finally found an empty space. ''The public doesn't know what it looks like, either. Now that I think about it, *I* don't even know what it looks like.''

''But you have met the man?''

''Well, sure. Sort of.'' She unhooked the seat belt, then turned and flashed him a smile. ''It's show time!''

KYLIE COULDN'T BELIEVE what she found in the bookstore. Women. A long, sprawling line of women that started at the table stacked with Harry's book and wound through the fiction section, around the audiotape display case, and into the towering stacks of reference books.

The manager hurried over to them. ''Hi, I'm Bob, and I'm so glad you're finally here. I was afraid I'd have a riot on my hands if Mr. Hanover was a no-show.''

Bob was thin and balding, with a straggly goatee that he kept rubbing between his fingers.

Dexter looked around the store in disbelief. ''All

these women are here to see Hanover...I mean, me?''

"That's right," Bob affirmed.

"I never expected this kind of turn out," Kylie exclaimed. "It's wonderful!"

Bob blushed. "This manager gig is only temporary. I actually have a degree in marketing and came up with this fabulous idea...."

He was cut off by the chant of the women in line.

"We want Harry! We want Harry! We want Harry!"

"Looks like you're in demand," Bob said as he ushered them to the table at the front of the store.

Dexter leaned toward Kylie. "What exactly is going on here?"

"I'm not sure," she replied, noting that each woman held a copy of *How To Jump-Start Your Love Life.* "Let's just enjoy the moment."

Dexter sat down behind the table as the store manager clapped his hands together.

"If I can have your attention please, ladies. Mr. Hanover has arrived."

A joyous cheer arose from the back of the line, along with several wolf whistles. Kylie could see heads bobbing in the back, craning to get a better look at him. The women in the front of the line were staring at Dexter and whispering excitedly to each other.

Kylie felt a curious mixture of pride and protectiveness.

Bob cleared his throat to get their attention once

more. "On behalf of The Book Attic, it is my pleasure to introduce Mr. Harry Hanover, author of *How To Jump-Start Your Love Life*. But Mr. Hanover goes by another name as well."

Dexter glanced up at her, obviously confused. Kylie held her breath, wondering what the manager had up his sleeve. There was no way he could know the truth.

Bob turned and picked up a large box, setting it on the table beside Dexter. Then he reached inside and pulled out a rhinestone crown. "It is my pleasure to present the King of the Kiss!"

The women cheered as Bob placed the crown on Dexter's head. Kylie forced a smile, aware that Dexter looked, and no doubt felt, ridiculous. The crown was too large and slid off his temple, hanging haphazardly on his head.

She pulled the bookstore manager aside. "Will you please tell me what's going on here?"

"It's a marketing ploy," he said, his face flushed with excitement. "I've inserted a raffle ticket into each copy of the book. The winner gets a fifty-dollar gift certificate and a kiss from Hanover. I coined that King of the Kiss moniker. Don't you love it?"

That wasn't exactly the word she wanted to use, but she was too confused at the moment to come up with a more polite term.

"I appreciate you ingenuity," she said, trying to remain calm. "But it might have helped if you'd given us a little advance notice."

He shrugged. "I just came up with it this yesterday, shortly after you called to tell me the signing was a go. I had to find some way to get buyers here.''

"How did you do it?'' she asked, grudgingly impressed with the number of women crowding the store.

"The local radio disc jockey is a friend of mine and gave it a plug on his show. I also handed out flyers at the grocery stores, then sent one of my clerks to the mall. I really played up the King of the Kiss angle. And I might have alluded to the fact that Hanover could pass for Mel Gibson.'' He looked over at Dexter. "If you squint your eyes just right there is sort of a resemblance.''

In her mind, Dexter certainly had as much appeal as Mel Gibson. Maybe not that shining star quality and rogue charm that practically oozed from the movie star, whom she'd met at a number of Hollywood parties. Dexter's attraction was definitely more subtle. The kind that made you want to peel off his glasses and rumple his perfect hair, and fluster his rock-steady demeanor.

Of course he wasn't wearing his glasses anymore. A decision she still wasn't sure she agreed with.

"I appreciate your enthusiasm,'' Kylie said at last. "I suppose the important thing is that it brought buyers into the store.''

The manager rubbed his hands together. "Exactly! Now we'll proceed with the drawing, then Mr. Hanover can start autographing books while I man the cash register.''

"What's going on?" Dexter asked, while the manager retrieved a big jar stuffed with ticket stubs from behind the counter.

"Don't worry," she whispered, giving him a re-assuring smile. "Just go with it."

The manager stood on top of a stepstool, his hand dipped inside the wide-mouth jar. "Now for the moment we've all been waiting for."

Kylie attempted to straighten the crown on Dexter's head, wishing she had some bobby pins in her purse.

"And the lucky winner is," the manager shouted, "number 432855!"

A high-pitched scream indicated that the winning ticket holder was located near the back of the line. After a little jostling, a short, rotund woman with bleached blond hair and dark roots elbowed her way to the front. She wore a gold lamé tunic top over black stretch pants that looked as if they'd been stretched well beyond their capacity.

"That's me," she trilled, handing her ticket to the bookstore manager. Then she grabbed Dexter by his shoulders and pulled him toward her. "Plant one on me, King!"

"Wait a minute," Dexter began, "I'm not sure what's going on here..."

The woman cut him off by slapping her thick lips over his mouth. She grasped the front of his shirt to tug him closer and he came halfway out of his chair. Strangled gurgles emanated from his throat.

Kylie shifted on her feet, itching to rescue him

from this ravenous customer. Then again, the man did work as a gigolo. Surely he was used to dealing with women's appetites.

At last the woman broke the kiss. Dexter fell back in his chair, the crown slipping off the top of his head and banging onto the table in front of him.

"What, no tongue?" the woman complained. "You'd think for a book that costs fifteen bucks I'd at least get a little tongue."

"You bit me!" Dexter pulled a white handkerchief out of his pocket and dabbed at his lower lip.

"It was a love nip," she huffed. "Straight from page forty-seven in your book." She turned to face the crowd of women. "Save your money, girls. The King just fell of this throne."

The manager hurried to her side. "Here is your gift certificate, good for one year at The Book Attic."

"Well, at least this day isn't a total waste." She stuffed the gift certificate into her gold lamé purse.

Kylie's heart plummeted as she saw the line of women in front of Dexter's table slowly begin to disperse. Some tried to be subtle about it, turning their attention to the books on the shelves in front of them and surreptitiously laying down their copy of *How To Jump-Start Your Love Life* before walking away.

Perhaps most of them were only in it for the gift certificate and had never intended to buy the book. But something told her that if the kiss had been a success, the bookstore would have sold out.

To Kylie's relief, one elderly woman did toddle up to the table and laid a copy of the book down in front of Dexter. He smiled up at the woman, flashing that sexy dimple in his chin. Kylie's heart warmed. What woman could resist that?

"Your name, please," he said, picking up a pen off the table.

"Oh, you don't need to go to the trouble of signing it, young man. I just want to buy it."

Kylie moved toward the table. "You'll have to pay for the books at the cash register, ma'am. It's right over there. But I'm sure Harry would be happy to autograph it for you. There's no extra charge."

"It would be my pleasure," he said, opening the front cover.

The old lady smiled. "Well, if you insist."

"What's your name?" he asked, the pen poised over a crisp, blank page.

"Mrs. Herbert Dalrymple."

Dexter began writing in a neat, even script. "It's a pleasure to meet you, Mrs. Dalrymple." He signed the name Harry Hanover with a flourish, then handed it to her. "I hope you enjoy it."

"Oh, I won't be reading it," she explained. "My refrigerator has been sitting crooked for over a year and I believe this little book is just the right size to even it out."

Dexter's smile faded. "I see."

Mrs. Dalrymple reached out to gently pat his hand. "If I ever buy a new refrigerator, perhaps I'll read it then. I'm sure it's very good."

"Thank you," he mumbled, as she walked away. Then he looked up at Kylie. "Just *go with it?* Did you know that woman was planning to kiss me?"

"Not until a few minutes ago. Bob just told me about the raffle. Besides, I assumed that you've kissed lots of women in your profession, so you wouldn't need any advance notice."

"Thanks," he said, dabbing at his lower lip. "Thanks a lot."

"It will be better next time. We'll be more prepared."

"How?" he asked, shoving his handkerchief back into his pocket. "It should be obvious by now that I don't know anything about *How To Jump-Start Your Love Life.*"

"Don't worry, Harry," she said, resisting the urge to scrub that woman's lipstick off his mouth. "I'll teach you everything you need to know."

4

"HOW LONG HAVE YOU BEEN working for Studs-R-Us?" Kylie asked, handing him a glass of wine.

They hadn't said a word about the disaster at The Book Attic on the drive back to Pittsburgh. Dexter had wondered if Kylie was rethinking her plan to have him impersonate Harry Hanover, until she invited him up to her apartment to review the next week's schedule.

"We're not allowed to reveal any personal information." He sat sprawled on a blue beanbag chair in her living room, his long legs bent at an uncomfortable angle. Kylie and her roommate had an eclectic array of inflatable furniture and beanbag chairs scattered around the living room. Which only reinforced his belief that Kylie had sunk more money than she wanted to admit into her brother's floundering business.

She blinked at his terse reply. "Oh."

"It's company policy."

She took a seat on the purple inflatable sofa. "Well, I suppose I can understand that. Although, I have to say that for a gigolo, you're not quite what I expected."

He didn't like her tone.

"What exactly did you expect?"

She cleared her throat. "Well, please don't take offense, Harry. I'm not criticizing you. I suppose I had a certain stereotype of a gigolo in my mind and you're...not it."

Harry. She insisted on calling him that name, even when they were alone together. He didn't like it. "That doesn't mean I can't do the job."

"But look what happened this afternoon."

His jaw tightened. "That woman caught me completely off guard. But I can assure you I do know how to kiss, if that's what you're worried about."

"I'm not worried," she assured him with a smile. "I have faith in you, Harry."

His irritation faded under glow of her smile. He took another sip of wine and told himself to relax. Kylie might be disappointed in his job performance, but at least she was willing to give him another chance.

She set down her wineglass. "I think we should practice kissing. Just so you're fully prepared if it happens again."

His pulse picked up a notch as his gaze fell to her lips. They were full and pink. Inviting. And he'd just been issued an invitation. "You're the boss."

"Good. Let's start with a refresher course." She picked up a copy of Hanover's book and flipped through the pages. "There are some great pointers in chapter three."

"Pointers?" Dexter echoed, realizing he must

have misunderstood her. "You think I need pointers?"

"I think you should be familiar with Harry's tutorial on kissing. We want your method to match the book."

Tutorial? This was ridiculous. He'd been mauled by a strange woman in a bookstore and Kylie was concerned because he hadn't seduced the woman on the spot. But before he could explain that he'd never had any complaints about his kisses, she began reading aloud from *How To Jump-Start Your Love Life.*

"The right kiss will make your lady purr like the engine of a Lamborghini," Kylie looked up at him. "Harry likes to draw a lot parallels between romance and auto mechanics to make it more comprehensible to male readers."

"Fascinating," Dexter said dryly.

"There are three key components to remember when striving for the perfect kiss. Proximity, pressure and pizzazz."

"Should I be taking notes?" he asked, finding this entire conversation ludicrous. He was twenty-eight years old. Did she really believe he that needed remedial lessons in romance?

"That's not a bad idea," she replied, then pointed to the end table. "There should be a pencil and notepad in the drawer."

Well, at least that answered his question. He didn't move from the beanbag chair. "I think I can keep it all in my head. I just have to remember the three Ps. Proximity, pressure and pizzazz."

"Very good," she replied, then turned back to the book and continued reading. *"Proximity is the most important of these three vital components. A man should immediately establish the dominant role, invoking the image of both protector and pursuer."*

"Okay, now we're up to five Ps." Dexter said, leaning back in the beanbag chair. "Proximity, pressure, pizzazz, protector and pursuer. I take it Hanover is a big fan of alliteration."

Kylie dropped the book in her lap. "I'm not sure I agree with that bit about the dominant role. And I certainly don't remember reading anything about it in the first draft. Maybe there was an editing mistake."

"It sounds fine to me."

She frowned. "You believe men should play the dominant role in a relationship?"

"That's not what the book says," he replied evenly, warming up for a good debate. He'd been a state champion in forensics in high school. "Hanover clearly states that the man should establish the dominant role during the kiss. That he should take on his natural role of pursuer. Since the beginning of time, men have been the hunters, pursuing their prey. A thousand years ago they hunted the water buffalo. Today it's the woman."

She arched a brow. "And you don't find that attitude at all sexist?"

"Hey, you're the one who hired a gigolo. Don't you think that's sexist? You even gave me a makeover so women would find me more appealing."

"You were appealing before," she countered, her cheeks turning a becoming shade of pink. "But image is everything in this business, and you looked more like a power broker than the author of a book on romantic relationships."

"So who do you like better?" he asked, taking a sip of his wine. "The old Dexter Kane or the new Harry Hanover?"

She picked up the book and held it in front of her, making it impossible for him to see her face. "I think we've gotten off the subject."

Dexter opened his mouth, then closed it again. Maybe he didn't really want to know her answer. "Then let's move on to the next P. It's presumptuous, isn't it?"

"Pressure," she replied, lowering the book. "Are you sure you don't want to take notes?"

"Positive."

"All right, but pay attention."

Dexter watched her lick her lips and wished he could *stop* paying attention. Stop watching the way her fingers trickled through her silky nutmeg hair when she tucked it behind her ear. Stop noticing the way her eyes sparkled when she smiled. Stop his gaze from falling to the enticing curves outlined by her hot pink sweater. Or even lower, to appreciate the way her black capri pants hugged her long legs.

He reached for his wine, suddenly wishing it was something stronger.

"There are two kinds of pressure," she read aloud, *"that should be applied to achieve a penul-*

timate kiss. The first is bodily pressure. If you've achieved the correct proximity, it should simply be a matter of leaning close enough to make physical contact with the length of her body. Like cables clamped on a car battery, you need a good connection to generate electricity.''

Dexter set down his wineglass, suddenly growing very warm. It was possible the sheen of sweat on his brow wasn't due to the wine. In fact, he knew with a growing certainty that his body was reacting to the sound of Kylie's soft, throaty voice describing the way to turn a woman on.

She shifted on the inflatable sofa, tucking one leg underneath her and stretching the other long leg in Dexter's direction. *''Second is mouth pressure. This should vary during the length of a kiss. Seduce her into submission. Too much pressure will cause the kiss to stall out. Too little won't even get her engine started.''*

"Exactly what kind of relationship does Hanover have with his car?" Dexter asked, trying to break the tension building up inside of him.

"I know it's a little heavy on the automobile references," she replied. "Harry started out writing car repair manuals. But I think one of the great things about this book is that it will appeal to men. There aren't many romance self-help books out there that relay information in this kind of language."

"That I definitely believe."

"Okay, on to the third P," she said, flipping to the next page. *"Pizzazz in a kiss is like racing stripes on your car. That little something extra that really makes it stand out from the crowd. So how do you put pizzazz in a kiss? By using both verbal and nonverbal communication to convey your attraction. Use your body, your hands and your words to ignite the passion between you. Just like you talk to your car, talk to your lady. Make her know how much you care about her. And how good she makes you feel.''*

Kylie closed the book. ''That's it.''

''Okay.'' He picked up his wineglass and drained it. Then he set it down and took a deep breath. ''I'm ready to go for a test drive.''

KYLIE SMILED AS SHE watched Dexter struggle out of the beanbag chair. It obviously wasn't designed for someone over six feet tall.

She stood up and held out her hand. ''Need a lift?''

He looked up at her, the expression in his molten gray eyes sending a shock wave throughout her body. *It must be the wine.*

Only the wine didn't explain the strange sensation that enveloped her when his hand closed over hers. Her heart skittered in her chest as she helped him to his feet. She was suddenly aware of how big Dexter Kane was compared to her. At five feet seven inches, she'd never considered herself petite. But she barely reached his chin. His shoulders were so broad they blocked the view of the hallway, though she knew Amy's door was closed and her roommate fast asleep.

Kylie swallowed, her throat suddenly dry. Dexter was still gazing at her with those penetrating gray eyes and his hand still held hers. He had strong, broad hands and the shirt they'd picked out for him emphasized his well-honed biceps. The combination made her believe that he could lift her off the floor with the slightest effort. Not that she wanted him to lift her, she told herself firmly. But the image was undeniably thrilling.

"Are you ready?" he asked huskily, their palms growing warm.

"Ready?" she echoed dumbly.

"To practice that kiss."

She blinked. "Oh, yes. Of course."

"I've got the three Ps memorized. Proximity," he murmured, moving a step closer to her. "Pressure." Another step. "Pizzazz." He stood so close she could barely breathe.

"All right," she replied, taking a deep breath. "Let's do it."

Then she whirled around and raced across the living room. She pulled the dressmaker's dummy from the corner and rolled it over to him. "This is Gertrude. She'll be your date for this evening."

Dexter stared at her. "You want me to kiss a plastic woman?"

"You can start with Gertrude and work your way up from there," Kylie replied, still trying to regain her equilibrium.

But Dexter didn't give Gertrude a second glance. He turned to Kylie, slowly advancing on her. "I don't think so."

Kylie backed up a step, then another, until her back met the wall. "What are you doing?"

"I'm establishing the dominant role." He stood directly in front of her, then planted one hand on either side of her shoulders. "Is it working?"

She swallowed. "Yes."

His expression softened. "Are you scared of me?"

She wasn't certain how to answer that question. Her knees were shaking, but not out of fear. "No."

"Good." Then he leaned his head closer to hers and inhaled deeply. "You smell so good. It's been driving me crazy all day long."

"I use…raspberries," she stuttered, then realized she sounded like an idiot. "I mean raspberry-scented body lotion. The soap and shampoo, too."

His gray eyes darkened. "I like it."

She licked her lips, then noticed his gaze fall to her mouth. If he was determined to play this out, she wished he would just get it over with.

He took a step closer, his face now so close to hers she could smell the bouquet of the red wine on his breath. Then his lips feathered over one eyebrow and burned a trail down the length of her cheek. She closed her eyes as he kissed the corner of her mouth, then she found herself parting her lips and turning her head toward him.

He didn't wait for any further encouragement,

closing his mouth over hers with a low, guttural moan. Her arms circled around his neck as he deepened the kiss, the silken thrust of his tongue making her pull him closer.

His hands were on her shoulders now, his fingers gently kneading her skin until she thought she would collapse from the exquisite sensation. His lips molded against her own, teasing and tasting and tempting, until he drew a long moan from deep within her throat.

At last he lifted his head and stared into her eyes, his breathing as ragged as her own. "There's one thing you should know about me, Kylie."

"What's that?" she whispered, her lips still tingling.

"I'm a very fast learner." Then he turned and walked out the door without another word.

5

"YOU WOKE ME UP TO BRAG about a kiss?" Amy Kwan yawned behind her hand, her eyelids drooping.

"I'm not bragging," Kylie said, pacing back and forth across the living room floor. Dexter had left over an hour ago, but she still couldn't get that kiss out of her mind. Her heart raced just thinking about it. "I mean it was a stupendous kiss. I have never been kissed like that before in my entire life!"

"I know," Amy murmured sleepily. "You already told me three times. He made you see stars, yada, yada, yada. So what's the problem?"

Kylie stopped in front of her roommate, who lay stretched across the inflatable sofa. "The man is a gigolo. A male escort. A professional seducer of women. You don't see that as a problem?"

Amy's delicate brows drew together. "But you knew he was a gigolo when you hired him. In fact, that's the *reason* you hired him. You wanted the fake Harry Hanover to be able to sweep a woman off her feet, didn't you?"

"Yes," Kylie exclaimed, flopping down into the beanbag chair. "Of course. I want him to dazzle every woman he meets. But not me!"

Amy sat up. "Kylie, you're doing it again."

"Doing what?"

"Letting your heart lead you instead of your head. Or in this case, your hormones. How long has it been since your last date?"

"I've been busy," Kylie hedged.

"Six months?" Amy guessed. "Seven?"

She sighed. "Twelve months and thirteen days."

"So you agree it is possible that you're overreacting to that kiss?"

"Anything is possible at two o'clock in the morning." She rubbed her face with her hands. "Maybe you're right. Maybe I am overreacting."

Amy grinned. "You do have a tendency to leap before you look. Remember Tony?"

Kylie felt a blush crawl up her cheeks. Amy knew all about her years in Hollywood. She'd been as impulsive in her relationships as she had in every other aspect of her life. "That was my fault for getting involved with an actor. They love themselves too much to love anyone else."

"And Adam."

"A director. Even worse, when you consider the size of their egos."

"And now there's Dexter."

"Okay, okay," Kylie conceded, holding up both hands. "You've made your point. And I know you're right. I've always been too impulsive. I wouldn't be in this mess if I hadn't scheduled a book tour for Harry Hanover without getting his approval first. But Dexter is...different."

"Just be careful," Amy admonished. "The man is a gigolo. A professional babe magnet. Kissing is his stock and trade. He probably has this affect on all his women."

All his women. She needed to remember that she wasn't his first and certainly wouldn't be his last. No doubt there was a long line of women Dexter D. Kane had kissed until their toes tingled.

But had it ever meant anything to him?

Kylie nibbled her lower lip. "You know, now that I think about that kiss, he did go strictly by the book, hitting every high point in chapter three. Establishing his dominance. Applying just the right amount of pressure."

"Chapter three?"

"It's the kissing tutorial in *How To Jump-Start Your Love Life.*"

Dexter's husky words echoed in her mind. *You smell so good. It's been driving me crazy all day long.* She closed her eyes, realizing he'd added a dash of pizzazz as well. "I'm an idiot."

"Now I think you're definitely overreacting," Amy said gently.

Kylie shook her head. "Here I am swooning over Dexter's kiss and he was just playing his part. He's probably forgotten it already. Especially since he just turned around and walked out the door while I, on the other hand, could barely stand up."

"Well, you wanted the man to practice kissing, didn't you?"

"On Gertrude, not me!"

Amy snorted. "*Gertrude?* Okay, I hate to admit it, but Dexter is starting to grow on me. Any man who would choose a real flesh-and-blood woman over a plastic mannequin can't be all bad."

Kylie folded her arms across her chest. "That's not the point. Dexter needs to remember that I'm the one in charge of this operation. I did hire him, after all, not the other way around. If I want him to kiss a plastic woman, then I think he should do it. There will be several last-minute decisions I have to make on the book tour and I need to be certain he'll follow through."

"And what happens if he tries to kiss you again? Can you keep from swooning at his feet?"

"Of course. I simply won't let it affect me."

"Uh-huh." Amy looked skeptical.

"No, really," Kylie said, firming her resolve. "First thing in the morning, I'm going to make it clear to Dexter that I'm in charge. Which means from now on, he keeps his lips to himself."

"I WASN'T EXPECTING YOU so soon." Dexter stood in the doorway of his apartment, a towel wrapped around his waist and his face covered with shaving lotion.

Kylie walked inside, a box of doughnuts in her hands. "I called to tell you I was coming over early."

He closed the door, then turned to face her. "You called me thirty seconds ago on your cell phone. I didn't realize you were standing right outside my door.''

Her gaze dropped to his chest, then to the towel hanging low on his hips. "Dexter, we need to talk."

"Can I get dressed first?"

A pink blush suffused her cheeks. "Please do."

He walked into his bedroom, closing the door firmly behind him. He wasn't sure why Kylie had made a beeline for his apartment this morning, but after that kiss last night, he wasn't exactly in a talking mood. Even after a second icy cold shower, he still hadn't been able to stop thinking about her.

He tossed the towel onto the bed, then quickly dressed in an outfit that would meet Amy Kwan's approval. He ran a comb through his wet hair, slicking it back. Then he walked into the adjoining bathroom and finished shaving. The man looking back at him in the mirror had bloodshot eyes caused by staying up half the night doing research on the Internet.

He had finally figured out that the way to succeed at this gigolo gig was to approach it just like he'd approached the other challenges in his life—by learning everything he could about the subject until he mastered it. It had worked with accounting. And business law. So why not with romance?

He'd found myriad Web sites pertaining to romance, along with several chat rooms populated by people who offered some very interesting variations on how to properly seduce a woman. Not that he actually intended to seduce anyone, especially Kylie, but he'd mentally filed the information anyway.

Dexter had learned a long time ago that information was power. So the more he knew about romance, the more successful he'd be at imitating the author of the latest fad book on the subject.

He'd thumbed through *How To Jump-Start Your Love Life* last night, too, but he intended to give it a much more thorough examination on the car ride from Pittsburgh to Columbus, Ohio, today. Kylie had arranged an interview for him there on an early bird radio show tomorrow morning.

Dexter wiped off the remnants of shaving cream from his jaw with a towel, blinking rapidly to moisten his dry eyes. The optometrist had warned him that he should let his eyes adjust gradually to the contact lenses or risk irritation and possibly infection. He'd obviously worn the new contact lenses for too many hours yesterday.

He reached for his glasses, then changed his mind. Kylie had hired him to portray Harry Hanover, and Harry didn't wear glasses. At least, that's the reason he told himself as he unscrewed the contact lens case and placed a lens into each eye. It had nothing to do with the fact that she'd melted in his arms while he was in his Harry Hanover persona. If she wanted Harry, then he'd give her Harry.

By the time he returned to the living room, Kylie had the doughnut box open and half empty.

"Your eyes are red," she said, licking vanilla glaze off her fingertips.

"They're fine," he replied, blinking away the sting. "Now what did you want to talk about?"

"Sit down, Dexter."

"Harry."

She frowned. "What?"

"You called me Dexter. I thought you wanted to refer to me as Harry from now on to avoid any confusion while we're on the book tour."

"Oh. Right."

"Can I get you a glass of orange juice?" he asked, moving toward the small, open kitchen. "Or I can make you a cup of coffee?"

"Orange juice will be fine." She picked up another doughnut out of the box, this one drizzled with chocolate glaze and covered with colorful candy sprinkles.

He poured them each a tumbler full of juice, then sat down across from her at the breakfast bar. It occurred to him that Kylie was the perfect guinea pig to test his newfound knowledge of romance. Not only did she think he was a gigolo and expect him to flirt and flatter, but it was crucial to the success of the book tour.

Taking a sip of his juice, he regarded her over the rim of his glass. According to the information he'd gleaned, small compliments made a woman feel both attractive and special. "I like your ears."

Kylie stopped chewing and swallowed. "What?"

"They're just right. Not too big, not too small. And they don't stick out at all."

"No one's ever really mentioned that before."

He smiled, pleased that he'd been the first. "Your teeth are great, too. Very white."

She brushed the crumbs off of her fingers. "Thanks."

"But do you know what my favorite part of you is?"

She stilled, then looked up into his face, her gaze wary. "What?"

"Your laugh," he hesitated, wondering if he should go on. But something about the way she was looking at him impelled him to keep talking. "It reminds me of my first-grade teacher. Miss Ames. She had a laugh like yours. Light. Infectious. It always made me think of sunshine."

Her gaze softened. "That is so sweet, Harry. Did you have a crush on her?"

He shrugged. "It was a long time ago." Dexter found himself reluctant to reveal his single-minded devotion to Miss Ames, even after all these years. Despite the small gifts he'd given her, along with a sappy love poem he'd copied out of a library book, the young teacher had always preferred his brother. Sam had been a perennial teacher's pet, enchanting all the female teachers from kindergarten through high school.

Miss Ames had just been the first in a long line of the fairer sex who had been more interested in his brother than in him. They liked Sam's roguish charm and impulsive nature. The exact opposite of Dexter.

But he wasn't Dexter anymore, he was Harry Hanover. And Harry made women fall at his feet.

Kylie glanced at her watch. "We don't have much time. Are you packed?"

He hitched his thumb over his shoulder.

"My suitcase is by the door."

"Good." Then she hesitated, tucking a stray curl behind her perfectly curved ear. "We need to talk."

He looked at her for a long moment, wondering if she realized she had a smudge of chocolate on the corner of her mouth. He was tempted to lean over and lick it off, just to see her reaction. He hadn't come across such a method while doing his research, so maybe he shouldn't improvise. Then again, spontaneity had been encouraged. His gaze fell to chocolate on her mouth again and blood pooled low in his body just thinking about it.

"So are we in agreement?"

He blinked, startled out of his fantasy. "About what?"

"That I am completely in charge from here on out. Your boss at Studs-R-Us assured me that her employees were quite adept at following orders."

He arched a brow. "Exactly what kind of orders do you have in mind?"

Her gaze flicked to his mouth, then back up again. Which made Dexter discover something else he liked about Kylie. She blushed beautifully.

"I'll tell you when we get to Columbus."

6

"YOUR ROOM IS RIGHT THROUGH here, Miss Timberlake." The bellman indicated the door adjoining Dexter's hotel room. He opened it to set her suitcases inside, then closed it again. "Will there be anything else."

"No, thank you," Kylie said, digging in her purse for money to pay the tip. But Dexter beat her to it, pulling some crisp bills out of his billfold and handing them to the bellman.

"That kind of thing is my responsibility," Kylie informed him once they were alone in the room. "So how much do I owe you?"

"Forget it," Dexter replied, tossing his suitcase on top of the king-sized bed. "I'm not letting you pay for everything on this trip."

She arched a brow. "Isn't that what a gigolo does best?"

"Male escort," he amended, unzipping the suitcase, then lifting the lid. Inside were three piles of neatly stacked clothing. "I don't know about other male escorts, but I pay my own way."

She folded her arms across her chest, deciding this was as good a time as any to make her point. "Remember what I said about following orders?"

He carried a stack of clothing from his suitcase to the dresser and laid it inside the top drawer. "I remember you told me to follow your orders, but I don't remember agreeing to do so."

She took a deep breath. "Then maybe I should get another male escort."

Dexter straightened and looked at her. "You'd really do that?"

She licked her lips, hoping he wouldn't call her bluff. She didn't have time to find another fake Harry Hanover. Besides, she liked Dexter. The thought of firing him made her stomach go a little queasy. "I'll do whatever is necessary to make this book tour a success."

He was across the room in three strides. "So will I."

Kylie had to tilt her chin to look up at him, and she was struck once again by the sheer presence of the man. Dexter didn't have to worry about establishing dominance. It radiated from his powerful body.

"I mean it, Kylie," he continued, his gray eyes dark and earnest. "This job is important to me. I can't tell you how important." He stopped for a moment, then took a deep breath. "I'll even agree to follow your orders. As long as they make sense."

She rolled her eyes. "Is that supposed to reassure me?"

He smiled, the dimple in his chin once again catching her off guard. "It's the best I can do. I've never been very good at letting anyone boss me around.''

A knock at the door forestalled her reply. She looked up at Dexter. ''Are you expecting someone?''

''Yes, but considering how you feel about taking charge, I'm not sure I should answer it.''

''Answer the door, Harry,'' she replied, giving her first order. For some reason, her body tensed as she considered the possible identity of the person on the other side of the door. Had he made a date with an old flame? Or an old client? Was Dexter moonlighting to earn some extra cash?

He moved toward the door and opened it. But it wasn't a woman on the other side. It was a waiter pushing a room service cart. He rolled it inside the room and over to the small table in the corner.

''What's this?'' Kylie asked, as the waiter covered the table with a white linen tablecloth. She watched as he briskly set the table with two plates, silverware and wineglasses, then placed a vase with a single red rose in the center.

''Dinner for two.'' Dexter slipped the waiter a generous tip, then turned to her. ''I thought we'd probably be too tired to go out to eat after the long car trip, so I took the liberty of ordering something for us. I guess I should have checked with you first.''

''You certainly should have.'' She walked over to the table, her stomach growling. ''It smells delicious.''

Dexter joined her, removing the silver covers from both plates. "Amy told me you like filet mignon."

She looked up at him, inordinately pleased that he'd cared enough to ask. "It's my favorite."

He nodded. "Good." Then he pulled out a chair for her. "Shall we?"

Kylie sat down, still a little stunned. Dexter had not only been thoughtful enough to order dinner, but he'd called Amy to find out her favorite food. It made her feel a little tingly inside and…special.

"Wine?" he asked, holding up the carafe of merlot.

"Yes, please," she replied, handing him her glass. "And I insist on paying for dinner."

"Too late," he said, filling her wineglass, then his own. "This is my treat."

She arched a brow as he took a seat across from her. "I thought you just agreed to follow my orders."

"True. But I ordered this dinner before our agreement, so it doesn't count."

She sighed. "You're not going to let me win this argument, are you, Harry?"

He smiled. "No. But I will let you make a toast."

She picked up her wineglass. "To the success of *How To Jump-Start Your Love Life*. May it sell a gazillion copies and make Handy Press a household name."

"To success," Dexter said, an enigmatic gleam

in his eye. Then he lightly clinked his glass against hers.

Kylie took a sip of the wine, the smooth bouquet telling her it was an expensive label. Then she picked up the white linen napkin and laid it on her lap. "So tell me, Harry, what made you become a gigolo?"

Dexter froze, his fork halfway to his mouth. After a moment, he said, "Why do you ask?"

She shrugged as she dabbed butter onto her baked potato. "I'm just curious. You're the first male escort I've ever met. You have to admit it's quite an unusual occupation."

"You can say that again," he muttered.

"Do you like the work?"

He looked up at her, his gaze lingering on her mouth. "It has its moments."

She knew he was remembering that kiss last night and she wondered if it had affected him at all. "So how many women have you…worked for."

He gave her a smile that made her toes curl. "I'm afraid that information is confidential."

"You mean gigolos don't ever kiss and tell?"

"Something like that."

As Kylie ate her dinner, she wondered why Dexter seemed so reluctant to part with any information about himself. She knew nothing about him except that he worked for Studs-R-Us and his first-grade teacher was named Miss Ames.

Did he have any family? Friends? Women he saw outside of work? The last thought sent an uneasy chill through her, even though it was entirely possible. The only reason Dexter was having dinner with her right now was because she was paying him to do so. True, he'd paid for the dinner, but for all she knew he could be using money from an expense account. Mrs. Brubaker had told her Studs-R-Us had a commitment to making certain all their customers were completely satisfied.

"So what made you become a publicist?"

She looked up at him, startled from her thoughts by his question. Then she gave a small shrug. "I like people. And I love being able to bring out the best parts of them. So many people have good qualities that they can't see for themselves. Like you, for instance."

"Me?"

"You're very handsome, Harry."

He gaze dropped to his plate. "Since my makeover, you mean."

She shook her head. "No, you were handsome before. But you almost seemed to be hiding it. As if you didn't want the world to know anything about the man underneath the glasses and the three-piece suit."

He stared at her for a long moment. "That's who I really am."

"Is it?"

He set down his fork. "I learned a long time ago that it doesn't do any good to pretend to be someone else. You're not only fooling other people, you're fooling yourself. The one thing I refuse to be is a fool.''

Kylie could hear a strange undercurrent in his tone, but couldn't place it. Was it anger? Pain? Or just naked honesty. His words made her more confused than ever. Was there really such a thing as an insecure gigolo?

She picked up her wineglass. ''I think you're forgetting that a lot of women are attracted to the strong, shy, silent type.''

''Are you?'' he interjected, his gaze fixed intently on her face.

She opened her mouth, then closed it again. Admitting that she'd been very drawn to him from the first time she saw him would definitely be crossing the line from professional to personal. And she'd made a vow to herself not to do that anymore. A lesson learned the hard way.

''I'm speaking as a publicist,'' she replied at last. ''In my experience, women find something inordinately sexy about a man who doesn't try to flaunt his sexuality.''

He reached for his wineglass. ''Or at least they say they do.''

His implied rebuke stung. ''And I suppose men are the epitome of honesty when they say they're looking for a witty, intelligent woman rather than a set of measurements?''

His eyes twinkled. ''Can't we have both?''

She laughed in spite of herself. ''You sound just like Adam.''

"Adam?"

"My ex-client. And ex-fiancé." She reached for her wine, wondering what had induced her to bring him up.

"You were engaged?"

"For a very short time. Adam proposed, but he failed to mention our engagement was merely a publicity stunt." She took a sip of wine, not quite meeting Dexter's gaze. Despite the lightness of her tone, she knew he'd be able to see the old pain in her eyes. "Although I learned a valuable lesson. Two, actually. The first one is that romance sells, especially in Hollywood. The press was wild about the story."

"And the second?"

She put down her wineglass and made herself look at him. "The second was that too many men put themselves and their careers first. Adam loved me in his way, but he loved his image more."

"Then Adam is an idiot."

"Agreed," she said with a smile. "And on that note, I think I'll say good-night." She placed her napkin on her empty plate, then pushed her chair away from the table. "We have an early day ahead of us tomorrow."

He rose quickly to pull her chair out for her. "Thank you for having dinner with me tonight."

"It was my pleasure," she replied, wondering why she was blushing.

He escorted her to the door adjoining their rooms. "Good night, Kylie. Sweet dreams."

"Good night, Harry." Then she walked into her hotel room, closing the door firmly behind her.

The first thing she saw were the flowers. Half a dozen bouquets of all kinds of flowers spread throughout the room. Puzzled, she walked over to the closest vase and plucked the note card off the holder.

She smiled as she read the message. "Amy told me you like filet mignon, but Gertrude told me you like flowers. I hope I can make this book tour everything you want it to be. Yours truly, Dexter."

"IT'S TIME TO ROCK IN THE morning on 1240 KROC," boomed the radio disc jockey who went by the name of Doogie. "And to get your day started right, we've got the sultan of sexuality. The high priest of horniness. The lusty ladykiller. That's right, boys and girls. Author Harry Hanover is here to tell us about his sizzling hot new book, *How To Jump-Start Your Love Life*."

Dexter adjusted his headphones, his gut tied into a knot. Kylie had been thrilled about landing an interview spot on the morning show at KROC, but he didn't share her excitement. Sending flowers and ordering a romantic dinner for two was one thing. Broadcasting his newfound knowledge about romance to thousands of listeners was quite another.

The young disc jockey turned to Dexter. "Okay, Harry, I don't need any passion pointers. I've got the babes lined up at my bedroom door. But what about those pitiful yokels who can't even turn on a vibrator, much less a woman.''

Doogie was one of those shock jocks so popular on radio talk shows. He reminded Dexter of the loudmouthed jerks in high school who had made themselves feel good by tearing others down. The same jerks who were responsible for christening him with those stupid nicknames. But Dexter wasn't Frankenbrain today, he was Harry Hanover, official stud. And it was time for him to step into the role.

Fortunately, he'd read Harry's book a second time last night. Not only had he memorized the title of each chapter, but he'd practiced incorporating Hanover's automobile references in response to potential questions.

Dexter leaned toward his microphone. ''You can't rev the engine until you warm up the car, Mr. Doogie. So I suggest any men out there who have their eye on a particular lady try to warm her up with small romantic gestures to show her how much he really cares.''

Doogie waggled his hairy eyebrows. ''I know all kinds of gestures to make a woman melt right into my arms, Harry. The Doog-Master has all the right moves. In fact, my friends call me the magician because I can make a woman's clothes disappear.'' He snapped his fingers into the microphone. ''Voilà!''

''That's not exactly what I meant by gestures. Men need to…''

''Answer me this,'' Doogie interjected, ''how

many sexy babes have you scored with since you published this book?''

Dexter glanced at Kylie through the Plexiglas window separating the booth from the control room. Her small white teeth worried her lower lip and she kept glancing at the clock. No doubt hoping as much as he that this so-called interview would end soon.

Doogie followed his gaze. ''Speaking of sexy babes, who is that hot number you brought with you today?''

''She is *not* a hot number,'' Dexter replied, irritated by way Doogie was ogling Kylie. ''She's a publicist with Handy Press.''

''Well, she could definitely come in handy around here,'' Doogie said with a smirk. ''I may have an opening in my babe schedule if she's interested.''

''Sorry, Doogie,'' Dexter said wryly. ''She only dates men with class.''

''Ouch,'' the disc jockey exclaimed. ''The Doogster obviously stepped on some testy toes. So what's the scoop with you and that spark plug publicist, Harry? And have you revved up her engine yet? Come on, spill. Just between you and me.''

And thousands of his listeners. Dexter leveled his gaze on the disc jockey while his fists curled in his lap. ''I guess you'll need to read my book to find out the answer. Who knows, Doogie, you might even learn something.''

''The Doogster doesn't need lessons on how to do the horizontal hustle,'' he chortled into the microphone. ''But for you losers out there who are tired of those blowup dolls, check out Harry Hanover's new guidebook, *How To Jump-Start Your Love Life*. It might be a waste of money, but it could fill up another lonely Saturday night. This is 1240 KROC, rockin' you in the morning.''

Then Doogie flipped a switch and loud music reverberated from the speakers. He turned a dial, then swiveled his chair to face Dexter. ''That's a wrap. Thank you so much for coming in this morning, Mr. Hanover. I'm sure my listeners will enjoy your book.''

Dexter blinked, surprised by the transformation. ''You're welcome.''

Then Doogie nodded toward the control booth. ''So is your publicist unattached?''

Despite the fact that Doogie might not really be as bad as his shock jock persona, Dexter wasn't about to let him anywhere near Kylie. ''Sorry, she's not available.''

Doogie picked up a copy of the book. ''Good stuff here. I especially like chapter sixteen.''

''Why Men Can Cry?'' Dexter asked in disbelief. ''You actually read it?''

Doogie smiled, placing a hand over his heart. ''Hey, I'm a sensitive guy. Ask anyone.''

Dexter shook his hand, the urge to punch Doogie in the jaw gradually fading. But he found Kylie wasn't ready to be so forgiving.

''Can you believe that?'' she asked, as they walked out of the radio station. ''He ripped you and the book to shreds! We'll be lucky if anyone in Columbus buys it now.''

''Aren't you the one who said any publicity is good publicity?''

''He made you sound like a pimp!''

''Not me. Harry.'' He slowed and turned toward her. ''There is a difference.''

She took a deep breath. ''I know that. I just wish the *Doogster* would have been a little more supportive of *How To Jump-Start Your Love Life* instead of making it sound like it was just written for losers. Ridiculing the author and the book certainly isn't going to help sales. I should have complained to the station manager.''

He clasped her arm, pulling her to a stop. Her cheeks were flushed and her brown eyes glowed with angry sparks. He wanted to tell her she was beautiful when she was angry, but Hanover's book had specifically warned against using tired clichés. So he tried to calm her down instead. ''Look, anyone who listens to Doogie's show expects him to act that way. That's the reason they tune in. If he had gushed over the book, they never would have believed him. This way they got a few laughs at the same time they got exposed to the information.''

''Exposure is good,'' she conceded grudgingly.

''Right. And the next time they're in a bookstore and see *How To Jump-Start Your Love Life,* they'll remember it. More importantly, they'll probably buy it just to see what Doogie was making such a fuss about.''

She smiled up at him. "You're pretty smart, Harry, did you know that?"

He thought about his decision to kiss her instead of Gertrude.

"I have my moments."

Kylie squared her shoulders. "Okay. Doogie set the ball rolling. So now I just need to think of some way for us to take advantage of it."

7

THREE DAYS LATER, Dexter sat in a Cleveland shopping mall at a table piled high with copies of *How To Jump-Start Your Love Life*. So far he hadn't sold a single book, although he had given several people directions to the rest room.

Kylie had spent most of the last three days on her cell phone, although she had brought him a chocolate ice cream cone a few minutes ago to relieve his boredom. Dexter licked the top layer of the cone, wishing he could apply the frozen treat to his eyes instead of his mouth. They were dry and itchy, despite the fact that he'd added the lubricating drops the optometrist had given him when he'd purchased the contact lenses.

He glanced at his watch, suppressing a groan when he realized he still had over an hour to go before this interminable book signing came to an end. And twenty-one more days to go until his mission was over. This last week, spending every day with Kylie and dreaming about her every night had been sheer torture.

By the time Kylie reappeared at his table, he'd finished the ice cream cone and had counted all the holes in the ceiling tiles above him.

"How's it going?" she asked, looking expectantly around the mall.

"I think the people in Cleveland are satisfied with their love life," Dexter replied. "Is there any way we can ditch this thing early?"

Kylie shook her head. "I have a reporter from the *Cleveland Plain Dealer* coming down to do a story. She should be here any minute."

"I'm afraid the story is going to be that the book is a bomb."

Kylie sat down in the chair next to him. "Actually, I've got a different story in mind."

"Care to clue me in?"

"What if *How To Jump-Start Your Love Life* was responsible for a real-life romance? Undeniable proof that the book really does work."

"It might help sales, but where do you intend to find this proof?"

She smiled at him. "Right here."

"In the mall?"

"No, I mean right here." She waggled her forefinger between the two of them. "You and me, fella. What do you think?"

His body tightened. "I think it has possibilities."

"I got the idea from our conversation the other night. Remember when I told you about Adam?"

"Your ex-fiancé?"

She nodded. "He announced our engagement as a publicity ploy. And it worked. Our picture was plastered all over the newspapers."

"I thought you were upset about it."

"That's because I didn't know it was a ploy. I thought he really loved me."

"And if you had known?"

She shrugged. "Who knows? I might have gone along with it. I used to do a lot of crazy things."

"It sounds like you still do," Dexter replied, aware of a woman walking purposely toward them.

"I talked to Amy and she thinks it's a great idea."

"That's supposed to make me feel better? She's the same woman who wanted to exfoliate me."

Kylie grasped his hand. "Here comes the reporter. Just follow my lead."

"What exactly do you want me to do?"

She took a deep breath, then looked into his eyes. "Kiss me."

Despite his reservations about her plan, Dexter was happy to oblige. He placed his hands on Kylie's shoulders and pulled her close, not caring if this was just another publicity ploy. He'd been wanting to kiss her again ever since that night in her apartment. To prove to himself that the jolt that had shot through him was just a fluke. A natural reaction to a stressful day.

But as soon as his mouth touched her succulent lips, he knew it hadn't been a fluke. Awareness prickled throughout his body and his pulse began to race. Her lips parted for him, allowing his tongue to enter her sweet mouth. He groaned under his breath as she circled her arms around his neck and leaned even closer to him.

Then her palms smoothed up the back of his neck and ruffled his hair. Heat spiraled through his body, threatening to boil over as her tongue tangled with his. He forgot about the reporter. About the fact that they were sitting in the middle of a shopping mall. About everything except how soft and supple Kylie felt in his arms.

All the information he'd gathered on romance hadn't mentioned how powerful one kiss could be. Or what the hell he should do about it. Then he pulled back, realizing he couldn't do a damn thing. It was forbidden by his employer. If he wanted to keep his job and have any chance of becoming the new owner and CEO of the Kane Corporation, then he had to do his thinking above the neck, not below.

Kylie blinked up at him, her breath coming in short, quick gasps. Then he saw her lick her lips and he leaned forward, unable to stop himself from kissing her again.

But the reporter intruded before he had a chance. "So the rumor is true?"

"Rumor?" Dexter echoed, still perplexed by the power of that kiss.

The reporter sidled closer to the table and lowered her voice. "I got an anonymous tip that the author of *How To Jump-Start Your Love Life* had something hot and heavy going on with his publicist."

Dexter looked at Kylie, somewhat surprised to find her blushing. She was obviously the one who had planted that rumor. And from the interested gleam in the reporter's eye, it had worked.

The reporter held out her hand. "I'm Mara Hayden, feature writer from the *Plain Dealer*."

Dexter shook it, noting the way her approving gaze flicked over him. Despite the fact that he'd been in his Harry Hanover persona for a week he still wasn't used to the female attention it garnered him. Only Kylie still treated him the same.

Or did she?

Would she have fallen into his arms like that if he'd been plain old Dexter Dependable Kane instead of the new and improved Harry Hanover? Was he just a walking impersonation of her fantasy man?

"I did a review of your book a couple of weeks ago for my paper," Mara continued. "We got some great letters about it. More than usual, in fact. So I contacted Handy Press about doing an in-depth interview with you tomorrow before you leave Cleveland. But once I got this tip, I decided I didn't want to wait that long."

Dexter glanced at Kylie, impressed with her quick thinking. The newspaper reporter had already expressed an interest in the book tour, so why not spice it up with rumors of a romance?

Only Kylie didn't look like she was thinking at all now. She hadn't said one word to the reporter, just kept staring at Dexter with a dazed expression in her big brown eyes. Was she already regretting this romance charade?

He looped his arm around her shoulders and pulled her closer. They'd come this far already, so they might as well play it out and see what happens.

"I'm glad you're here, Mara, because we really can't keep it a secret any longer. We're in love."

"That's right," Kylie said, her throat sounding a little hoarse. She cleared it, then gave the reporter a tremulous smile. "Harry swept me off my feet. I've never felt this way about a man before."

The reporter's eyes gleamed as she pulled a notepad and pen out of her purse. "So tell me, Miss Timberlake. What exactly is it about Mr. Hanover that you find so intriguing?"

Kylie turned to him. "It's hard to explain. I really didn't expect anything like this to happen. This book tour is simply business after all. But the first time he kissed me..." Her voice trailed off.

"We just knew," Dexter finished for her.

The reporter hastily scribbled into her notepad. "And a question for you Mr. Hanover. Did you use any of the concepts in your book to win the lady's affections?"

"Absolutely," he replied. "Kylie mentioned our first kiss. I have a very detailed tutorial on how to deliver a dynamite kiss in chapter three of *How To Jump-Start Your Love Life*. I'd say that chapter definitely had a significant effect on our relationship."

"Harry's right," Kylie agreed. "But it's more than his kisses. He is every inch a male, strong and determined. But he's also thoughtful, kind and considerate. He makes me feel special."

"Which is all outlined in chapter six of my book," Dexter intoned. "But you must understand, Mara, that my feelings for her come from my heart, not a book. *How To Jump-Start Your Love Life* certainly gave me the confidence and skills to pursue a woman as wonderful and beautiful as Kylie. But I had to do the rest on my own.''

''This is great stuff,'' Mara said, flipping over a page of her notepad. ''So where do you two go from here? Is this book tour going to end in a wedding chapel?''

Kylie shook her head. ''I think it's a little too early in our relationship to talk about making that kind of commitment.''

Dexter smiled at her. ''Not for me, sweetheart. And I intend to do everything in my power to make you change your mind. Because I'm already hearing wedding bells.''

''This is so cool,'' the reporter exclaimed. ''I know my readers are going to eat it up.''

''I hope so,'' Kylie said softly.

The reporter double-checked the spelling of their names and took down some more information about Handy Press, then hurried off to write her story.

Neither one of them said a word for several long moments. Then Kylie glanced at the big clock suspended from the ceiling of the mall. ''Looks like your time is up. The book signing is over.''

He sighed at the stacks of books in front of him. ''And I didn't sell a single one.''

''Maybe this new angle will help publicity.'' Her small white teeth nipped her lower lip. ''If it doesn't...''

''Then we'll think of another angle,'' he assured

her. "We'll make this book a success, Kylie, no matter what it takes."

"Even wedding bells?" she teased, although he heard an odd undertone in her voice.

"Did I go too far?"

"Of course not. I mean, you were just playing up the story, right?"

"Right," he agreed, wondering how she'd feel if he denied it. If he told her that she did have him thinking about things he'd never really considered before. A woman in his life. A family. Suddenly the thought of waking up with Kylie every morning was incredibly appealing.

Of course, once she met Sam, she'd want the real thing, not an imitation. He wasn't the man she saw now. He wasn't Harry. Beneath the clothes and the haircut was plain, old Dexter Kane.

His eyes began to itch again and he knew he needed to apply more lubricating drops. "Are you ready to go back to the hotel?"

She nodded. "As soon as you sign all these books. The store manager will be less likely to return them for a refund if they're autographed. And maybe Mara's newspaper story will bring in some customers." Her brow furrowed. "Do you think we should stay in the same room at the hotel, just for appearances' sake?"

His body tightened at the thought of sharing a hotel room with her. A bed. He swallowed convulsively, then reached for the first book on top of the pile. "We've got adjoining rooms. I think that will give people enough to speculate about."

"You're probably right."

He certainly hoped so. Because this charade of being wild about Kylie had the disturbing possibility of becoming all too true.

TWO DAYS LATER, Kylie had just finished putting the finishing touches on her makeup when she heard Dexter call out to her from the other room.

She opened the connecting door and stuck her head through the crack. "Is there a problem?"

He sat in a chair in the dark, holding his head in his hands. "As a matter of fact there is. I can't see a damn thing."

She walked into the room. "What do you mean?"

"I mean there's something wrong with my eyes. They itch like crazy and the light makes it ten times worse."

So that's why he had the drapes closed and all the lamps turned off. She knelt down by his chair, worry twisting her stomach into a knot. "When did this happen?"

"My eyes have been bothering me for a few days. I thought it was just part of the normal adjustment to wearing contact lenses. But I don't think this is normal."

She rose to her feet and moved to the phone. "I'll call an eye doctor."

"I'm sorry, Kylie," he said. "I know we have

that book signing this morning. I might be able to tough it out until then.''

"Forget it, Dexter. Your eyes are much more important than some book signing.'' She swallowed her exasperation as she looked up the telephone number for the nearest eye doctor. Were all men determined to be martyrs? Her brother had been the same way. Brushing off his early symptoms and refusing to go to the doctor until he couldn't deny something was wrong with him anymore.

A shiver passed through her when she thought about how lucky Evan had been. Despite his delay in seeking treatment, they'd still caught the Hodgkin's disease in the early stages. He'd had to go through radiation treatment and have his spleen removed, but his prognosis was excellent.

Still, there had been times of uncertainty during his health crisis. Times when Kylie had almost gone crazy with waiting and worrying. Those same sensations gnawed at her now, even though her common sense told her Dexter's condition was probably nothing serious. But she'd seen the redness in his eyes. Noticed him blinking a lot. She should have realized there was a problem.

Now she definitely intended to do something about it.

8

"ACUTE CONJUNCTIVITIS." Dr. Cardoza announced his diagnosis, then pulled out his prescription pad. "I'm going to prescribe you some antibiotic drops. I want you to apply them to your eyes three times a day. There's an analgesic in there too, so that should help with the discomfort."

"Should he stay in bed?" Kylie asked, relieved that the diagnosis wasn't anything more serious. Dexter sat beside her in the opthamologist's office, wearing a pair of sunglasses to keep the light out of his sensitive eyes.

"That's not necessary," Dr. Cardoza replied. "But I don't want you to wear those contact lenses for at least a week. Give your eyes time to heal."

Dexter glanced at Kylie. "Can I wear them a couple of hours a day? Just when I'm out in public?"

"No way," Kylie interjected before the eye doctor could reply. "I like you better in your glasses anyway."

The doctor tore off the prescription and handed it to Dexter. "This should take care of it. But if the discomfort increases or you start having vision problems, come back and see me."

Dexter thanked him, then he and Kylie stopped

by the pharmacy counter to get the prescription filled.

"Did you reschedule the book signing?" he asked, looking both mysterious and sexy in his sunglasses.

"Yes, it's on for this afternoon." Despite how well he looked, she knew he felt awful. Which just increased her guilt. "But I'm still not sure it's such a good idea. Maybe you should just rest today."

"I'm fine," he assured her. "But you look tired. Didn't you sleep well last night?"

She'd barely slept at all. Memories of that kiss kept invading her mind, leaving her tossing and turning in her bed. Her empty, lonely bed.

The chirp of her cell phone saved her from answering his question. "Will you excuse me for a minute?"

"Sure."

Kylie walked a few aisles away, thankful for the distraction. She just hoped it wasn't another Cleveland bookseller wanting to make arrangements for a signing. Despite Dexter's reassurances that he was fine, she didn't want to push him too hard until he was feeling better.

Only it wasn't a bookseller on the phone, it was her brother.

"What the hell is going on, Kylie?" Evan asked, a suspicious inflection in his tone.

A warm glow suffused her when she heard his voice, despite the fact that he didn't sound happy. He was alive. That's all that mattered. Especially since she'd come much too close to losing him. "Hi, Evan. How are you?"

"Confused. I just talked to Harry Hanover on the phone. The *real* Harry Hanover. He's not with you in Ohio. So just exactly who is?"

"His name is Dexter Kane and he's doing Handy Press a small favor."

"What kind of favor?"

She took a deep breath. "He's playing the part of Harry Hanover."

Evan didn't say anything for three long beats. "Oh, Kylie, what have you done now?"

She smiled at her brother's question. He'd been asking it with the same exasperation in his tone for as long as she could remember. Evan and she were opposites, he was steady and pragmatic while she tended to act on her impulses and consider the consequences later. But despite the differences in their personalities, they'd always been close. Never more so than when he'd been diagnosed with his illness.

But, thankfully, that was all behind them. And despite the fact that he was going to become a lot more irritated with her before this conversation was over, she was thrilled that they didn't have anything more serious to worry about than a small difference of opinion.

"It will work, Evan," she assured him. "Dexter is doing a super job of impersonating Harry. You should have heard him on the radio yesterday. He was terrific. Not even you would have known he wasn't the author of *How To Jump-Start Your Love Life.*''

"The radio?'' Evan gasped. "Oh, crap, this is worse than I thought. Does the word fraud mean anything to you, Kylie? You can't just pick up some guy off the street and pretend he's someone else.''

"I didn't pick him up off the street,'' she countered. "I hired him from Studs-R-Us.''

"He's a gigolo?'' Evan's voice cracked over the line.

"He prefers the term male escort.''

"I don't care what he prefers! In the first place, he has no business pretending to be an author. In the second place, I'm not crazy about the idea of my big sister spending day and night with a gigolo.''

"We have separate hotel rooms.''

"And that's supposed to make me feel better? Especially since I got a call last night from some reporter in Cleveland wanting the inside scoop about the hot romance between one of my authors and the Handy Press publicist.''

Kylie winced. "She called you?''

"Yes. She also faxed me a copy of her article in this morning's *Plain Dealer*. Have you seen it?''

"No, I've been tied up this morning.''

"I hope you don't mean that literally.''

She blinked, shocked by her brother's innuendo. "Why would you say something like that?''

"Because according to the newspaper, you two can't keep your eyes or your hands off of each other.

This article makes it sound as if you were practically having sex in the middle of the mall.''

"That's an exaggeration," she replied, as a tingle of excitement rushed through her. If the newspaper article provoked this kind of reaction from Evan, how would the public respond? She couldn't wait to find out.

"Kylie, just come home. We can cancel the rest of the book tour. Handy Press is never going to make it into the big league. Let's just cut our losses. I really think that would be the best thing for all of us."

"No." Her refusal was immediate and automatic. She could hear the resignation in her brother's voice, but she refused to let him quit. His unwillingness to battle for what he wanted had scared her the most when he was sick. She'd been so afraid he would just give up. But he'd fought for his life. And now she was ready to fight for his business. Evan deserved success. And she'd do everything in her power to make it happen.

Evan sighed into the phone. "And what if the press finds out this book tour is all a big lie?"

"Harry Hanover wrote a great book." Kylie lowered her voice a notch as a customer passed her in the pharmacy aisle. "That's not a lie. It has the potential to become a bestseller. That's not a lie either. Handy Press is simply using Dexter as a promotional tool. If he encourages people to buy the book and they benefit from it, then what exactly is the harm?"

"I don't know, Kylie." Evan's outrage had

turned to uncertainty. "I still think it could backfire on us."

"Just leave everything to me," she assured him. "I'll make it work. I promise."

After she hung up, she found Dexter paying for his prescription eyedrops at the cash register.

"I'll take care of the bill," she said, reaching into her purse.

He stuffed the receipt in his shirt pocket. "Already done."

She was tempted to argue with him, but had already learned in their time together that Dexter could be as stubborn as Kylie herself. If he wouldn't allow her to pay for items along the way, then she'd just keep a record of all the expenses and add it to his paycheck at the end of the month. She just hoped Handy Press would have enough cash on hand to pay him. It all depended on the success of this book tour.

He looked at his watch. "We only have about twenty minutes until the book signing is due to start. Are you ready to go?"

"Are you sure you're up to it?" she asked, still concerned about pushing him too hard. She knew she could probably juggle his appearances for the next day or two, although the schedule was pretty tight.

"I'm fine," he assured her, nudging his sunglasses down his nose so she could see his gray eyes. They were still a little red, but at least he could keep them open now. "I've already put some of those drops in and they helped quite a bit."

It hit her then that he hadn't complained once, despite the fact that the conjunctivitis was her fault. She was the one who had insisted on the makeover, which included the contact lenses. He'd worn them without a single gripe until he literally couldn't keep his eyes open. In her experience, most men didn't take minor aches and pain well. Adam, her phony ex-fiancé, had once stood her up on a date to celebrate her birthday because of an ingrown toenail. But Dexter was already anxious to get back to work.

Her opinion of him went up another notch.

"All right." She smiled up at him. "Let's go make everybody wild about Harry."

DEXTER STOOD IN THE rest room of the book store, his hands braced on either side of the sink. The book signing was due to start in ten minutes and his eyes hurt so damn bad he didn't know if he could stand sitting there and smiling for the next three hours. The analgesic effect of the eyedrops had faded and he wasn't supposed to reapply them again until bedtime.

He glanced into the mirror, squinting at the bright halogen light emanating from the ceiling. It was no use. He'd have to wear his sunglasses inside the store. Pulling them out of his pocket, he slid them on his nose, the discomfort reduced substantially now that the glare of light wasn't irritating his eyes.

A soft knock sounded on the door. "Harry, are you all right?"

Kylie's voice carried a note of worry. He hated acting like such a wimp in front of her. Maybe he should have just toughed it out this morning, pretended his eyes were fine. Although she might have started getting suspicious when he started walking into walls.

He moved to the door and opened it. "I'm okay."

She looked up at him. "Your eyes hurt."

"They're fine. Just still a little sensitive to the light. Do you think it will be a problem if I wear these sunglasses during the signing?"

If she said yes, then he'd take off the sunglasses and ignore the pain. Dexter wasn't about to disappoint her. Not after she'd worked so hard to pull this thing off.

"Actually, they make you look rather mysterious," she mused. "Women like mystery. Keep them on."

He nodded, though part of him wondered if she was just saying that out of concern. "Anybody here yet?"

"Several reporters." She couldn't hide the note of excitement in her voice. "That newspaper article obviously generated some buzz. Lucky for us, it's been a slow news week in Cleveland."

He reached out and snagged her by the waist, pulling her closer. "Then I guess we'd better give them something to report."

Her eyes widened. "What are you doing?"

"Generating some buzz," he replied, then captured her mouth with his before she could tell him why this wasn't a good idea.

Dexter wanted to kiss her to distract himself from the pain in his eyes. At least, that's the excuse he told himself. She tasted like honey and cinnamon, a delicious combination that sent every nerve ending in his body into high alert. Her hands came up and curled over his biceps as if to push him away, but instead her fingers flexed on his arms, then pulled him even closer.

Her tongue slid into his mouth, catching him by surprise. Dexter had initiated this kiss, but Kylie had definitely taken control of it. He let her set the pace, aroused by the assertive movements of her tongue and her hands.

Her arms slid around his neck and a soft moan reverberated from deep in her throat. Dexter hoped she wasn't a good actress, because this moment was very real for him. The discomfort in his eyes faded with each second the kiss went on, but he couldn't say the same about the discomfort in certain other portions of his anatomy.

The flash of a camera startled them both and they pulled away from each other. Kylie's cheeks were flushed and her lips deliciously red.

Dexter swallowed once, then twice, before turning to the cameraman and giving him a grin. "Looks like you caught us."

The reporters peppered them with questions about their budding romance as they made their way to the signing table. Dexter was surprised to see a line already forming. This time he hoped it was because of Kylie's publicity stunt rather than another raffle.

Dexter sat down in the chair and picked up a pen, half wishing he and Kylie could have continued that kiss in private. Even if he couldn't let it lead anywhere.

The first customer walked up to him and laid two copies of *How To Jump-Start Your Love Life* on the table. "I'm buying one for my husband and one for my newly married son." She was a plump, middle-aged woman with bifocals propped on her nose. "I think every man in America should read this book."

Dexter signed both copies, then turned to the next customer, a young woman with books stacked so high in front of her that her face was partially concealed.

"Let me help you," he said, rising half out of his chair and taking the books out of her hands.

"Thanks," she said, after they were safely on the table. "I'm a teacher at South High School and I'm making *How To Jump-Start Your Love Life* required reading in my Sex Education class."

Kylie moved closer to the table. "Do you mind telling me how you heard about the book?"

The teacher smiled. "One of the boys had his radio tuned to an obnoxious disc jockey on some morning show before class. I demanded he turn it off, but not before I heard what Mr. Hanover said about the right way to treat a woman. Judging by the behavior of some of the kids in my school, I'm convinced they need to learn that love is about a lot more than hormones.''

A reporter sidled up the table. ''Can I quote you on that? And could you spell your name for me please?''

While the enthused teacher walked off with the reporter, Dexter finished signing her books, then turned to the next customer. An elderly man with a snow-white goatee and thick Coke-bottle glasses stood reading *How To Jump-Start Your Love Life*.

''How do you do, sir,'' Dexter said, as Kylie beamed at the growing line of customers. ''Would you like me to sign that for you?''

''I would be honored, Mr. Hanover. My name is Cooper. Cecil Cooper.'' He set the book in front of Dexter. ''There's a lady I'm courting at the local seniors center and the tips in this book might just be the ticket to get her to accept my marriage proposal.''

''Good luck, Mr. Cooper,'' Dexter said, handing him back his book.

The old man winked. ''I don't need luck. Just some privacy so I can try out some of these wonderful kissing techniques on her.''

After he left, Kylie reached over and gave Dexter a hug. ''Isn't this wonderful?'' she whispered. ''Everybody loves this book, young and old. Even teachers!''

Dexter nudged his sunglasses up on his nose. ''Maybe you should start planning some of these book signings at school assemblies and seniors centers."

Kylie got a speculative gleam in her eyes. "That's not a bad idea."

Dexter smiled, then turned to the next customer. She was young and on the thin side, with her strawberry-blond hair drawn back into a simple ponytail. She wore a loose-fitting black sweatshirt and matching sweatpants and held *How To Jump Start Your Love Life* clutched to her chest. Oddly enough, she also wore sunglasses. Perhaps conjunctivitis was more common than he'd realized.

"Can this book really help me?" she asked, her voice so soft he could barely discern her words.

Something in the woman's tone made Dexter hesitate. If he had to define it, he'd call it desperation. "You need help?"

She stepped closer to the table and lowered her voice another notch. "I just want something that tells me how to make my husband love me more. I've tried everything, but he still gets so frustrated with me sometimes...."

Uneasiness stirred in Dexter's gut. "And what does your husband do when he gets frustrated?"

"Sometimes he loses his temper. He's always been very...emotional." She held on to the book like a lifeline. "If I can just figure out some ways not to make him so angry, I think it will help our marriage."

Dexter knew the woman didn't suffer from conjunctivitis. Her condition was much worse. "Has he ever hit you?"

She swallowed convulsively. "No. Hardly ever. And only if I do something to really make him mad. He tries to be patient, but he's under a lot of stress at work."

Dexter could feel Kylie tense beside him. She knew, too, that this woman needed more than the newest fad book on injecting a little romance into your life. He cleared his throat. "Have you ever talked with anyone about your…problem?"

She shook her head. "No. But lately it seems to be getting worse. So when I read about you in the newspaper, I thought your book might be able to help me."

"What's your name?" he asked gently.

"Debbie." She licked her pale lips. "Debbie Gunderson."

"Debbie, I'm going to let you take that book home with you for free," he said, reaching for a promotional bookmark. "But you have to promise to do something for me. Are you a woman who keeps your word?"

"Always," she said without hesitation. "My mother always said people can take everything away from you but your word. It's the most important thing you have."

Dexter wrote a name and phone number on the bookmark. "I want you to call the woman at this number. Her name is Michelle Parr. She's a lawyer and a friend of mine. I know she'll want to talk to you."

Debbie took the bookmark, but looked uneasy. "Why would she want to talk to me? She doesn't even know me."

"Because she volunteers for a foundation that helps women who have problems like yours. I think she'll help you even more than my book. Just tell her what you've told me today."

Michelle worked on the legal team of the Kane Corporation and she and Dexter had co-chaired a charity drive for battered women shelters. He'd been impressed with her highly successful methods of convincing abused women to leave hopeless, destructive relationships and make new lives for themselves.

"Okay," Debbie said tentatively.

"Promise me," Dexter insisted.

Debbie took a deep breath. "I'll call her. I promise."

After the woman left, Kylie turned to him, tears shining in her brown eyes. "You were perfect."

He nodded, his chest tight. "I hate men that make a woman feel like that. Ashamed. Helpless. It's a sick power trip."

"Is this Michelle you referred her to one of you regular clients?"

"No, she works with me," Dexter replied, then realized Kylie meant a client at Studs-R-Us, not the Kane Corporation. But his answer seemed to satisfy her anyway. No doubt she assumed Studs-R-Us employed female escorts, too.

Dexter looked around the bookstore as the next customer approached the table. "What happened to that reporter?"

Kylie shrugged. "He was just here a minute ago. Maybe he had to meet a deadline."

"Do you think the paper will do another story on us?"

Kylie held up both hands, her fingers crossed. "We can only hope. The teacher angle was a good one. And his photographer got a picture of us kissing. I guess we'll find out when the morning paper hits the stands."

9

THE SHRILL RING OF THE telephone woke Dexter out of a sound sleep the next morning. He pulled the pillow over his head as sunlight streamed through the curtains drawn over hotel room window. His eyelids scraped like sandpaper over his sore eyes and a dull headache throbbed just behind his left temple. He and Kylie had stayed up late last night with a bottle of champagne to celebrate the success of the book signing.

The telephone rang again. He reached out from under the pillow and fumbled for the receiver, knocking it off of the cradle. It clanked against the nightstand before he wrapped it in his grip and pulled it under the pillow. "Hello?"

"May I speak to Harry Hanover, please?"

"Who?" he asked, his voice rough. Then it clicked. "Oh, Hanover. Yeah, Harry Hanover. That's me."

"Mr. Hanover, this is Paige Miller from the 'CBS Morning Show'. We'd like to extend an invitation for you to appear on our program tomorrow, via satellite, from our local Ohio affiliate station."

He sat up in bed, wondering if he was still half asleep. Had she really said the "CBS Morning Show"?

"Kylie Timberlake is in charge of scheduling all the media appearances. You really need to talk directly with her."

He heard a frustrated sigh over the line. "Ms. Timberlake's phone has been busy for the last hour. If you could just give us a verbal commitment, we can fax a contract to your hotel in Cleveland. Ms. Timberlake can then negotiate any details she wishes."

"I can't commit to anything without Kylie's approval," he replied, wondering why the woman was pushing.

"Can you at least tell me if you've already agreed to appear on a rival network?"

"I haven't even eaten breakfast yet," he said, squinting at the digital clock next to the bed.

The woman was instantly contrite. "I'm sorry to have disturbed you so early, Mr. Hanover. Our station will be happy to send you a complimentary fruit basket for any inconvenience we may have caused you. And I can promise that you will get star treatment if you agree to appear on our show."

He reached for the pencil and notepad next to the telephone. "I'll take your number and have Kylie give you a call."

She tried to push for a definite commitment, but finally gave up and recited her telephone number, along with once again emphasizing the urgency of her request.

Dexter had just hung up the telephone when the

adjoining door to his room flew open and Kylie rushed inside.

"Did you see it?" she exclaimed, her pink silk robe billowing around her.

"See what?" he asked, too enamored of the way her hair fell in unruly waves around her head to even comprehend her question. She looked as if she'd just gotten out of bed.

"The newspaper?" She unfolded the morning edition of the *Plain Dealer* and held it in front of her so he could read the bold headline.

"Love Mechanic Repairs Abusive Relationship." His brow furrowed. "What's that all about?"

"That woman in the bookstore," Kylie replied. "Debbie Gunderson. The reporter must have overheard your conversation. She's referred to as Jane Doe in the article, but he quoted everything you said as well as your advice about calling Michelle Parr. There's another story on her in here, too. She works for some company that started a foundation to help battered woman."

Dexter didn't tell her that company was the Kane Corporation. Soon to belong to him, if he didn't blow it. And he'd never been so tempted to blow it as at this moment. He could glimpse Kylie's nightgown through the opening of her robe. It was a satin pink number that clung to her delectable curves and was cut low enough to reveal the creamy expanse of her cleavage.

She followed his gaze, then pulled her robe together, her cheeks flushed. "I'm sorry."

"I'm not. You're a beautiful woman, Kylie."

She smiled. "I'll bet you say that to all the girls. Especially since you're a professional gigolo."

"You don't believe me?"

"I believe you're in the business to make women feel good. And I'll give you credit, Harry, you're certainly much better at it than I ever anticipated. But we don't have to pretend anymore."

He got an empty feeling in his gut at the thought of never kissing her again. "Even in front of the cameras?"

She gave a small shrug, not quite meeting his gaze. "I think our focus should be on this new angle. I've had twelve calls already this morning from media outlets interested in interviews and feature stories about you and *How To Jump-Start Your Love Life.*"

"Oh, that reminds me. A woman from the 'CBS Morning Show' called and wants me to appear on their program via satellite. I told her you'd return the call."

Kylie blinked. "'The CBS Morning Show?'"

"That's right." He reached over to the nightstand and handed her the number. "She's a producer. Her name is Paige Miller."

"'The CBS Morning Show,'" she said again, her voice cracking. Then she bent over at the waist, her hands on her knees. "I can't breathe so good."

"Sit down." Dexter reached out and pulled her down onto the edge of the mattress. "Now put your head between your knees."

She did as instructed until her breathing resumed a normal rhythm. Then she sat up and turned to face him, her brown eyes wide and her face pale. "I don't believe it. This is it. This is the big break I've been dreaming about for Handy Press. For Evan. We're talking national exposure here."

He smiled. "So this is a good thing. I was worried there for a minute when you looked as if you were going to faint."

"I've never fainted in my life," she assured him, as color flowed back into her cheeks. "It's just that this is all coming together so fast. We're barely half-way into this book tour and look at everything that's happened already."

He studied her face. "Are you sure this is a good thing?"

Her brows drew together. "What do you mean?"

He hated to put a damper on her jubilation, but his pragmatic side couldn't help but see the possible consequences of national fame. "What if all these reporters start digging deeper into Harry Hanover's life? What if they find out I'm not really Harry Hanover?"

Her smile faded. "That would be a disaster."

"Damn straight. So we need to figure out how to keep that from happening."

"I'll write up a bio," Kylie announced. "And make it available to all the press. I'll call Harry this morning and get all the interesting details about his life. We'll put it all out in the open. Then maybe the media won't be so inclined to go digging for it."

"Just make sure you show it to me first, in case I'm questioned about it."

"Definitely." Then she looked up at him, her eye gleaming. "I don't know how to thank you, Harry." She reached out one hand and laid it on his bare chest. "This is all because of that wonderful advice you gave to that poor woman. All because of you."

His breath hitched at her touch. Suddenly, he was all too aware that he was alone in a hotel room with the woman he'd been dreaming about almost every night since they'd met. She was on his bed, and precariously close to finding herself *in* his bed.

His gaze fell to her full lips, then to the graceful curve of her neck. His heartbeat kicked up a notch when he saw how her silk robe had fallen open again, revealing the delicate lace adorning the bodice of her nightgown.

He leaned forward and saw her eyes widen and her lips part. If he kissed her now, he couldn't pretend it was to practice the kissing lessons in chapter three of the book. Or for the benefit of the media. Kissing Kylie now could change everything between them. Worse, it could ultimately result in his losing the Kane Corporation.

Did he really want to take that chance?

He pulled back, confusion and desire warring within him. "You'd better go back to your room."

She stood abruptly, pulling her robe more tightly around her. "You're right. I have a lot of calls to make."

He took a slow, deep breath, willing himself not

think about the more pleasurable consequence he just denied himself. There was no reason to think Kylie wanted him. She might be attracted to the new and improved Harry, but she didn't even know the real Dexter Kane. The one who wanted to pull her into his arms and make her forget the book tour and the media and any man but him.

Nineteen more days to go.

Kylie stopped by the door, the sunlight penetrating through her thin lingerie to give him a perfect view of her silhouette. "Oh, Harry, one more thing."

He swallowed, wondering if she was trying to torture him. "What?"

"I owe you for this. If there's ever anything I can do for you. Anything at all, just ask."

He nodded, biting down hard on the inside of his mouth to keep from telling her exactly what he wanted. When she finally disappeared behind the door, he flopped back against the pillows and closed his eyes. He'd been dreaming about owning the Kane Corporation his entire life. But now he wondered if it could ever come close to making him feel the way Kylie made him feel.

And if it was worth the sacrifice.

THE NEXT WEEK PASSED IN a blur for Kylie. Her right ear literally ached from all the time she spent on the telephone. But the rewards definitely made it worth the pain.

Harry Hanover was a hit.

He appeared on radio and television talk shows both day and night. Newspapers wrote full-length feature articles on him. And bookstores everywhere sold out of *How To Jump-Start Your Love Life*.

She'd tried to contact her brother yesterday to suggest he do a second print run of the book as soon as possible. According to the local distributors she'd spoken with, the demand was unprecedented for a book from a small press. But Evan hadn't been in the office and so far, hadn't returned any of her telephone calls.

Now on this early Wednesday morning, she stood in the control room of the biggest radio station in Youngstown, Ohio, waiting for Dexter to finish up his latest appearance. It was a call-in show hosted by a female therapist who gushed over both Dexter and the book. So far, the woman had found an excuse to touch him twenty-seven times.

Not that Kylie was counting.

But despite the woman's hands-on approach to her radio show, the incoming calls had been running eight-to-one in support of *How To Jump-Start Your Love Life*. The positive buzz had definitely taken on a life of its own.

Kylie knew she should be happy about it. But the increased publicity had shortened the amount of time she and Dexter spent alone together. If she didn't know better, she'd almost think he'd been avoiding her since that morning in his hotel room when she thought he was going to kiss her. Or had that just been wishful thinking on her part?

She'd been doing too much wishful thinking lately. Wishing Dexter wasn't a gigolo. Wishing they had more time left together. Wishing she could trust her own heart. But she'd been burned too many times in Hollywood by perennial playboys who talked a good line until your back was turned. How could she know for certain that Dexter was any different?

Because you can see his soul in his eyes. The words appeared in her mind almost as if someone had spoken them aloud. And she knew in her heart it was true. Kylie had never had that kind of connection with a man before. She'd tried to deny it at first, but it had only grown stronger in the time they'd spent together on the road. But could she really trust her heart?

All her past mistakes with men jumbled together, forming one big red light. She'd acted on her feelings before and found out the hard way that they were one-sided. So this time she intended to keep her mouth—and her heart—shut until Dexter made the first move.

"We've got time for one more call." The therapist punched a flashing button on the panel. "Welcome to 'Love Lines'. You're on the air with our guest, Harry Hanover."

"Hi, Harry." The voice was low and smoky, obviously that of a woman. "This is Delores."

Dexter reached up to adjust his headset. "It's a pleasure to talk to you, Delores."

"Do you have a question for Mr. Hanover?" the therapist prodded, one eye on the clock.

"I certainly do. I've been a big, big fan of Mr. Hanover's for many years. In fact, I'm wondering if he recognizes my voice."

Kylie saw Dexter's eyes flick toward her. She shrugged her shoulders, hoping he could improvise for the last thirty seconds showing on the program clock.

"I'm so glad you've enjoyed my work," Dexter hedged.

"Oh, I've enjoyed much more than your work, Harry. We share so many wonderful memories."

Kylie glanced at the clock. *Ten seconds.* She had a sinking sensation in the pit of her stomach.

"You do sound a little familiar," Dexter improvised.

"That's because I'm not just your fan, Harry," the caller said, her voice sure and smug. "I'm your wife."

10

"IT WAS JUST A CRAZY PRANK," Kylie said, when they reached Dexter's hotel room. "It has to be."

He slipped the key card into the slot, then opened the door. "Maybe. But she didn't sound crazy. Or unsure of herself."

She held the cell phone up to her ear. "Harry's still not answering his phone."

Dexter swung the door to his hotel room and Kylie walked inside. She stopped so fast that Dexter bumped into her. He reached out to grab her shoulders before she hit the ground.

"Are you all right?" he asked.

"Harry," she said, her voice a little breathless. "Look."

He followed her gaze to the bulging mailbags surrounding his bed. "What is it?"

"Fan mail." She turned around and grinned up at him. "It's official. You're a hit!"

He stared into her big brown eyes, then unconsciously took a step closer to her. The smile faded from her face and he heard the quick intake of her breath. He was tired of playing the part of Harry Hanover. Tired of pretending that he wasn't attracted to Kylie. Tired of playing the game.

He circled his arms around her and pulled her tightly against his body. A low groan rumbled from his throat as he satisfied the desire that had been building inside of him ever since their last kiss. Her body felt soft and supple against him. Just right.

Kylie's head tilted back and her lips parted, giving him access to her delectable mouth. He leaned down to kiss her, savoring the taste of her. Inhaling the scent of her skin and her hair. His hands molded to her slender waist, barely resisting the impulse to explore uncharted territory.

But when she moaned low in her throat, a sound that was both an invitation and a plea, Dexter couldn't resist anymore. His palms slid over her ribs, then cupped her breasts.

Kylie leaned into him, her fingers flexing on his biceps. Dexter had never felt so hungry for a woman before. So out of control. He wanted to touch and taste every inch of her. He broke the kiss, then swung her up into his arms and carried her to the bed.

Her eyes widened as he lowered her to the mattress, then she circled her arms around his neck and pulled him on top of her. Dexter moaned at the sensation of her body beneath his. They fit perfectly.

"Kiss me," she whispered. "Kiss me like you never want to stop."

Dexter complied with her wish, realizing he couldn't stop. For the first time he understood how the power of addiction must feel. His craving for Kylie was insatiable. Nothing else mattered. He kissed her lips, her cheeks, her silky eyebrows. His hands never stopped moving over her body, his desire heightened by the soft, sexy sounds she made in the back of her throat.

Her fingers found the buttons of his shirt, hastily slipping them out of the buttonholes until it gaped open far enough for her to splay her slender hands over his bare chest.

He tore his shirt off, and for the first time in his life, flung it to the floor. He didn't care about wrinkles. All he cared about was Kylie touching him. Everywhere.

She reached out to kiss him, one palm sliding around the back his neck, her fingers tangling in his hair. "Oh, Harry. I want you so much."

Harry. He froze, his desire fading with the realization that she didn't want Dexter Kane. She wanted Harry. The man she'd created. The man who didn't really exist. How many times had he been attracted to a woman, only to find she wanted another man—his brother—instead?

"What's wrong?" she whispered, her brows furrowed as he held himself stiffly above her.

"Nothing," he bit out. Then he rolled away from her and climbed off the bed.

"Harry?"

Dexter didn't reply or even turn around. He just walked straight to the bathroom and closed the door behind him. His body still pulsed with need for Kylie. Bracing his hands on the porcelain sink, he stared into the mirror. He'd almost risked everything for a woman who didn't really want him. She wanted a mirage.

He took a deep breath, realizing how close he'd come to breaking his employer's cardinal rule. Not to mention his own. Years ago, when yet another woman had shown her preference for Sam over him, he'd tried to change his style. Endeavored to be more like his brother. Charming, easy-going, carefree.

And failed miserably.

That's when he'd vowed never to let anyone or anything try to change him again. He was Dexter Dependable Kane. And proud of it. He just wished Kylie could be proud of him, too. Wished she really wanted him instead of the phony Harry Hanover.

A wish that didn't have a chance in hell of coming true.

KYLIE LAY ON THE BED for ten minutes before she realized that Dexter wasn't coming back. At first, she thought he'd bolted into the bathroom in search of birth control. But the sound of the shower running had quickly dissuaded her of that notion.

She sat up, more confused than ever. When Dexter had kissed her, all common sense fled. She'd wanted him with a passion she'd never felt before. And he'd wanted her. That was a fact he hadn't been able to hide. And then...

And then he'd simply stopped.

She chewed on her lower lip, wondering if this was some ploy on the part of gigolos that she didn't know about. Leave the client wanting more? Only when Dexter had been kissing her, she hadn't thought of him as a gigolo. He'd simply been a man. Her man. Her Dexter.

Kylie smoothed back her tousled hair, growing angry with herself. Dexter didn't belong to her. He'd been with hordes of women. Most of whom probably had more experience than her. Was that the problem? Had he simply decided she wasn't worth his time?

Her cheeks burned when she remembered the way she'd melted under his touch. The big, dumb, handsome jerk had turned her to mush. Then he'd just left her wanting more. Wanting so much more.

Kylie heard the sound of the shower turn off, then hastily straightened her clothes. She wouldn't let him know how much his desertion bothered her. Dexter wasn't the only one who could play games.

By the time he emerged from the bathroom, Kylie had straightened her hair and clothing and was calmly seated at the small table by the window, reviewing the fan mail. He wore only a pair of blue jeans, his wet hair slicked back on his head and his bare chest still noticeably damp from his shower. She swallowed hard and forced herself to look away.

Dexter adjusted his glasses. "I didn't realize you'd still be here."

"I wanted to take a look at your fan mail." She reached for an envelope and slit open the seal with more care than necessary. She didn't want to discuss what had just happened between them. Or hear his lame excuses about why he didn't want her.

"Anything good?" he asked, walking over to the table. Fortunately, he seemed just as willing to ignore their short outburst of lust.

"All of them are good," she replied, shuffling through the letters. The scent of his aftershave wafted toward her and her mouth grew dry. He smelled as good as she knew he tasted. A virtual beefcake buffet.

She cleared her throat as she pulled a handful of letters from the pile. "Here. Have a look."

Dexter took a seat across from her at the table, then read the first letter aloud. *"I'm so hot for you, Harry. You can rev my engine anytime. Love, Kiki."*

"That one included a picture," Kylie said, sorting through the envelopes.

"Where is it?"

"I threw it away. Kiki forgot to put her clothes on for the photo. But you can dig it out of the trash can if you're interested."

"I think I'll pass," he said, picking up another letter.

"My dearest Harry," Dexter began reading aloud. *"You're the man of my dreams. I sleep with your book under my pillow and hope someday we can meet in person so you can jump-start my love life."* He flipped the letter over in his hand. "She didn't sign it."

"How do we know the writer is a *she?*" Kylie asked.

Dexter frowned at her. "Very funny."

"Here's another one." She handed him a pink letter from the pile.

"You're the perfect man, Harry. Witty, charming and handsome. Almost too good to be true." He tossed the letter on the table. "I've read enough."

She looked up at him. "What's wrong?"

"What's wrong is that Harry Hanover doesn't exist. At least, not this plastic model you've turned me into. These women are looking for an ideal. But no man is perfect. I think we're doing them a disservice by pretending that I'm the perfect man."

She blinked at him. "You're upset."

"Damn right I'm upset. Maybe *I* should write a book. Maybe the women of the world would be interested to know how some men really think."

"How?" she asked, mesmerized by his intensity. This was a side of Dexter she'd never seen before. One she found oddly appealing.

"Well, take my brother, Sam, for instance. He's everything you want me to pretend to be. Charming. Fun. Romantic. Every woman's dream. Only he's got a very short attention span. I've seen him go out with three different women on the same night. He's always certain the perfect woman is just around the corner. And he's bound and determined to run after her as soon as he kisses his current woman goodnight."

"Not all men are two-timers," she countered, though her own dating experiences proved otherwise. "Are they?"

He shook his head. "You've got it all wrong. Sam isn't a two-timer. He never makes any promises. But the women he attracts read all kinds of things into his words and his actions. They want so badly to believe he's the one, that they don't realize he's already moved on."

"Sounds like he's a real jerk."

"Actually, he's great. Everybody loves him. Including me. And there's not one woman he's dated who wouldn't go out with him again if he asked. Although, Sam makes it a practice never to date the same woman for very long."

"And what about you?"

"Me? Or Harry?"

She wrinkled her brow. "What are you talking about?"

"Forget it."

"No. I want to know."

He sighed. "I just wonder if you really want my opinion, or the opinion you think Harry would have."

"Yours," she said, wondering why he suddenly seemed so sensitive about playing the part of Harry Hanover. It had never bothered him before. "I want yours."

He stared at her for a long moment. "When I find the right woman, she'll be the only woman in my life. Forever."

"Is that why you're a gigolo? Because you're searching for that one, right woman?"

"Not exactly," he hedged, picking up another envelope off the table. He tore it open, then pulled out the letter, signaling their discussion was over.

Kylie stared at him, wondering if she'd ever figure him out. He seemed disgusted with playboys, yet he'd practically made it his profession. But she truly believed him when he said he was looking for one woman. *The right woman.* And Kylie couldn't help but envy her, whoever she might be.

He frowned as his gaze scanned the letter. Then he looked up at her. "I think we have a problem."

"Your first hate mail?"

"Worse. It's from that woman."

Kylie wrinkled her brow. "What woman?"

"The woman who called the radio show this morning claiming to be Harry Hanover's wife. Delores. She wants to meet us. And she wants us to bring lots of money."

———————

"I THINK THIS IS A MISTAKE." Dexter sat across from Kylie in the corner booth of a truck stop just outside of Youngstown. Honky-tonk music blared from a jukebox and a ceiling fan whirred noisily above them. They were the only two people sitting in the row of booths in the narrow diner. Truckers filled the stools at the counter, hunched over the blue plate special of spaghetti, garlic bread and lima beans.

Dexter had ordered a slice of homemade peach pie, but his gut was too tied up in knots to eat it. He had to find some way to convince Kylie that this was a bad idea.

"We've got to at least meet her," she replied, picking up her fork and reaching over to nab a bite of Dexter's pie. "Find out if she's telling the truth."

He scooted the pie plate closer to her. "You're planning to take the word of an extortionist?"

"I'm hoping to prove she's a fraud." Kylie reached out to fork off another bite of pie. "I still can't reach Harry, but I had Evan fax me the man's bio and there's not a wife mentioned anywhere. She has to be lying."

Dexter leaned forward. "I think we should just ignore her."

"Now *that* would be a big mistake. What if she goes to the newspapers? Can you imagine the publicity?"

"If she's lying, they won't print the story."

She rolled her eyes. "You don't know the media. All they need is a whiff of a scandal about this mysterious Mrs. Hanover to print it. Harry Hanover has become a household name around here. The only thing the press likes better than building someone up is tearing them down."

"And what if it's true?" he challenged. "What if Harry really does have a wife? Do you think we can convince her to keep it a secret?"

Kylie nibbled her lower lip. "It can't be true. I'm sure Harry would have told me. If it is...then I guess we'll both be out of a job."

Dexter's eyes darkened. "That can't happen."

Kylie leaned toward him across the table. "Look, I don't believe this Delores woman is really Harry's wife. But if she is, we need to find out before the press does. Especially after the way we publicized our supposed romance. Finding out that the author of *How To Jump-Start Your Love Life* is a lying two-timer isn't going to sell many books. In fact, it very well might tank my brother's business."

Dexter's gaze wavered, then fixed over her shoulder. "I think she's here."

Kylie turned to see a flashy redhead in a snug, green polyester pantsuit walking toward them. She wore too much makeup and held a cigarette in one hand, oblivious to the No Smoking signs posted on the walls. But even more disturbing than the cigarette was the ring on her left hand. With a diamond the size of a basketball.

The redhead stopped at their table, her thin lips curved into a lascivious smile as she ogled Dexter. "Hi, honey. You're looking better than ever."

Dexter stood up. "You must be Delores."

"Smart as ever," she replied, sidling into the booth next to him.

Kylie couldn't wait to blast this woman out of the water. Delores couldn't be married to Harry Hanover because she didn't even realize that Dexter wasn't the real Harry. Her anxiety dissolved and she flashed Dexter a reassuring smile.

"Anybody want a beer?" Delores asked, hailing the waitress.

"No, thank you," Kylie asked, then got right to the point. "How exactly did you and Harry meet?"

Delores placed her order with the waitress, then turned to answer Kylie's question. "It was love at first sight. I brought my car into his repair shop for a tune-up." She took a long drag from her cigarette. "The rest, as they say, is history."

Kylie smiled. "It sounds more like fiction to me."

Delores returned her smile, looking as confident as ever. "It *was* like a storybook romance. We dated for three weeks, then eloped to Reno and were married at the Ding Dong Wedding Chapel by an Elvis impersonator. He sang the most beautiful rendition of 'Love Me Tender.'"

Dexter pushed away his pie plate. "Maybe we should talk about your letter."

Delores leaned back, both arms outstretched across the top of the booth. "To tell you the truth, I didn't expect to hear from you so quickly. Although, the sooner we can come to some kind of arrangement, the better off we'll all be."

He frowned. "You do realize this arrangement you're talking about is blackmail. And that it's a felony."

Delores looked at Kylie, chuckling under her breath. "Harry knows all about felonies. Automobile repair and romance aren't his only areas of expertise."

Time to put an end to this nonsense once and for all.

Kylie leaned forward. "We're calling your bluff, Delores. We all know you were never married to Harry."

"No," Delores said calmly. "What we all know is that this man isn't really Harry Hanover."

Kylie blinked, panic welling inside of her. "I don't know what you're talking about."

"Oh, I think you do." She took another long drag from her cigarette, then blew a stream of smoke in the air above her. "I told you I was married to Harry, but I never said this hunk was the same man. I'll admit he's a lot sexier, but he's not the real Harry Hanover. I knew it didn't sound like Harry on the radio, but I had to see him in person to be sure."

"That's quite an accusation. Can you prove it?"

Kylie wished she'd listened to Dexter and never agreed to meet this woman. She felt as if the faded linoleum floor was shifting underneath her feet.

"I've got wedding pictures and a marriage license. I've also got a signed copy of Harry's first book, *Spark Plugs and You*. I'm sure a handwriting expert would be happy to compare the signatures."

Dexter cleared his throat. "I don't think that will be necessary."

Delores turned and waggled her red eyebrows at him. "I'm glad to hear it. I'm sure we can come up with an arrangement that is mutually satisfying."

"What do you want?" Kylie asked baldly.

Delores took another long drag on her cigarette. "Ten thousand dollars."

Kylie's jaw dropped. "That's outrageous!"

Delores blew a lungful of smoke at her. "That's peanuts compared to what you're hauling in on this book. Look, I don't know if you're just using Harry's name because he's got a following from all his car books, or if that sly snake is behind this masquerade. The real Harry Hanover left me high and dry five years ago. So I'm not about to sit back and watch this gravy train pass me by."

Kylie looked at Dexter. "I think we should leave."

The woman gave a careless shrug. "Hey, if you don't want to pay me, I'm sure some tabloid will. I'll just sell my story to the highest bidder."

"Please don't be hasty," Dexter said. "I'm sure we can come up with something. It just might take awhile."

Kylie saw no sympathy in Delores's cold green eyes. "I don't have ten thousand dollars just lying around."

A muscle flexed in Dexter's jaw. "I do."

KYLIE FOLLOWED DEXTER into a Youngstown branch of the Wells Fargo Bank. "This is crazy. You can't give that woman your money."

"What choice do we have?" he said, approaching the front counter. "If we don't pay her, she'll go to the tabloids."

The teller behind it gave him a quick once-over, her mouth curving into a flirtatious smile. "May I help you?"

"I'd like a money order, please," he said, reaching for his wallet. He pulled out a card with his account number on it and slid it across the counter. "Make it out for ten thousand dollars to Delores Hanover."

She watched in disbelief as the teller began filling out the form.

"Dexter, what are you doing?"

He turned to look at her. "I can't afford to lose this job."

"That doesn't make any sense. Ten thousand dollars is a lot more money than you'll be paid for this job."

He turned back toward the counter. "It's worth it to me."

She stared at him, more confused than ever. Was it possible he was doing it for her? "This won't do any good, Harry. Delores won't stop here. She'll eventually want more money."

"All we need to do is hold her off for a few more days. Then it will all be over."

She took a step closer to him. "I can't let you do this."

"Here you go, sir." The teller handed the money order to Dexter. "The ten thousand dollars has been deducted from your primary account."

"Thank you." Then he turned to Kylie. "It's already done."

"Dexter..."

He clasped her elbow and pulled her to a secluded area of the foyer. "Please let me do this, Kylie. Don't you think it will be worth it to save Handy Press?"

So he was doing it for her. Kylie's heart melted. "I don't know what to say."

He leaned closer to her. "Don't say anything. And don't thank me. I have my own selfish reasons for wanting to keep Delores quiet."

"Reasons you care to share?"

He hesitated, then reached out and trailed his knuckle over her cheek. "Maybe someday."

Kylie knew she should push him for answers. But part of her was so relieved to know the Delores problem was solved, at least temporarily, that she let it go. Besides, if the sales of *How To Jump-Start Your Love Life* continued to soar, Handy Press should be able to easily reimburse Dexter. That comforting thought took the edge off of her guilt. But another thought still niggled at her.

"What if Delores isn't the only one?" she ventured.

Dexter's brow furrowed. "What do you mean?"

"I mean, what if Harry has been holding out on us. Could there be more than one ex-wife waiting in the wings, ready to sell her story to the highest bidder?"

"I suppose it's possible."

She reached up and rubbed her temple with her fingertips. The smoke from Delores's cigarette had given her a headache. "I'm going to call Harry again."

Dexter leaned against the white brick interior wall of the bank as she dialed the number on her cellular phone. She got a recorded message saying the number had been disconnected.

"No answer?"

"No," she said. "The number's been disconnected."

"Maybe he moved."

She shook her head. "This doesn't make sense. He's a hermit. He's been shut up in that house for the last six years."

"According to Delores, he was in Reno, Nevada, five years ago."

"But why would he lie about something like that?" Kylie's head began to pound. "Maybe Delores is the one lying. Maybe Harry's telephone is disconnected because he forgot to pay his bill."

"Money shouldn't be a problem with the sales of *How To Jump-Start Your Love Life* going through the roof."

"Except that Hanover Press pays royalties quarterly. He won't receive a check for two more weeks." She nibbled her lower lip as another, more ominous possibility occurred to her. "I hope he's all right. He does live all by himself in a fairly remote area."

"How remote?"

"A cabin in a wooded area in the foothills of the Alleghenies. About an hour east of Altoona."

"Which would only make it about a three-hour drive from here."

She looked up at him, wishing she'd thought of the idea first. "We don't have any book signings scheduled for tomorrow. And we're not due in Altoona until noon on Friday."

"A break might do us both good." He reached out one finger and gently traced her cheekbone. "You've got circles under your eyes."

Is that why you didn't want to sleep with me? But Kylie didn't say it out loud. It was a question she couldn't ask him without looking like a fool. Her skin tingled as his finger gently stroked her face. Then she took a step away from him, determined not to fall under his spell once more.

"Then it's settled," she said. "We're off to the Alleghenies to find Harry."

Dexter nodded. "To find the truth."

12

DEXTER PEERED OUT THE window, his brow furrowed. They'd been driving nonstop for the last five hours. "Are you sure you know where you're going?"

"Positive," Kylie said, checking the gas gauge. It was hovering perilously close to the danger zone. "I had a map last time I came out here, but I know his cabin is on this road somewhere."

The car hit a deep rut in the graveled surface, causing Dexter to bounce up and graze his head on the roof. "Are you sure this is a road?"

"Pretty sure," Kylie said, leaning over the steering wheel. The sun was starting to set, casting long shadows from the numerous fir trees bracketing both sides of the narrow road.

Dexter peered through the trees on his right. "What does his house look like?"

"It's more of a log cabin, really. With a big front porch." She steered around another sinkhole in the road. "And a big dog."

"Is the dog a Doberman pinscher?"

"How did you know?" she asked, turning toward him.

He hitched his thumb toward the window. "Because it's right over there."

She slammed on the brakes, causing Dexter to brace both hands against the dashboard.

"Finally," she cried, a note of triumph in her voice. "I knew I could find it."

They both climbed out of the car and were greeted by a low, menacing growl.

Dexter hesitated. "The dog doesn't look too happy to see us."

"Eugene is a real sweetie," Kylie said, marching through the brush toward the cabin. "He won't bite."

Dexter reluctantly followed her, hoping she knew more about Harry's dog than she knew about the man himself. Eugene's bared white teeth gleamed in the fading twilight as he watched them approach.

"Hello, Eugene," Kylie said, reaching out to ruffle the dog's thick fur coat. "How's my favorite puppy?"

Eugene's wet tongue lapped her forearm. Kylie turned to Dexter with a grin. "See, he likes me."

Dexter smiled and started forward, until the big dog whirled on him and began growling again. "I don't think Eugene likes me."

Kylie grabbed hold of the dog's thick leather collar. "I'll hang on to him until you're safely inside. If you can get inside, that is. Harry is a little…shy about receiving visitors."

Dexter didn't need any further encouragement, much more willing to face whatever obstacles Harry put in his way than Eugene's sharp fangs. He wheeled and headed up the porch steps toward the door. Venetian blinds completely concealed both windows and no sound emanated from inside the cabin.

He knocked once, then three times, his ear cocked toward the door for the sound of footsteps. Nothing. No movement, no blare from a television set or a radio. He turned back toward Kylie. "I don't think he's home."

"He has to be," she replied, scratching Eugene behind the ears. The dog had his eyes closed, ignoring Dexter now to enjoy the bliss of the moment. "Harry's agoraphobic. He never leaves his house."

Dexter turned back toward the door and tried the knob. To his surprise it wasn't locked. He let the door swing wide open, revealing a modest but neatly arranged living room. A blue-striped sofa and matching armchairs formed a cozy seating arrangement in front of a cold hearth. A small, portable television set sat propped on an old cream can. The bookcase on the east wall only had one shelf filled, all books authored by Harry Hanover. The rest of the shelves were empty but free of dust. Harry might be an eccentric hermit, but he was a neat eccentric hermit.

Kylie had left the dog and followed Dexter inside. She looked around the empty living room, her brow furrowed. "Harry?"

Her call went unanswered. She turned to Dexter. "Something's not right."

He walked toward the kitchen. It was empty, too. The old refrigerator hummed in one corner, but all the shades were pulled, shrouding it in darkness. "Looks to me like Harry made a full recovery and decided to go on vacation."

Kylie walked up behind him. "But why would he leave Eugene here alone?"

"Maybe he hired a neighbor to come over and feed and water him."

She shook her head. "You saw how few houses there were on the way up here. The nearest neighbor has to be at least three miles away." Slowly spinning on her heel, she looked around the small cabin. "I wonder if he ever gets lonely all by himself up here."

"A man can be lonely anywhere," Dexter replied. "Even in a city of over three hundred thousand people."

She nodded. "Hollywood was one of the loneliest places I've ever known."

He turned to face her, suddenly struck by how easy it was to talk to Kylie. It was an odd revelation at an even odder moment, but it suddenly occurred to him how comfortable he felt around her. That was not normal for Dexter Kane. He'd always been stiff and tongue-tied around women. Especially when it was a woman he admired. Always saying the wrong thing at the wrong moment.

Only ten more days. Then I'll never see her again. That thought created an ache deep inside his chest. Even the knowledge that his dream of owning the Kane Corporation would come true in eleven days didn't ease it.

But perhaps he could see Kylie again. They both

lived in Pittsburgh after all, They could meet for lunch. Or even date. Once he had the business firmly in his control, he'd be free to pay more attention to his social life. Although, running a multimillion dollar corporation rarely left a man with much free time on his hands. And there would be more chaos than usual with the change of ownership.

Even worse, he'd have to find some way to explain to Kylie how a gigolo could suddenly become owner and CEO of a Fortune 500 company. Which meant telling her he'd been deceiving her from the moment they'd met.

And she'd already made it perfectly clear how she felt about men who put their own interests first.

Kylie stared up at him. "Is something wrong?"

Everything. "No. Why?"

"You have a strange look on your face."

The sound of glass shattering forestalled his reply. They both bolted into the living room, then Kylie pointed toward a closed door. "I think it came from in there."

Dexter pulled her behind him. "Let me go first."

She didn't argue, but kept her hand wrapped around Dexter's arm as he slowly turned the doorknob. The door creaked open to reveal a man tied to chair. Masking tape covered his mouth. His wrists were bound together behind him, secured with the tape. Masking tape also secured each ankle to the front legs of the chair. Shards of glass covered the floor around him.

"Evan!" Kylie catapulted around Dexter, but he grabbed her before she could go to her brother.

"Wait," he commanded. "There's glass everywhere."

Evan blinked at them, relief shining in his eyes.

"Are you all right?" Kylie cried.

Her brother nodded, then made mumbling sounds through the tape.

Dexter grabbed a thick woven throw rug off the floor and tossed it on top of the splintered glass. Then he stood back while Kylie ran to her brother.

"This is going to hurt," she said, carefully peeling one corner of the tape off his cheek.

"Do it fast," Dexter advised. "It will hurt a lot more if you take your time."

She took a deep breath, then ripped the tape off of his mouth.

"Ouch," Evan exclaimed.

"Sorry," she murmured, now working to free his hands.

"It's all right," Evan assured her. "It's not as bad as that time you dropped a bowling ball on my foot."

Dexter retrieved a Swiss Army knife from his jeans pocket and carefully sliced through the thick layers of tape binding his ankles to the chair.

"How do you feel?" Kylie asked, her brow furrowed with worry.

"Stupid." Evan reached up to rub the red, irritated area around his mouth.

"What happened?" Dexter asked.

Evan looked up at him. "And you are?"

"Dexter Kane." He held out his hand. "Also known as Harry Hanover."

Evan rose unsteadily to his feet. He had Kylie's dark hair and eyes, as well as her upturned nose. But he was unnaturally thin for a man of his height. No doubt a residual effect of his illness. "So you're the guy who's been romancing my sister."

His grip was strong, despite his apparent frailty.

"It was just a publicity ploy," Kylie assured her brother, reaching up to gently brush an unruly lock of hair off of Evan's broad forehead.

Dexter watched her, wondering if she still really felt that way. It had become much more than a ploy to him. Especially after that last intimate encounter in his hotel room. What if he hadn't stopped? Would she still act so nonchalant about their relationship.

"Just a publicity ploy," Evan echoed, his gaze flicking from his sister to Dexter and back again. His tone made it obvious that he wasn't buying it. "Right."

A blush rose to Kylie's cheeks. "Look, we can talk about all that later. I want to know what happened to you. And where's Harry? Is he all right?"

Evan snorted. "Harry's long gone by now. And he's the one who did this to me."

Kylie blinked. "Why?"

"Because after you asked me to fax you his bio, I realized how sketchy it was. So I decided to do a little investigating. And I found out the real story behind the myth. Harry Hanover isn't a hermit with agoraphobia. Hell, Harry Hanover isn't even the jerk's real name. It's an alias he uses to keep from getting caught."

"Getting caught?" Kylie echoed. "I don't understand."

"The man is a con artist, sis," Evan explained. "He's been married about twenty times. And you know all those car repair manuals he wrote for Handy Press?"

"Yes."

"Well, guess what, he never wrote them. He plagiarized them. The real author is a mechanic who's been living in Europe for the past ten years, working for the Grand Prix. His wife made a visit to the States last month and bought a copy of *How To Jump-Start Your Love Life*. And guess what she saw on the cover page."

Kylie closed her eyes with a groan. "A list of all of Harry's past books?"

"That's right. The guy called yesterday and is threatening a lawsuit against us."

Her eyes flew open.

"But it's not our fault! Harry signed a contract stating that each book was his original work. He lied to us."

Dexter folded his arms across his chest. "Apparently that's the man's only true talent. But what about this latest book? Is *How To Jump-Start Your Love Life* another case of plagiarism?"

Evan shook his head. "Not according to Harry. He explained it all to me when he was taping me to the chair. His charm and charisma are the reason he persuaded all those women to marry him."

"Like Delores," Kylie murmured.

"Who's Delores?" Evan asked.

She sighed. "Never mind. It's a long story."

"Well, anyway, Harry decided to cash in on his knowledge of seducing the fairer sex by writing *How To Jump-Start Your Love Life.* Only he couldn't do the book tour because he's wanted in several states for fraud and petty larceny."

Kylie shook her head in disbelief. "You mean, we've been promoting the book of a felon?"

"That's right," Evan replied. "And it looks like Handy Press is going to pay the penalty for Harry's crimes. Once this news gets out, my business will be finished."

"Why does anyone have to know?" Kylie asked. "Maybe we can just end the book tour and keep quiet about Harry's criminal activities? Surely the police will catch him sooner or later."

"What about the plagiarism suit?" Evan asked. "Once that gets out, so will the rest of the story."

"And don't forget Delores," Dexter added. "She's one of Harry's wives. And she's determined to get a chunk of the royalties from *How To Jump-Start Your Love Life.*"

Evan raked one hand through his hair. "Can it possibly get any worse?"

"I'm afraid it can," Kylie replied. "Delores knows Dexter isn't Harry. She asked for ten thousand dollars to keep that little secret."

They all looked at each other, then Evan burst out laughing.

"What's so funny?" Kylie asked, her forehead etched in concern.

"This," he said, gasping for air as he sat down

beside her. "Us. Hell, what does it matter if Handy Press goes down the drain? And so what if the media has a field day with the scandal? We'll survive."

She reached for her brother's hand, a tender smile curving her mouth. "We've certainly survived worse."

Dexter watched them, still certain there had to be a way to save Handy Press. Just the thought of losing the Kane Corporation made his blood run cold. He couldn't let them just give up. Not when it was so important. "Maybe your business will survive this, too."

Evan shook his head. "Too late, Dexter. It's over. Once this story gets out, Handy Press will be finished."

"I disagree. Not if you're the one controlling the message."

Kylie looked thoughtful, but not too hopeful. "Maybe the public could handle the charge of plagiarism. Most people don't pay attention to those kinds of lawsuits anyway. But when they find out you've been impersonating Harry, and that the real Harry Hanover is a sleazy criminal, they won't be so understanding."

"Unless we put just the right spin on it."

Kylie looked up at him. "How?"

"I have an idea."

13

THREE DAYS LATER, DEXTER and Kylie lingered over dessert in the small bistro connected by a breezeway to their hotel. Dexter had noticed Kylie's lack of appetite during dinner, but hadn't nagged her about it. He knew she believed her brother's livelihood was hanging by a thread. And she was right.

"I hope it works," she said, swirling her spoon in the whipped cream of her brownie sundae.

"Evan seemed to like the idea," Dexter replied, pushing his cake plate away.

She smiled. "My brother is a fatalist. He believes everything happens for a reason. If he lost Handy Press, he'd just move onto something else. But I know how much his business means to him. He built it out of nothing and it's on the brink of becoming a huge success."

Dexter nodded, empathizing with her. He knew firsthand the importance of keeping a business in the family. "You've got to fight for what you want."

"Exactly." She squared her shoulders. "Okay, let's go over the plan one more time."

Despite the low lighting in the bistro, he could see the fiery sparks in her brown eyes. She was definitely a fighter. It was one of the things about her that appealed most to him. Along with her wit. Her intelligence. Her face. Her body. Her kisses.

Dexter cleared his throat, his thoughts definitely moving in the wrong direction. Along with his blood supply. This was business. Strictly business. And he knew better than anyone that nothing mattered more. He'd lived his entire life believing it.

"Tomorrow will give us the perfect opportunity to present our side of the story to the media," Dexter began. "The Stop Domestic Violence Foundation has invited me to sign books at their afternoon reception. The press will be there in full force."

She nodded. "And you'll be wearing a tuxedo, so you'll look fantastic."

"You think so?"

She blushed. "You always look fantastic, Harry. That's why all these women are crazy about you."

He stared at her for a long moment. "Considering the circumstances, maybe you shouldn't call me by that name anymore."

She shook her head. "We need to keep up the charade. At least until tomorrow."

"That's when I'll stand up and announce that I have a statement."

"No, not a statement. A surprise. We want to put a positive spin on this."

He nodded. "Okay, a surprise. I'll tell them I'm not the real Harry Hanover. That Handy Press decided to embark on a masquerade...."

"*Cleverly* decided to embark on a masquerade," Kylie interjected.

"Okay, cleverly it is. Then I'll say that we pulled this stunt to prove any man can learn how to jump-start his love life by reading Hanover's book."

"And we'll bring along all those bags full of fan mail to prove it. Testimonial after testimonial about how the book has changed peoples lives for the better."

"Good idea." He leaned back in his chair. "I'm sure the press will have some tough questions, but we'll field them as vaguely as we can. So far, no one knows about Harry's felonious past. But if that truth ever does come out, at least Handy Press won't be seen as trying to pull a fast one."

She frowned. "That's what I did, isn't it? I tried to rationalize my idea of hiring a gigolo to pretend to be Harry Hanover, but there was really no excuse for that kind of dishonesty."

"You did what you thought was right."

She smiled ruefully at him. "And just look where it got me."

Dexter reached for her hand. "This book tour hasn't been a total disaster. *How To Jump-Start Your Love Life* is still a hit."

She looked up from their clasped hands to his eyes. "This tour hasn't been at all what I expected. But then, neither have you."

Blood pounded in his veins. "What did you expect?"

She gave a small shrug of her shoulders. "All my preconceived notions about a gigolo flew out the door when I met you. I assumed I'd be hiring a cocky, swaggering egomaniac. Instead I found someone who was kind. Handsome. Generous. A little bit shy.''

"Disappointed?'' he asked, his voice barely above a whisper.

She slowly shook her head. ''Just the opposite.''

The waitress approached with the check, breaking the moment between them. Kylie signed it, then hastily got up from her chair. ''It's late and we have a big day ahead of us tomorrow.''

Dexter wasn't ready to say good night, but Kylie was already more tense than he'd ever seen her. It wouldn't be fair to pressure her at a time like this.

He stood up. ''I'm going to hit the exercise room and work off a little of this...adrenaline. Do you want me to walk you up to your room?''

She shook her head. ''No, I'll be fine. I'll see you in the morning, Harry.''

He watched her leave the bistro, wishing that just once she'd call him by his real name.

Wishing the exercise room could cure what really ailed him.

Two HOURS LATER, KYLIE stood in front of the connecting door leading to Dexter's hotel room. She'd heard the sounds of his footsteps earlier, so knew he was still awake even though it was close to midnight. She just hoped her reason for bothering him didn't seem too transparent.

She reached up and knocked on the door before she had time to chicken out. Time to remember that she'd vowed to let Dexter make the first move. Once again, Kylie was following her heart instead of her head.

The door opened and Dexter stood on the other side. He'd obviously just gotten out of the shower, judging by his wet hair and the towel wrapped around his lower body. He took more showers than any man she knew. And just like before when she'd seen him clad in only a skimpy towel, her mouth went completely dry and her head began to buzz. He was magnificent.

"Hello," he said, pushing his glasses up on his nose.

She swallowed hard. "I know it's late. I hope I'm not bothering you."

"Not at all. I couldn't sleep."

"Me either." She shoved the piece of paper in her hand toward him. "I've been working on the statement, I mean, the surprise announcement for the press. We want it to sound as polished as possible."

He took the paper from her. "Good idea. Come on in and we can rehearse it."

She followed him into his room, her legs feeling shaky. This was the craziest, most impulsive thing she'd ever done in her life. She hadn't knocked on Dexter's door because she'd wanted to rehearse his announcement.

She'd done it because she wanted him.

Kylie knew he was a gigolo. Knew she might never see him again after tomorrow. But she was tired of fighting her feelings. Despite her dismal history with men, she intuitively knew she'd regret it forever if she let Dexter slip out of her life without taking this chance.

He sat down on the bed and unfolded the sheet of notebook paper. Then he looked up at her. "It's blank."

She took a step toward him. "I know."

The paper fell out of his hand and fluttered to the floor as she moved closer. She could hear his quick intake of breath. She walked right up to him, then leaned forward, planting both hands on the bed, one on either side of his thighs. Her face was only a few inches from his own. The warmth emanating from his body made her heart race in her chest. She'd never done anything like this before. It was terrifying and exhilarating all at the same time.

"What are you doing?" he asked, his voice sounding a little strained.

"Establishing dominance." She leaned closer to him, aware of the desire that flared in his eyes. "Is it working?"

"Yes."

"Good. Because that aftershave you're wearing is driving me crazy. I think about you all the time. I want you all the time."

He swallowed. "Me...or Harry?"

"You," she said, leaning closer. "Definitely you."

His gray eyes flashed. "Then say it."

She licked her lips as her gaze fell to his mouth. "Say what?"

"My name." He moved his head to hers, his mouth a hairsbreadth from her own. "Say my name."

"Dexter," she whispered huskily. "Kiss me, Dexter."

He didn't wait for her to ask twice, clasping her in his arms and hauling her against his hard body for a soul-searing kiss. His damp skin was warm beneath her fingertips and she kneaded his broad shoulders, drawing a low moan from deep in his throat.

At last he pulled back. "Are you sure about this? About us?"

She shook her head. "I'm not sure about anything anymore, Dexter. All I know is that I want you. If you want me."

He closed his eyes and groaned, burying his face in the crook of her neck. "I want you so bad I think I'm going to explode."

She giggled. "Not yet."

Then he lifted his head and kissed her again, both of them tumbling back onto the bed. She'd wanted him for so long that all rational thought fled. All she could do was touch and taste and feel. Her hands were everywhere. So were his. It only took a moment for his towel hit the floor, and soon after so did her clothes.

He kissed the length of her body. Fervently. Reverently. She knew he probably had hordes of women in her past, but at this moment she felt like the only one in the world. The right one. Then his kisses became hotter, his caresses more intimate. She arched against his hand, wanting more. Wanting this moment between them never to end.

Dexter hovered over her, tenderly kissing her lips as his hands swept lightly across the tips of her breasts, then over her hips.

She sucked in her breath when his fingers began explore her most intimate places. "You don't know what you do to me, Dexter."

"Tell me," he said huskily.

So she did. Whispering her every desire in his ear. He fulfilled them all. And then some. Kylie closed her eyes as he worshipped her breasts with his mouth. His hands never stopped touching her, caressing her with the most exquisite tenderness. Dexter carried her higher, farther, and faster than she'd ever imagined possible.

"Wait for me," he said, fumbling for a condom in the nightstand. Then he was with her again. Inside of her. Part of her. She wrapped her arms around him, both of them soaring beyond thought and reason.

"I love you, Kylie," he whispered in her ear as he rocked against her.

"Dexter," she cried out, as her world exploded into a million bursts of light. Then the free fall began and she closed her eyes, lost in the pulsing, swirling ecstasy of the moment.

He collapsed against her, his breathed ragged. She held his body firmly to her, savoring the weight of him and way they fit so perfectly together. No matter what had happened before and what might happen in the future, he was hers in this moment. She lifted her head far enough to place a gentle kiss on his jaw, then whispered the words burning in her throat. "My Dexter. My love."

14

THE NEXT MORNING, Dexter lay in bed with his arms wrapped around Kylie's warm, supple body. The first rays of the sun were just beginning to peek through the window drapes. They'd made love all through the night, but he felt more exhilarated than exhausted.

A light tapping sounded on the hotel room door. Dexter carefully extricated himself from Kylie's embrace, then slipped on his terry-cloth robe and padded quietly to the door. He'd ordered room service a half hour ago, certain Kylie would be as famished as he was when she woke up.

He opened the door and picked up the tray off the floor, savoring the aroma of fresh-baked rolls wafting up from the covered platter. Carrying the tray back into the room, he glanced at Kylie and smiled. She hadn't moved a muscle, still fast asleep. Just the sight of her bare shoulders peeking over the white cotton sheet made his blood heat in his veins. She was the most incredible woman he'd ever met. Both in bed and out of bed.

Dexter quietly set the tray on the table, deciding breakfast could wait since he had in mind a more appetizing way in mind to wake Kylie. But a small envelope tucked in the top corner of the tray caught his attention. His name was neatly typed on the front of the envelope. Not Harry Hanover, the name he'd used to register at the hotel, but his real name— Dexter D. Kane.

Frowning, he picked up the envelope and broke the seal, drawing out the small card inside. It was a game card, exactly the same design as the ones used in the Chameleon board game. And this one had specific instructions on it. Instructions he must follow if he wanted to win the game.

> Go to the ferris wheel at Lakemont Park at exactly 9 a.m. Look for an operative wearing a blue coat and ask this question: What's the secret of winning the game?

The instructions on the game card made no sense, which wasn't exactly a surprise since his eccentric grandfather was involved. This must be one of the "surprises" Amos had mentioned. Dexter just hoped the answer to the question didn't involve more running around. His plan to spend the morning in bed with Kylie evaporated, although the urge to toss the game card into the trash was almost overwhelming. But he knew he couldn't ignore the summons. Not when his lifelong dream was at stake.

"Damn," Dexter muttered under his breath, glancing from the game card to Kylie. He barely had enough time to dress and make it to the park in time.

He threw on his clothes, choosing the gray flannel

suit he'd worn his first day on the job at Studs-R-Us rather than his Harry Hanover outfit. The errand would be completed much more quickly if no one recognized him. He slipped on his glasses, then paused long enough to scribble a quick note to Kylie, promising to be back soon. They'd have a few hours to spend together before the book signing this afternoon. Perhaps by then he'd have figured out some way to explain his brief disappearing act. He couldn't tell her the truth yet. Not while he was still playing the game.

He laid the note on his pillow, struck again by her wholesome beauty. But he resisted the urge to lean down and kiss her. She'd been exhausted these last few days and needed to sleep. Besides, if Dexter had his way, he'd be able to spend the rest of his life kissing her.

But first things first.

KYLIE WRAPPED HER ARMS around the pillow, sighing into the plump softness as she slowly awoke. Her body felt exquisitely relaxed under the warmth of the bedcovers and thoroughly rested for the first time in weeks.

All because of Dexter.

She smiled to herself as she remembered their heated embraces of the night before. He definitely didn't need romance lessons from Harry or anyone else. Her Dexter was just right.

Perfect, in fact.

She reached out for him, but couldn't find his

warm, hard body on the other side of the bed. Half-sitting up in bed, she blinked at the rumpled bedclothes and empty pillow.

Then she saw the note.

Tamping down the first wave of uneasiness, she picked it up and read it.

Had to go out for a while, but I ordered breakfast for you. I'll be back as soon as I can. Go ahead and eat without me.

Yours,
Dexter

She smiled at his thoughtfulness. She'd taken the biggest risk of her life last night, but instead of screwing up like she usually did, she'd found the love of her life.

Feeling energized, she hopped out of bed and put on Dexter's robe. Then she moved toward the table, lifting the silver lid off the big porcelain platter to see an enticing array of fresh croissants and muffins, along with an assortment of jams and jellies. She slid into the chair, her stomach rumbling, and reached for a cornbread muffin.

As she slathered strawberry jelly across one half of the muffin, she wondered where exactly Dexter had to go at this hour of the morning. And why he hadn't mentioned it last night. It would have been nice to wake up together. To share breakfast and blushes on the first day of their new life together.

"Hold it," she admonished herself aloud.

"You're getting ahead of yourself again. Dexter didn't say anything about a future together."

But after last night, she couldn't imagine her life any other way. She and Dexter belonged together. Still, prickles of uneasiness assailed her as she bit into the muffin. Building a life together wouldn't be easy. For starters, Dexter would have to give up his job at Studs-R-Us. She'd told herself his past didn't matter, but it did bother her to think of him with all those women. Had last night been special for him? Or just like any other job?

She put down her muffin, suddenly losing her appetite. She hated these doubts, knowing her past and her insecurities about men were to blame. If only Dexter had been here when she woke up. Her imagination always tended to run away with her when she had too much time alone to think.

A knock on the hotel room door made her heart jump in her chest. *Dexter.* She smiled to herself as she hurried toward the door. He probably forgot his key. She knew that as soon as she saw him, as soon as he held her in his arms, all her fears would disappear.

Her hand grasped the doorknob, then she hesitated, too safety savvy to open the door before she knew for certain who was behind it. She quickly finger-combed her hair, wishing she'd had time to put on a touch of makeup before seeing Dexter this morning. She wanted to look perfect for him.

Another knock sounded, louder this time.

Her heart beat a rapid tattoo in her chest and her

body began to tingle at the anticipation of Dexter holding her again. "Who's there?"

"Police. We'd like to ask you a few questions."

DEXTER RACED BACK TO THE HOTEL, furious with his grandfather for sending him on a wild-goose chase. He'd spent the last two hours at the park, approaching strangers wearing blue coats and asking them for the secret to winning the game. One woman had fled in terror, three people had made rude comments, and one had waved down a security officer who had strongly suggested Dexter leave the amusement park immediately.

Unable to flag down a taxi, he'd jogged the twenty blocks back to the hotel. Now out of breath, he paused by the side entrance to check his watch. He'd have just enough time to change into his Harry Hanover clothes and insert his contact lenses before the luncheon. And to kiss Kylie. From now on, he'd always make time for that.

Straightening his tie, he walked into the hotel lobby, already milling with crowds of people. Three hundred guests were scheduled to attend the Stop Domestic Violence luncheon and it looked as if half of them had already arrived.

He wove his way through the throng, slowly making progress toward the bank of elevators. Suddenly, a rush of people shot in front of him. He looked up to see Kylie emerge from the elevator, flanked on either side by a policeman. Her face was ashen and brown eyes wide. They flared with panic when cameras started flashing and hordes of journalists surrounded her.

"Is it true that Harry Hanover is a fugitive from justice?" one reporter shouted.

"Did you know about Hanover's criminal past before you hired him for this publicity tour?" shouted another.

A tall, bony blonde holding a microphone elbowed her way to the front of the crowd, bringing her nose to nose with Kylie. "Is Hanover charged with any crimes against women? Was his strong stand against domestic violence really just a ruse to seek out new victims?"

Dexter stood frozen in the crowd. All their plans to reveal the truth in their own way and time had come tumbling down. This was chaos, and unless he quickly found a way to minimize the damage, Handy Press was finished.

Obviously none of the press recognized him in his old clothes and glasses, or they would have descended on him, too. If the police didn't nab him first. Then he'd have to prove he wasn't the real Harry Hanover. They would ask him countless questions. Questions he couldn't answer if he wanted to win the game. To win his dream.

Which meant he had to choose between Kylie or winning the game. And suddenly it was the easiest choice he'd ever made. Winning the game simply didn't matter anymore. All that mattered in his life was Kylie and she needed him.

Dexter started forward, impeded by the crowd,

then stopped. He had to think. His sudden appearance at Kylie's side would only arouse more questions, more chaos. He'd have a better chance of figuring a way out of this mess if he wasn't under arrest.

His heart ached at the bewildered expression on her face and he wanted nothing more to go to her and shelter her in his arms. But that wouldn't help her or Handy Press in the long run.

Which left him with only one alternative.

KYLIE MOVED AS IF SHE WAS in a fog. The shock of finding the police at the hotel room door had been compounded by the realization that they knew all about Harry Hanover. Apparently, one of the reporters had contacted some of Harry's old friends who had been burned in a phony investment scheme. The story had snowballed from there. The only thing the reporter hadn't discovered was that Dexter wasn't the real Harry Hanover.

Kylie had tried to explain to the police about Dexter's charade, but they'd looked skeptical when she'd relayed the whole story. And more than a little suspicious that Dexter had disappeared.

Now they wanted to take her down to the station for questioning.

As the policemen herded her through the curious, boisterous crowd in the lobby, she replied to each question shot at her by firmly saying, "No comment."

She needed time to prepare an official statement

from Handy Press. Once this mess was straightened out, then she could move on to damage control. In her experience, shouting out denials and trying to fit explanations into small sound bites always led to disaster.

They were almost to the door when she saw him in the crowd. *Dexter.* Her heart leapt at the sight of his handsome face. She could handle anything with the man she loved by her side. Just knowing Dexter was nearby made her feel stronger. Safer.

Their gazes met and he mouthed three words to her. *I love you.*

Then a journalist jostled her from behind, causing Kylie to stumble. When she regained her balance, she looked back into the crowd for Dexter, but he had disappeared. The doorman hurried to swing the door open for Kylie and her police escort. She could see the shiny cruiser parked at the front curb, but she couldn't leave without Dexter. He was the missing part to her story. The missing part of her heart.

"Let's go, Ms. Timberlake," one of the cops said, nudging her elbow.

She turned and looked frantically back at the crowd, searching for some sign of the man she loved. Tears stung her eyes, blurring her vision. Her throat tightened as both cops finally grasped her arms and pulled her out the door and into the waiting cruiser.

I love you. If he'd really meant those words, why wasn't he here? Seated in the cruiser, she closed her eyes, certain this was a nightmare. If she just waited long enough, she'd wake up in Dexter's arms.

Leaning her head back against the seat cushion, she took a deep shuddering breath. The police radio crackled, announcing crimes in progress and dispatching units. The officers in the front seat were discussing where they should eat lunch today. The driver preferred Italian, his partner wanted Chinese.

Kylie opened her eyes as reality came crashing down on her. Last night had meant nothing to Dexter. She was obviously just a client to him. She'd given him her body, as well as her heart and soul. He'd given her good service.

Her stomach twisted into a tight knot when she thought of the way she'd thrown herself at him last night. In the light of day, Dexter hadn't been so willing to acknowledge her. He certainly hadn't come to her rescue. Instead, he'd just turned and walked away.

Just like every other man in her life.

15

KYLIE BREATHED A SIGH of relief when Evan entered the precinct, followed by a tall brunette carrying a briefcase. "What took you so long?"

"I had to track down the best lawyer in Pennsylvania," Evan replied, motioning to the woman beside him. "This is Chandra Coffman. Chandra, this is my big sister, Kylie."

Chandra smiled as she held out her hand. "I've heard a lot about you."

"Really?" Kylie looked back and forth between them. They seemed very comfortable with each other and Evan could barely take his eyes off of Chandra. Had her brother been holding out on her?

The attorney seated herself at the conference table and motioned Kylie to do the same. "Evan tells me you're in a bit of trouble."

She slumped back in her chair. "I think that's an understatement."

Evan pulled out a chair next to Chandra and sat down. "I don't understand why you're still here. Didn't you tell the police that the real Harry Hanover is long gone?"

"Several times," Kylie replied. "But since Dexter isn't here to back me up, they're not quite ready to believe me. They haven't actually placed me under arrest yet, but I think they're considering it.''

Chandra arched a brow. "Who is Dexter?"

"Dexter *Dependable* Kane," Kylie said wryly. "He's the gigolo I hired to play the part of Harry Hanover for the book tour."

Chandra brow furrowed. "Tall? Brown hair? Glasses?"

"Yes," Kylie replied, wondering if this woman had been one of his clients. A spark of jealousy flared inside of her. "Do you know him?"

"I certainly do. But Dexter Kane is no gigolo." She laughed. "He's more of a gigabyte nerd. He's also one of the heirs to the Kane Corporation."

"The game company?" Evan asked.

"That's right. It's owned by Amos Kane, a certified loon. But Crazy Amos is rich enough to get away with it. If Dexter is impersonating gigolos now, maybe he's every bit as crazy as his grandfather."

Kylie shook her head. "It can't be the same man. Dexter would have told me...." But would he? She realized how little he'd actually confided about himself or his personal life. She knew he had a brother, but he'd been deliberately vague when pressed for further details.

Chandra glanced at Evan, then turned back to Kylie. "Dexter chaired a state fund-raiser for a community service group I belong to. But he was AWOL at the last meeting, which definitely isn't his style. He is the most responsible, punctual man I know. The receptionist at the Kane Corporation was deliberately obtuse when I called there looking for him after the meeting. She refused to connect me to his brother Sam, too.''

Sam. Her heart sank to her toes. Sam was the name of Dexter's brother. Which meant they were talking about the same man. Worse, it meant that Dexter had been deceiving her all this time. He wasn't a gigolo, he was a business executive. The only question was why had he ever hired on at Studs-R-Us. Was it a lark? An early midlife crisis? The first signs of insanity?

Kylie closed her eyes, wishing she would have listened to her instincts. She'd known from the start that Dexter didn't fit the gigolo mold. But she'd been so desperate to find someone to play the role of Harry Hanover that she'd ignored her better judgment.

And look where it had gotten her.

''I still can't believe Dexter could actually pull off a stunt like this,'' Chandra said, slowly shaking her head. ''Stud is not the first word that comes to mind to describe Dexter Kane. Intelligent, yes. Driven, definitely. But he's always shown more interest in hard drives than sex drives.''

Kylie opened her mouth to defend the man she loved, but abruptly shut it again. The man she loved didn't exist. She'd created him in her mind just like she'd created Dexter's new image. Only new clothing and contact lenses couldn't change a person's heart. And Dexter had shown her his true identity when he'd abandoned her at the hotel.

Evan leaned forward in his chair and reached for her hand. "I know this comes as a shock, Kylie. But the important thing now is to get you out of here. If we need Dexter to corroborate your story before the police will let you go, then we'll simply have to find him."

"Good luck," she muttered, not certain she ever wanted to see him again. On the one hand, she'd like to give him a piece of her mind for playing her for a fool. Unfortunately, she feared the urge to throw herself into his arms would overwhelm the outrage she was feeling at the moment. Despite his lies and betrayal, Dexter Kane was the only man she'd ever given her whole heart to unconditionally.

And he'd probably be the last.

"I can try his cell phone number," Chandra said, hauling the black telephone on the conference table toward her. She picked up the receiver and started dialing.

Kylie shook her head. "He won't come."

"How do you know?" Evan asked.

"I just do."

"No answer." Chandra hung up the receiver and pushed the phone away. "If I could just find him and talk to him, tell him how important this is. The guy's a little shy, but he's always been dependable."

"It's worth a try," Evan concurred. "When did you last see him, Kylie?"

A blush burned in her cheeks. "Last night." She

didn't intend to tell her brother how much of Dexter she'd seen. Or the fact that they'd been in his bed at the time.

But from the glance Chandra and Evan exchanged, she sensed they'd already guessed as much.

The attorney rose to her feet. "Let me talk to the lieutenant in charge of the case. Maybe we can work something out."

Evan waited until Chandra had left the conference room before he turned back to his sister. "Well?"

She tipped up her chin. "Well, what?"

"Do you want to tell me what's really going on between you and Kane?"

"No. As a matter of fact, I don't." But to her horror, tears filled her eyes."

"Ah, hell." Evan got up and circled the table, then knelt down by Kylie's chair and wrapped his arms around her. "That big, dumb jerk hurt you, didn't he?"

"It's happened before," she said on a choked sob. "I'll get over it."

Evan stared at her for a long moment. "I don't think so. I saw the way you were looking at him in Hanover's cabin. This was more than a fling for you."

She swiped a renegade tear off of her cheek. "That's because I'm an idiot. An impulsive idiot. I don't have anyone besides myself to blame, Evan. Really. I practically threw myself at the man."

"Right," Evan said wryly. "I'm sure you had to drag Kane kicking and screaming the whole way."

She sniffed. "Not exactly."

"I didn't think so."

She shook her head. "But that still doesn't excuse my tendency to leap first and look later. I didn't even know the real Dexter! Will I ever learn from my mistakes?"

"Mistakes are just a part of life, sis," he said, tenderly brushing another tear off of her cheek. "They help make us strong."

She took a shaky breath. "I don't feel very strong at the moment."

"I know." He smiled. "But I've got just the thing to make you feel better."

"Mocha almond fudge ice cream?"

"That's right. Guaranteed to cure every ill in the Timberlake family. Hey, it helped me beat Hodgkin's disease, didn't it?"

She sat up in her chair, feeling a little foolish for falling apart over a ruptured romance. Evan had faced and conquered much worse. How could she give up on life now? No matter how empty it seemed.

"Can I have the whole quart?" she asked, swallowing down the last sob.

"We'll binge and buy a gallon if I can see a smile."

Kylie gave him a tremulous smile, hoping he couldn't see the heartbreak in her eyes.

The door to the conference room opened and

Chandra stuck her head inside. "You're free to go, Kylie. I promised the lieutenant you'd be available for questioning at any time. They're still in the process of gathering data on Harry Hanover, so the investigation is at somewhat of a standstill anyway."

Kylie rose out of her chair. "All they have to do is wait until the newspapers hit the streets tomorrow morning. I'm sure they'll be full of headlines about the story. And about Handy Press."

Evan handed Kylie her purse. "They say there's no such thing as bad publicity."

She shook her head. "This isn't going to be bad, Evan. It will be disastrous."

He sighed. "Then there's only one thing we can do.

"Buy two gallons of mocha almond fudge ice cream?" Kylie ventured.

"That's right." He put his arm around her. "Let's go home."

DEXTER SAT IN HIS OFFICE at the Kane Corporation and stared at his computer screen as the letters blurred together. He'd spent the last few hours trying to get the words just right. Only he kept seeing Kylie's face. Remembering the haunted look in her beautiful brown eyes. It literally made his chest ache.

"Concentrate, Kane," he admonished himself, revising the last paragraph. This was the most important thing he'd ever written. He had to get it just right.

Finally he slumped back in his chair and punched the print button. It was the best he could do. He just hoped it was good enough.

Rubbing one hand around his stiff neck, he checked the clock on the wall. He had a little over an hour left to change his mind. All it would take was one phone call. He looked at the telephone, testing himself for the temptation to reach for it. Surprisingly, it was easier to resist than he ever would have suspected.

Something had changed him these last few weeks. Or more specifically, someone. Kylie Timberlake had barreled into his life and turned it upside down. And now it would never be the same again.

He just hoped that when it was all over she'd give him a second chance.

All of Dexter's calls to her apartment had resulted only in reaching her answering machine. He'd left countless messages, but so far had received no return calls. But at least he'd been able to hear the sound of her voice, even if was just a recording.

She was probably furious with him. And he couldn't blame her. He knew she'd spotted him at the hotel. No doubt she'd thought the worst when he'd disappeared in the crowd. But he'd needed time. Time to make everything right.

Now there was no turning back.

The door opened and his grandfather walked inside. He blinked at Dexter. ''What are you doing here?''

''Just a little housekeeping to make sure the Kane

Corporation keeps running smoothly while Sam and I are away from the company." He briefly wondered how Sam was faring. Probably sailing smoothly through the game, knowing his brother.

Amos chuckled. "I take it you don't trust the old man to keep the company afloat long enough for you or Sam to take over. Don't worry, Dexter, the Kane Corporation will be strong and sound when one of you wins the game."

"I'm not worried," Dexter assured him. "I just wanted to save you a little work." He pointed to the stack of files near his computer terminal. "Those are the projection studies. You might want to take a look at them in your spare time. And I made an appointment for you with Dr. Baynes for a checkup on Tuesday next week. It's been almost a year since your last physical."

Amos cocked his head to one side. "Is something wrong, Dexter? You don't seem like yourself. Dependable as ever, of course, but...different."

"Watch the six o'clock news tonight, Grandpa," Dexter said, as he headed out the door. "You'll find out everything you need to know."

16

EVAN STOOD NEXT TO THE freezer in his kitchen. "There's about two scoops of mocha almond fudge ice cream left. Want it?"

Kylie shook her head, figuring she'd gained about twenty pounds in her efforts to drown her sorrows in ice cream. "You can have it."

His house was connected by a long hallway to the offices of Handy Press. She could hear the whir of the printer through the wall. How much longer until Evan was forced to liquidate all his assets and sell his business?

But Handy Press wasn't the only casualty of this debacle. Kylie had lost her heart and her reputation as a publicist as well. Would any amount of ice cream make up for the pain of her failure?

"Come on, Ky, cheer up," Evan said. "At least Dexter called you to apologize."

Amy had phoned Handy Press a half hour ago with the news that Dexter had left twenty-four messages on their answering machine.

"We don't know that," Kylie replied, "since he didn't actually apologize on the phone. According to Amy, he just asked me to call him as soon as possible."

"Well, what else could he want?"

She shrugged, trying not to get her hopes up. After the way he'd treated her, she couldn't afford to give him a second chance. "Maybe his clothes. I packed them up when you drove me over to the hotel to check out."

Fortunately, the press and the mob of people had been long gone by that time. Evan had waited in the car while Kylie had cleaned out her own room. Then, unable to resist temptation, she'd checked Dexter's hotel room to see if he had returned. But the room was empty. The maid hadn't even cleaned it yet.

The sight of the rumpled bedsheets had brought all the memories of last night rushing back. Kylie had even hugged Dexter's pillow, inhaling the familiar scent of his aftershave still clinging to it.

When would she ever learn?

"So where did you put his clothes," Evan asked.

She pointed to the fireplace, the flames burning brightly in the hearth.

Evan grinned. "Gives new meaning to the phrase 'burned by love.'"

"You know me and my impulses."

He got a spoon out of the kitchen drawer and began scooping spoonfuls of ice cream out of the gallon bucket. "You wouldn't be the same person without them, Kylie. That's what makes you so special."

"I don't feel too special at the moment. Although

I may give into the impulse to track down Dexter D. Kane and strangle the man.''

He walked over to the sink to rinse off his spoon, then stared out the window. ''So I guess that means you're not ready to forgive him.''

''Not until the next millennium,'' she declared.

''Too bad. Dexter's going to get cold standing out there on the porch for so long.''

She bolted off the sofa. ''He's out there?''

Evan nodded, still staring out the window. ''Right outside the door. Wonder why he hasn't knocked yet. Must be trying to work up his nerve.''

''Well, for his own safety, he'd better just turn around and go home. I'm not interested in anything he has to say.'' She began pacing back and forth in front of the sofa. ''If he wanted to talk to me, he could have done it at the hotel when the police showed up instead of leaving me there high and dry.''

''Should I let him in so you can tell him off in person?''

She whirled on him. ''No! I never want to see Dexter Kane again.''

Evan's eyes softened. ''Liar.''

Kylie sank down on the sofa. ''All right, I am lying. It's killing me not to go out there. But how can I possibly forgive him? How can I ever trust him again after everything that's happened between us?''

Evan shrugged. ''I don't know, Kylie. I guess you just have to follow your heart.''

She knew that would be a mistake. Her heart wasn't at all rational about this situation. She needed to use her head before Dexter found a way to hurt her even more. If that was possible.

"Is he still out here?"

Evan turned back to the window. "Yep. And he's not alone."

"What do you mean?"

"The press has arrived and they're setting up a bank of microphones on the front step. Looks like Dexter is planning to hold a news conference."

"What?" she exclaimed. "Here? Why in the world would he do such a thing?"

"How do I know? You're the expert on the man."

Kylie's heart began to pound, imploring her to give Dexter one more chance. But she hardened her resolve. "It's too little, too late. Nothing he says now can make up for what he's done."

Evan looked at her. "What has he done, exactly?"

"Well, in the first place, he lied to me about being a gigolo."

"But Chandra called the owner of Studs-R-Us and verified that Dexter was employed there."

"He never told me he was a business man or the heir to the Kane Corporation."

"That sounds more like a crime of simple omission rather than deceit."

She frowned. "Why are you defending him?"

"I'm not. I'm just trying to be the voice of reason."

"Then tell me why I should forgive him for abandoning me at the hotel after the police arrived? He saw me, then he just walked away!"

"I can't give you the answer. But maybe Dexter can, if you give him the chance."

She folded her arms across her chest. "Forget it."

"Why don't you admit the real reason you're so angry with him."

"You tell me."

"Okay, I will. You're head over heels in love with the guy."

Kylie's lower lip quivered. She'd never been able to hide the truth from her little brother. "You're right. And I'm not sure what to do about it."

"Well, let's see what Dexter has to say." He walked over to the television and turned it on. After flipping through the channels, he found a local news station.

"This is Darryl Starr, reporting to you live from Handy Press, the small company that published How To Jump-Start Your Love Life, *authored by the notorious Harry Hanover. Mr. Hanover will be giving a brief statement in just a moment."*

Kylie scooted closer to the set. "They still think he's Harry!"

"Shh, Dexter is coming on."

They both watched as the camera focused on Dexter's handsome face. He stood right outside the door, but Kylie felt as if he were a million miles away. Though her heart traitorously softened when she saw that he wore his glasses. And looked more than a little nervous.

Dexter cleared his throat. *"Am I on?"*

One of the reporter's shouted a question at him. *"Do you plan to turn yourself in to the police, Mr. Hanover?"*

"No," Dexter replied firmly. *"Because I'm not Harry Hanover."* He let that sink in for a moment, then continued. *"My name is Dexter Kane and I work for the Kane Corporation. But for the last few weeks, I've been masquerading as Harry Hanover."*

The press erupted into a firestorm of shouted questions. Kylie experienced a stab of empathy for him having experienced a similar verbal barrage only a few hours ago.

Dexter held up his hands to silence the crowd. *"If you'll just let me make my statement, I think it will answer all of your questions."*

A few intrepid reporters still shot questions at him, but were quickly shushed by their colleagues. Dexter looked straight into the camera.

"A few weeks ago, Handy Press hired me to portray Harry Hanover, author of How To Jump-Start Your Love Life. *They were duped by him into believing that he was agoraphobic, but they wanted to give this book,"* he held a copy high in the air, *"the kind of promotion that would make a difference in the lives of people everywhere."*

A derisive snort sounded in the background. Dexter ignored it and went on.

"When Handy Press's publicist, Kylie Timberlake, approached me to impersonate Mr. Hanover, she had no idea that I was associated with the Kane Corporation. You see, Harry Hanover wasn't the only one duping Handy Press. I was playing the role of a male escort and didn't reveal my real identity for one very simple reason. My grandfather had forbidden me from telling anyone that I was playing a real-life version of Chameleon, *the career role-playing game that made his company internationally famous. The rules were simple. Tell no one and play the game for one month. My only competition was my brother, who's playing a game of his own. The prize is ownership of the family business."*

A ripple of murmurs rose over the crowd of journalists.

Kylie looked over at Evan. "That's crazy."

"Amos Kane is crazy," he replied. "You heard what Chandra said about the man."

"Well, that month is up in five more days," Dexter continued. *"But I'm not going to play the game anymore. I'd rather lose that company, the one I've dreamed of owning my entire life, than lose the woman I love. I may not be the real author of* How To Jump-Start Your Love Life, *but it taught me that love is more important than business. Hell, it's more important than anything...."*

"I don't believe it," Kylie said to Evan, turning her attention away from the television set. "He's giving the book a plug."

"Shh." Evan took her chin in his hands and

turned her attention to the television screen once again. "He's not done."

Dexter looked calmly over the crowd. *"I've learned more about love in these last few weeks than in the previous twenty-eight years of my life, thanks to that book. And the most important lesson is not to give up. So, despite the fact that my one true love refuses to speak to me, I've got something to say to her."*

Kylie held her breath as Dexter looked straight into the camera.

"I love you, Kylie. You're the perfect woman for me. The only woman. And I intend to spend every day of the rest of my life proving that I'm the right man for you. Will you…"

The door of Handy Press flew open and Kylie rushed out onto the porch and jumped into Dexter's arms. "Yes! Yes, yes, yes!"

He laughed, pulling her close. "I haven't even asked the question yet."

She wrapped her arms around his neck. "Well, what are you waiting for…ask!"

He looked into her eyes. "Will you marry me?"

She leaned up to kiss him, her heart leading all the way. "Yes, Dexter. I'll marry you. I'll love you forever."

She could hear the sound of cameras flashing as Dexter kissed her, but she didn't care who was watching. Until he poured so much passion into the kiss that she didn't want anyone around. She just wanted Dexter all to herself so she could show him how very much she loved him.

At least he broke the kiss and smiled down at her. "Do you have any idea how great I feel?"

"You gave up your family business for me." Her heart contracted. "Oh, Dexter are you sure you won't regret it?"

He shook his head. "The only thing I regret is not coming to your rescue in that hotel lobby. But I knew I could help you more by leaving than by staying. Do you understand? And more importantly, can you forgive me?"

"Yes." Her eyes gleamed. "I had no idea you had so much at risk. Or that you would give it up for me."

"In a heartbeat." He reached up to tenderly caress her cheek. "I almost risked losing the woman I love for a pile of bricks and mortar. That doesn't keep a man warm at night. Believe me, I've worked enough all-nighters at the company to know."

Kylie pulled him closer. "Just make sure you don't pull any all-nighters at Studs-R-Us. In fact, I think resigning from that job would be the perfect wedding present for me."

His eyes twinkled. "I've got to work somewhere."

Evan appeared at the door. "Sorry to interrupt, but I just got a phone call from the distributor. He said orders of *How To Jump-Start Your Love Life* are coming in fast and furious." Evan grinned.

"Looks like Handy Press has just been resurrected, thanks to Dexter here."

"That's wonderful," Kylie exclaimed. She turned to Dexter. "Maybe you could work here. I'm sure as Handy Press grows we'll need someone to handle all the contracts and legal business."

"Not so fast, sis," Evan interjected. "That wasn't the only phone call. There was one for Dexter."

Dexter looked up. "From who?"

"Your grandfather."

"What did he want," Dexter asked.

"It was a long message," Evan said. "So I wrote it down." He handed the note to Dexter, then walked back into the house.

"What's it say?" Kylie asked, reading over his shoulder.

"The secret to winning the game of life is that sometimes you have to break the rules. I'm proud of you, Dexter. You finally learned what's really important. Love trumps business every time. Congratulations. See you at midnight next Saturday."

Her brow furrowed. "I don't understand. What does it mean?"

Dexter grinned. "I think it means I'm still in the game."

Operation Beauty

Kristin
Gabriel

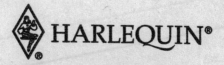

HARLEQUIN®

TORONTO • NEW YORK • LONDON
AMSTERDAM • PARIS • SYDNEY • HAMBURG
STOCKHOLM • ATHENS • TOKYO • MILAN • MADRID
PRAGUE • WARSAW • BUDAPEST • AUCKLAND

1

SAM T. KANE KNEW HIS DAY was only going to get worse when he parachuted onto a pile of fresh cow manure. Standing in a pasture surrounded by a herd of curious Holstein cows, he yanked off his parachute harness, then looked around the pasture for his brother, Dexter. He'd last seen him thirteen thousand feet ago, when they'd both jumped out of the airplane at the request of their grandfather.

But his brother was nowhere in sight. He'd probably floated into some other pasture. Sam wasn't really worried about him. Dexter always managed to land on his feet. Ever since he could remember, his older brother was always succeeding at something. High school valedictorian. National Honor Society. A full ride to the highest caliber Ivy League school. Success seemed to come as easily to Dexter as breathing.

But not for Sam.

He scraped his boots in the knee-high grass, trying to remove the pungent cow manure. But this time he wasn't going to lose. Not when the playing field was finally level between them. Their grandfather, Amos Kane, was ready to hand over the family business. And true to his eccentric reputation,

Crazy Amos had devised a competition to make his grandsons earn it.

Sam still couldn't believe his grandfather was staking the family business on a real-life version of a board game. Chameleon was a career role-playing game where players take on different occupations to embark on the road to success. And it had definitely catapulted the Kane Corporation to success, selling into the millions around the world.

Sam had always assumed his brother, Dexter, would inherit the Kane Corporation by default. After all, he was the one with the college degree and the computer brain. Sam, on the other hand, was a high school dropout who had drifted from job to job until he'd finally landed a position at the Kane Corporation as a creative consultant.

It was the perfect job for him. Free to brainstorm new ideas, he wasn't bogged down with number crunching or endless reports. It had paid off, too. Since Sam had hired on, his department had seen a twenty-percent increase in productivity.

But all that had changed when Amos announced his retirement and arranged to hand over the business to whichever grandson could succeed at the real-life version of Chameleon. And it was winner take all.

While his older brother might have the diplomas to qualify him for the job, Sam believed he could do it just as well. A good leader knew how to delegate the duties that might cause him problems. Besides, running a business involved more than cash flows and financial projections. It took creativity and good people skills. And a little bit of luck.

Leaving the neon-blue parachute in the pasture, he waved to the cows, then began jogging toward the gate. Thunder rumbled in the sky above him, an ominous warning that this game might not be easy to win. But Sam wasn't about to back down now. It seemed as if he'd always been about three steps behind Dexter, never able to catch up. He'd quit trying years ago, pretending it didn't matter.

But it did matter. Sam wanted to make his mark in the world. And now, thanks to his grandfather, he had the chance to do just that. If he could win the game, he'd be the owner of a Fortune 500 company. The thought terrified him as much as it thrilled him. There was a reason he'd never been able to keep up with Sam academically. The same reason that had kept him from trying to compete with Dexter in the business world. But he'd take it one step at a time. Just like he'd done every day of his life.

Lightning flashed when he reached the aluminum gate and unfastened the chain. Big, fat drops of rain pelted him as he walked through the gate, then closed it behind him. There was no farmhouse in sight, just a lonely gravel crossroad. He looked down one road, then the other, wondering which one led into Pittsburgh. But before he could flip a coin to decide which road to take, an ancient blue Ford pickup truck appeared over the crest of a hill.

Sam hailed it as he walked to the side of the road. Three young women in halter tops sat in the front seat. They slowed down, craning their necks to look at him. Then the driver hit the brakes, the pickup truck sliding to a stop.

He approached the truck as the driver rolled down

her window. They looked like twenty-somethings with too much time on their hands. "Good afternoon, ladies."

"Hi there," the driver said, as one of her passengers giggled. "Need a lift?"

"As a matter of fact, I do. Which way are you headed?"

The driver looked at her friends, then back at Sam. "Wherever you're going. I'm Mandy." Then she pointed to the girl beside her. "This is Angie, and next to her is Shannon. But everybody calls her Squeak."

He nodded, wondering if he should wait for another car to come by. The three of them looked as if they'd be happy to provide the kind of distraction he couldn't afford right now.

"What's your name?" Angie asked.

"Sam." Lightning crackled over his head. "Can you tell me how far is it into Pittsburgh?"

"Only another five miles," Mandy replied, her gaze making a slow journey down his body. "We're going to a great Mexican joint for enchiladas and strawberry margaritas. Care to join us, Sam?"

"Maybe another time." He hitched his thumb toward the bed of the pickup. "But do you mind if I just jump in the back until we hit the city limits?"

Angie leaned forward. "Oh, there's room up here for you, Sam. Really. We can all squeeze together."

"Besides," Mandy said, "you'll get wet back there."

"No problem," he said, hopping into the back of the pickup truck. "I like rain."

As if the clouds could hear him, they let forth a

torrent, soaking him to the skin before the pickup had even gone a mile. But Sam didn't care. The game had begun, and he'd been lucky enough to get a good head start. But then, Sam had always been lucky.

He needed luck to keep his secret.

LAUREN MCBRIDE HELD UP A red velvet garter in her hand. "When you want to make that romantic dinner extra special," she said, stretching the garter over the rim of a white ceramic bowl. "Add a little spice to the appetizers by dressing up your serving dishes."

The women gathered at the Ladybug Lingerie party oohed and aahed as Lauren added the bowl to the other items on the counter. Decorative lingerie was the latest creative solution to expanding the market of Ladybug Lingerie, a popular home-party business that was just starting to move its products in the retail sector.

Lauren had been skeptical about adorning dishes and other furnishings with artfully arranged panties, bras and assorted intimate apparel, but it seemed to be a hit at every party she worked.

If only decorative lingerie could solve the problems in her life.

Like her car, which had refused to start this morning. And her rent, which was a week late. She forced a smile as a headache throbbed behind her eyes. No doubt a result of staying late at the college library last night to read class assignments out of the textbooks she couldn't afford to buy.

The bills were mounting up and her job at Ladybug Lingerie just wasn't enough to make ends meet. Even if the schedule did allow her the flexibility to attend college full-time.

Fortunately, college coeds, like the four roommates hosting this party in their tiny off-campus apartment, were some of her best customers. Even if they did make Lauren feel older than her twenty-seven years.

The age difference didn't seem to bother her best friend, Becky Wittley, who had driven her to the party. Then again, Becky was engaged to be married in three short months and had other things on her mind.

Lauren finished her presentation, encouraging the guests to peruse the catalog and examine the sample items she'd brought with her. Then she turned to Becky, who sat in a chair beside her. "Find anything you like?"

Becky heaved a wistful sigh, gazing at a picture of a lovely white peignoir in the catalog. "I like everything. But the wedding is already costing Don and I a fortune, so I'd better just look instead of buy."

"I have an idea," Lauren said, straightening the stack of order forms in front of her. "Why don't I give you a Ladybug Lingerie party for a bridal shower?"

Becky's eyes widened. "You can do that?"

"I don't see why not. I'm one of your bridesmaids, after all. Just write up a list of who you'd like to invite and I'll set it all up."

Becky smiled. "That would be perfect. Wait until Don hears about this." Then her smile turned to a mischievous grin. "On the other hand, maybe I'll keep it a secret. Then he can find out on the honeymoon."

"My lips are sealed." Relief flowed through Lauren at Becky's enthusiasm for the idea. She'd come up with it a few days ago, after weeks of worrying about how she'd possibly be able to afford giving her best friend a bridal shower. This way, her party earnings would pay for the shower, and since Lauren received a generous discount on any Ladybug merchandise she purchased, she could afford to give Becky the white peignoir that she had her eye on as well.

The guests began to line up and place the orders, keeping Lauren and her calculator busy for the better part of an hour. At last the room began to clear, leaving Becky to help Lauren pack up the display cases.

"So how would you like to meet the perfect man?" Becky asked, sliding the red garter off the ceramic bowl.

"Is this a trick question?"

"I'm serious. His name is Leroy."

"He doesn't sound like my type."

"Don't you think you should at least meet him before you decide? I know, I'll invite him to my Ladybug Lingerie bridal shower! Then he can see you in action."

"Forget Leroy," Lauren said firmly. "A Ladybug Lingerie party is no place for a man. Besides, I'm still recovering from the last blind date you set me up with. Remember Harold?"

"I thought you liked Harold."

"I did. We went out on one date, then I never heard from him again. But at least he was better than Brian, who disappeared during the movie intermission on our first date. I never saw him again either."

"Harold and Brian were your transitional men. Leroy could be the one."

Lauren shook her head. "Where do you find these guys?"

"They're everywhere," Becky assured her. "You just have to look around. Be open to the possibilities."

"I'm open."

"Okay, then how about that guy?" she asked, pointing out the window. A painter stood on an eight-foot scaffolding at the adjacent apartment building, wearing a pair of worn blue denim overalls and a ball cap. "Would you go to bed with him?"

"How do you know it's a guy?"

Becky looked at her. "Wow, it has been a long time for you, hasn't it?"

Lauren shook her head. "There are women painters, too. Besides, we're too far away to tell."

"Okay, then hypothetically speaking, if that painter is a man, would you sleep with him?"

"Of course not. I don't even know him."

"Let's say you hit the scaffolding with your car when you backed out of the parking lot and he fell and broke his leg."

"You drove today, remember? Besides, I'm not quite desperate enough to maim strange men with my car just to meet them. At least, not yet."

"Just go with me on this. His leg is broken. You

feel guilty, so you offer to bring him dinner every night until he's back on his feet.''

''You know I'm not a good cook.''

''Night after night,'' Becky continued undaunted, ''you visit him in his apartment, the attraction between you is building, until one night you arrive to find him out of his cast. And out of his clothes.''

''That's a little presumptuous on his part, isn't it? Answering the door naked?''

''He gave you a key.''

Lauren laughed, packing the last of the lingerie. ''Okay, I give up. If he was a nice guy, and if I really, really liked him, then I might sleep with him.''

''*Might?* How are you ever going to fulfill your New Year's resolution with a *might?*''

Lauren swallowed a groan, wishing she'd never shared her New Year's resolution with her friend. Especially since fulfilling that particular goal was the least of her problems.

''It's already September,'' Becky reminded her. ''You've got less than four months left.''

''Celibacy isn't a terminal disease, you know. The only reason I made that silly resolution was because I decided it was time to get over Chuck once and for all.''

Becky's face darkened at the mention of Lauren's ex-husband. ''Well, sleeping with another man would be a good start. And so much fun to rub into Chuck's face.''

''You know I'm not into revenge,'' Lauren said softly. As much as she appreciated Becky's outrage on her behalf, she'd gotten over her ex-husband's infidelity a long time ago. But his betrayal had hurt, and made her insecure about her own appeal. Even two years after their divorce, she was still suffering from rejection-phobia. And her last two dates certainly hadn't helped.

"Lucky for Chuck," Becky mused, a note of disgust in her voice. "He used you to pay for his college education, then he just dumped you."

"I dumped him," Lauren reminded her. It had been the day he'd gotten the news that he'd passed the bar exam. She could still remember how hard it had been for her to say the words—to ask him to leave. He'd cracked a joke that she could hire him for her divorce lawyer.

"So don't you think it's about time you start wearing some of this lingerie you sell so well?"

"I will...someday."

"You're too picky." Becky stuffed a handful of silk camisoles into the case. "You've been divorced for two years and gone out with, what, three guys?"

"Four," Lauren replied. "If you count Brian."

"Brian was an idiot, so he doesn't count."

"Okay, then three. That was more than enough. And the sad thing is, I wasn't really sorry to see any of them go."

Becky shook her head. "What am I going to do with you?"

Lauren shrugged. "So maybe I am picky. What's wrong with that? Besides, I'm more interested in earning my teaching degree than in romance."

"Can't you have both?"

Lauren wasn't so sure anymore. She'd believed it once. When she and Chuck had met as freshmen at

Penn State, they had both been full of big plans for the future. Chuck wanted to be a lawyer and Lauren wanted to be an elementary school teacher. They'd fallen in love quickly and married over spring break. That was her first mistake.

Her second was dropping out of school and working full-time. They agreed that once Chuck was through with law school, it would be Lauren's turn. She could go back to college and earn her teaching degree while Chuck supported them.

But it hadn't worked out that way. Their divorce had come on the heels of Chuck's graduation from law school. Now Lauren was on her own, still determined to get her college degree. Her divorce attorney had pushed her to sue for alimony, but her pride wouldn't let her take one penny from her ex-husband.

So she'd found a job at Ladybug Lingerie with a schedule flexible enough to allow her to take classes full-time at the University of Pittsburgh. It paid fairly well, but her small budget was still stretched well beyond its limit. She cut corners wherever possible, including her grocery list. Unfortunately, the bills were still piling up and Lauren didn't see a solution in sight. But that didn't mean she was ready to give up.

Thunder rumbled in the sky, signaling the release of a downpour. Becky smiled as rain pelted the window. ''I'll bet that poor painter is going to get soaked.''

''He's a man,'' Lauren said with a wry smile. ''He probably deserves it.''

2

SAM HAD STARTED HIS afternoon surrounded by cows, but now, three hours later, he was in much more familiar environment. He sat in an office at Midnight Lace surrounded by bras.

Big bras, skimpy bras, lacy bras and leather bras. Bras of every color, style and texture. The only problem was they were worn by headless mannequins instead of warm-blooded women. But that might be a blessing in disguise, since Sam was determined to keep his mind on business for the next four weeks.

According to his game card, that business was working as a salesman for Midnight Lace. Sam glanced at his watch, wondering when the interview would begin. He was confident that the company would hire him. For one thing, Midnight Lace was a subsidiary of the Kane Corporation, so he knew his name would carry some weight. For another, he'd become an expert at separating ladies from their lingerie. How hard could it be to operate in reverse?

But despite his optimism, his palms were damp and he kept looking at the door. Escape was still an option.

Three hours ago, he'd jumped out of an airplane

to start the game that could change his life. The problem was that Sam had never won a game of Chameleon—never stood a chance of winning given his liability. But his older brother, Dexter, had always goaded him into playing and Sam had usually put an end to the game with his fists before he could be mocked as a loser. At least in a fistfight he had a fifty-fifty chance of coming out on top.

But he wasn't ten years old anymore. Now, at age twenty-seven, his entire future hinged on beating his brother at this real-life version of Chameleon. Dexter was probably already hard at work, impressing his new boss. It was true his brother had balked a little when he'd discovered his new career was as a male escort. But Sam didn't have any doubts about Dexter's abilities. Sam had spent too many years living in his big brother's overachieving shadow.

The door opened and a short, plump man with thinning brown hair walked inside. "Good afternoon, Mr. Kane. Hope I haven't kept you waiting too long."

"No problem," Sam replied, rising up to shake the man's hand.

"I'm Howard Cooper, marketing director here at Midnight Lace." He sat down heavily in the chair behind the desk. "Your grandfather told me you'd be coming."

"I see." This was news to Sam. Had his grandfather done the same for Dexter? Or was he trying to give Sam a little extra help?

Cooper smiled as he leaned back in the chair. "I'm so glad you accepted this assignment. It's a

little delicate, of course, but Amos Kane assured me
that you're the perfect man for this position."

"When can I start?" Sam asked, assuming he'd
learn the details along the way.

Cooper held up one of the bras displayed on his
desk. "As soon as you can fit into one of these."

Sam blinked. "Excuse me?"

"You're welcome to choose any style you wish,"
Cooper said, motioning to the other bras around the
room. "I recommend the cotton/spandex blend with
hidden underwire, but perhaps we should leave the
final decision up to the fashion consultant I hired.
You've got an appointment scheduled with her this
afternoon...."

Sam held up both hands. "Hold it. I am not wearing a hidden underwire bra or any other kind of bra.
I'm supposed to sell the lingerie, not model it."

Cooper's brow furrowed.

"I see we have a slight communication problem.
Didn't your grandfather fill you in on the details of
this assignment?"

"Obviously not. Because this sounds crazy. Why
would I possibly want to wear a bra?"

"Because that's the only way to infiltrate the Ladybug Lingerie company."

"I thought I was supposed to work here, at Midnight Lace."

"You *will* be working for us, but not as a salesman. Your job is more of an undercover assignment." Cooper chuckled. "In more ways than one."

"You want me to spy on the competition?"

Cooper leaned forward, his face sober now. "We
want you to get your hands on the Seductress."

"Who?"

"The Seductress isn't a who, it's a what. A bra, to be exact. Ladybug Lingerie plans to launch their new Seductress bra during the Christmas season. The reports we've received so far indicate that it has the potential to become the hottest bra on the market. But we don't know enough about it. Certainly not enough to come up with a good, competitive product of our own."

"You want me to steal a bra?"

"Steal is such an ugly word. And we would certainly never condone anything illegal. But if you become an employee of Ladybug Lingerie and obtain possession of one of the prototypes of the Seductress, there's no reason you couldn't let our designers take a look at it for an afternoon or two. All in the name of research, of course."

"Is this some kind of joke?" Sam asked, his head spinning.

Howard looked affronted. "I can assure you that our company's position as a leader in the lingerie market is no joke. And we intend to keep it that way."

"But you still haven't explained why it's necessary for me to wear a bra."

"Because the founder of Ladybug Lingerie insists her company hire *only* women in its sales department. There are two reasons for that. One, they're just beginning to explore retail outlets, preferring to go into people's homes to sell their products. A man going door-to-door with a trunk full of sexy women's lingerie might cause a few problems—with both the women and their husbands or boyfriends."

"And the second reason?"

"Ladybug Lingerie touts itself as a progressive company that hires women who have difficulty finding jobs elsewhere. Women in transition, such as widows or those adjusting to life after divorce. That's how the founder apparently got the business started over twenty years ago. Her husband bailed out on their marriage, so she began making and selling nightgowns and negligees to support herself. Her business took off from there and now she wants to give that same opportunity for a new start to other women."

"Fascinating," Sam said wryly. "I'm not doing it."

Cooper sighed. "That is certainly your choice, Mr. Kane. However, your grandfather did ask me to pass on a message. If you refuse the job, you're out of the game. Whatever that means."

Sam scowled. "You're certain my grandfather knows about your plan to turn me into a woman?"

"It was his idea. According to the memo he sent over to our office, you took quite a few drama classes in high school." Cooper reached around his desk and picked up a file folder. "And it sounds as if you made something of a name for yourself impersonating a woman called Philomena Gallagher."

"You know about Mrs. Gallagher?" he muttered, wondering what else the man knew. Mrs. Philomena Gallagher had taught English at Jefferson High during Sam's junior year. A strict disciplinarian, she demanded high standards of achievement and terrified most of the students.

Except for Sam, who could crack her up with his

voice impersonations. He had a talent for it and could mimic Mrs. Gallagher's low, imperious tone to a T. Even going so far as to develop a silly classroom comedy routine for the school's radio station. He didn't realize his grandfather had even been aware of it. Especially since Sam had dropped out of high school in the middle of his junior year.

"I hope you'll reconsider," Cooper said, tossing the file folder back on the desk. "We've already invested a considerable amount of money into this project. Not only have we hired a top makeup artist and fashion consultant to assist you in the transition, but we have custom wigs, professional cosmetics and a full wardrobe ready to go."

Sam slumped back in his chair, wondering if all the rumors questioning his grandfather's sanity were true. How could masquerading as a woman possibly prove that Sam was capable of taking control of the family business? It didn't make sense. But then, neither did this game. So he'd either have to play along—or let Dexter win again.

"I'll do it," Sam said, before he had time to change his mind.

Cooper nodded his approval. "Good. We've already laid the groundwork and sent a fictional résumé and job application for Philomena Gallagher to Ladybug Lingerie. All you have to do is show up for the company seminar tomorrow morning."

Sam's jaw dropped. "That soon? How will I ever convince anyone I'm a woman if I don't have time to get used to the idea? Much less figure out how to pull this off."

Cooper shrugged. "We're working on a tight

schedule here, Mr. Kane. But you won't be totally on your own. Ladybug Lingerie assigns each new saleswoman a mentor to teach her the ins and outs of the business. These mentors are their most trusted employees and have access to all their new proto-types before they hit the market. Find a way to get close to your mentor and you'll find the Seductress bra.''

"There's got to be an easier way to get our hands on that bra.'' He cleared his throat. "I do have a certain way with women....''

Cooper shook his head. "We've already tried that approach. Company loyalty runs high at Ladybug Lingerie. The only way to acquire the Seductress is to become one of them. And do not, under any cir-cumstances, reveal your true identity. That's imper-ative. If you do...''

"I'm out of the game,'' Sam finished for him, realizing he didn't have any wiggle room to avoid this particular job assignment. "And if I accomplish my mission before the four weeks is up?''

"We'd like you to stay on at Ladybug for the full month, just to keep from raising suspicions.''

Sam sat back in his chair as doubts began to sink in. He had to work as a woman for the next for weeks. He'd never be able to pull it off. He loved women, but he didn't begin to understand them. And he sure as hell didn't act like one.

"I'll be your only contact at Midnight Lace. The only one who knows what's really going on,'' Coo-per said, obviously not sharing Sam's doubts about his ability to do the job. "Everyone else will be in the dark.''

Sam couldn't believe he was actually going to go through with this ridiculous charade. But what choice did he have? "This might be more fun than you think." Cooper leaned back in his chair. "Hey, if you're lucky, you might even get a Bug."

Sam nodded, wondering if a fake bout with a nasty virus would keep him in the game but out of a dress. He gave a weak cough, then rubbed his chest. "Actually, I am feeling a little congested."

"Not that kind of bug," Cooper said wryly. "A Volkswagen Beetle custom-painted like a ladybug. You know, orange with black dots. It's one of the incentive prizes the company uses to reward their most productive saleswomen."

Sam realized he'd seen some of those odd-looking cars zipping around Pittsburgh. He'd always wondered who would be nuts enough to own something like that. "I think I'll just concentrate on finding the Seductress."

"Good. That's why I knew we needed a man for this job. Someone who isn't afraid to get his hands dirty."

"And who would agree to wear a bra."

"That, too." Cooper waved his hand around the room. "Go ahead and pick one out. You're going to need it."

Sam surveyed the array of bras surrounding him, realizing they didn't look so bad on the mannequins after all. The question was, how would they look on him?

3

LAUREN WALKED INTO THE Verandah Café, her mouth watering at the savory scents that met her at the door. She'd left class early to attend this lunch meeting, knowing it would be foolish to turn down an invitation from the owner of Ladybug Lingerie. Especially since food had become a luxury item on her budget.

The hostess approached her. "Table for one?"

"I'm meeting someone here," Lauren replied. "Mrs. Tina Chavez."

The hostess checked her reservation book. "Oh, yes. Mrs. Chavez has already arrived. Follow me, please."

Lauren's curiosity was almost as strong as her appetite. Mrs. Chavez was known for her generosity and frequently hosted lavish lunches for her employees. She also tended to provide doggie bags for the leftovers. With careful planning, one of those doggie bags could last Lauren a week. She wondered if it would be in poor taste to ask for a doggie bag at a place like the Verandah Café.

Mrs. Chavez looked up as Lauren approached, a wide smile wreathing her wrinkled face. She had a salt-and-pepper beehive and wore a huge diamond ladybug brooch on the lapel of her black silk jacket. "Hello, Lauren. I'm so glad you could come."

"It's my pleasure," she replied, taking a seat across from her. Her gaze fell on the basket of crusty rolls in the center of the table, their fragrant, yeasty aroma making her stomach rumble loudly.

Mrs. Chavez pretended not to notice. "I'm starving. Shall we order right away?"

"Our special today is the pan-fried chicken," the hostess said. "It comes with mashed potatoes and gravy, stuffing, cole slaw and baked beans."

"That sounds delicious," Lauren said, tucking a stray curl behind her ear.

"We'll take two specials." Mrs. Chavez said. "And a pitcher of your raspberry iced tea."

The hostess nodded. "I'll give your order to your waitress."

"Have a roll." Mrs. Chavez held the basket out to Lauren. "This is one of my favorite restaurants, but their cooks never get in a hurry. It could be awhile before our food arrives."

"Thank you," Lauren said, taking a roll and tearing off a corner. It melted in her mouth. She tore off another chunk, then hesitated, reminding herself to eat slowly.

Mrs. Chavez took a roll also, breaking it open and slathering on a generous helping of butter. "I asked you here today because there are two items that we need to discuss. The first is your promotion."

Lauren froze, the roll halfway to her mouth. "Promotion?"

Mrs. Chavez nodded. "I realize you've only been with the company a little over a year, but your sales numbers are outstanding. I think you're ready to move up the ladder and become a mentor.''

Lauren didn't know what to say. But she did know that sitting there with her mouth hanging open wouldn't impress Mrs. Chavez. "Thank you for giving me the opportunity. I promise not to disappoint you."

"Please understand that you'll have to go through a probationary period. Each new mentor must bring her first protégée successfully through the seven-week Ladybug training program. Some of our Ladybugs, though wonderful at sales, simply aren't cut out to be teachers."

Lauren nodded, sincerely hoped that wasn't true in her case since teaching was her chosen profession.

"So the pay increase for your new position won't be in effect until your protégée successfully completes the Ladybug Lingerie training program."

Lauren set the half-eaten roll on her plate. "May I ask how much that pay increase will be?"

Mrs. Chavez scribbled a figure on the paper napkin in front of her, then slid it across the table. "I hope you'll find this satisfactory."

Lauren stared at the number, unable to argue with her. "More than satisfactory."

"Good." Mrs. Chavez licked the buttery crumbs off her fingers. "Of course, becoming a mentor includes another perk in addition to a salary increase. And I don't think we should make you wait for it."

Lauren watched in disbelief as the older woman pulled a set of car keys out of her purse.

Mrs. Chavez smiled. "Your new Volkswagen Beetle is out in the parking lot."

Her throat grew tight as she took the keys out of her hand. The increase in salary would unlock the stranglehold on her budget. She could actually pay her rent. Afford to buy clothes again. Splurge on fast food once in a while. But best of all, a Ladybug of her very own would finally allow her to consign her twenty-five-year-old lemon to the junkyard where it belonged. "I don't know what to say."

"Say—pass the honey. Your roll looks a little dry to me."

Lauren choked on a giggle, her elation making her a little giddy. "Pass the honey, please. And thank you, Mrs. Chavez. Thank you so very much."

"You don't have to thank me," Mrs. Chavez replied, handing her the small honey pot. "You still have to earn the promotion, Lauren. But you're a hard worker, so I have no doubt you'll succeed."

"Are you sure you're not my fairy godmother in disguise?"

Mrs. Chavez laughed. "If I had a magical wand, I'd have a body like a supermodel and a lover who looked like Sean Connery. No, I'm just a businesswoman. But I will admit this is one of my favorite parts of the job."

Lauren wrapped her hand around the car keys, the metal warm against her palm. She'd struggled for so long in pursuit of her dream to become a teacher. To prove to herself that she could make it on her own. Now everything was falling into the place. The reality of it all made her eyes sting and her throat tighten. Part of her feared this was all some incredible dream and she'd wake up to find another eviction threat under her apartment door.

Of course, she still had to bring a protégée through the Ladybug Lingerie training program before she'd see that increase in her salary, but how hard could it be? Lauren had completed the seven-week program without any problems. And she looked forward to the chance to give another woman a helping hand.

Her life was definitely taking a turn in the right direction. A new car. A new promotion. A new chance to make her dream of becoming a teacher finally a reality.

What more could she possibly want?

Becky's reminder about fulfilling her New Year's resolution niggled in the back of her brain, but she ignored it. What were the chances of meeting the right man in the next three months? Besides, she needed to concentrate on her new job until the probationary period was over.

Lauren wasn't about to let anything or anyone stop her now.

THAT AFTERNOON, SAM PUT himself into the hands of two sadists who were disguised as a fashion consultant and a makeup artist. He stood on a dais in a salon trying to decide which part of his body hurt the most. They'd plucked his eyebrows, shaved his legs and wrangled him into a gel bra.

Now they were circling him like two fashion vultures, ready to draw blood if necessary to transform him into a believable woman.

"I'm glad we went with the peplum jacket,"

Amy Kwan said to Marco. "It makes the padding we added to his hips and waist more flattering and hides the width of his shoulders a little better."

Marco nodded. "The pantsuits are a must. His legs are hideous."

Sam frowned. "That's because I've got bandages all over them from all the nicks you inflicted with that damn razor."

Marco tutted under his breath. "My, aren't we testy this morning. Must be that time of the month."

"Let's not fight, girls," Amy chided, then looked back up at Sam. "How does the wig feel?"

"It itches like crazy," Sam replied.

"You'll get used to it," Amy assured him. Then she turned to Marco. "He looks pretty good. I don't think I could tell if I saw him on the street."

Marco wrinkled his nose. "I don't find him very attractive."

"Well, that's a relief," Sam said, shifting on his feet. His toes were pinched by the low-heeled pumps Amy insisted he wear. "The less attractive, the better."

"Wait a minute. I have an idea." Amy turned and rushed over to the walk-in closet.

Sam held his breath, fearing the worst. Her last idea had been to insert wax pads in his cheeks to make them plumper. If Marco tried to corral him into a girdle again, he was drawing the line. A man could only take so much.

"Here we go," Amy said, holding out a pair of translucent pink plastic-rimmed eyeglasses. "These have clear lenses, so they shouldn't affect your vision. But I think they'll add just the right touch."

Sam put them on, then waited for their reaction.

Marco gasped in appreciation. "This is why they pay you the big bucks, Ms. Kwan. Those glasses are the pièce de résistance."

Amy nodded, a satisfied smile curving her mouth. "We did it, Marco. He's a woman."

Marco walked over to the corner and pulled a full-length mirror out into the center of the room. "Take a look, Sam. Or should I call you Samantha?"

But Sam didn't even hear the question. He gaped at the woman in the mirror. She looked about forty and a little on the heavy side. Her hair was cut in short blond bob and she wore too much makeup.

He stepped off the dais for a closer look, wishing the glasses he wore did have corrective lenses in them, because he simply couldn't see himself anymore. Sam Kane had disappeared. And in his place was a stranger. A *female* stranger. "Damn."

"That, my dear Samantha, is an understatement," Marco replied. "But you've got to do something about the voice. It's too deep."

Sam cleared his throat, then spoke in the distinctive voice that he'd impersonated so often in high school. "My name is not Samantha," he replied, nailing the high-pitched inflection perfectly. He saw Amy's eyes widen. "It's Philomena. Philomena Gallagher."

Amy burst into laughter. "I can't believe it. That's perfect! How do you do it?"

"I'm a man of many talents."

"Not anymore," Marco replied, leaning against a counter and folding his arms across his narrow chest. "You're a woman. And now that we've worked our magic, would you mind telling us what this is all about? Mr. Cooper was marvelously mysterious about it all. Are you in the witness protection program or something?"

"Sorry, that's confidential," Sam replied, trodding carefully across the room. He felt as if he were walking on ice.

"Try to glide," Amy suggested. "And take shorter steps. You'll get used to it after a while."

Sam wasn't so confident. He'd admired women for as long as he could remember, and certainly enjoyed spending time with members of the opposite sex. But he hadn't realized that everything about them was so complicated. From their shoes to their hair to their makeup. And that was just on the outside.

What if he made a major blunder? Blew his chance to win the company before he ever had a chance to prove to his grandfather and himself that he could handle the job?

He began to pace back and forth across the room, imagining all the worst possible scenarios.

"That's better," Amy said, watching him walk. "I think you're getting the hang of it."

He paused, taking a deep breath and pushing his worries away. He'd pulled off tougher charades than this. Hell, he lived a lie every day of his life. The key was confidence. If you portray a strong belief in yourself and your abilities, other people tend to naturally follow along and believe it, too.

"I think I'm ready," Sam announced.

"I'm not so sure," Marco said, scowling at Sam's chest. "I think his breasts are all wrong."

Sam looked down at the two foreign lumps sticking out under his collarbone. "Are they too big?"

"No, too small," Marco said, moving toward the counter. "They're out of proportion with the rest of your body. Makes you look a little hippy." He turned to Amy. "Do we have a bigger gel bra?"

"What size?" Amy asked, digging through the box full of bras Sam had brought with him from Midnight Lace.

"Let's try a 40D."

She pulled out a big white bra and approached Sam. "Maybe you should put this one on. You're going to have to get dressed on your own from now on."

"Sure." He shrugged out of his jacket, then removed the blouse. It couldn't be any harder to put on a bra then to take one off. And he'd had years of experience doing just that with more women than he could count.

The bra was huge, the two cups filled with a gel-like substance designed to give it a natural look and feel. But he had to contort his arms at an uncomfortable angle around his back to pull the two straps together. It took three attempts before the hooks finally caught and the bra was on.

"Your boobs are riding a little high," Marco commented, watching the show.

Sam looked down and bumped his chin against his new breasts. Grasping the elastic band on the bottom edge of the bra, he tugged it down farther on his chest.

"That's better," Amy said. "I think you're ready."

He was exhausted. Becoming a woman was hard work. The clothes, the padding, the bra. And the makeup. Marco had written down instructions on how to apply the heavy layer of cosmetics that hid his whiskers and softened the hard angles of his face. Tomorrow Sam would have to do all of it on his own.

That's when the real test would come. He had to convince everyone he met, especially his new Ladybug Lingerie mentor, that he was a woman. The clock on the wall showed he had less than twenty-four hours to prepare himself for the toughest challenge he'd ever faced. Or, at least, the second toughest.

One that could change his life forever.

4

THE NEXT MORNING, Sam stood outside the meeting room at Ladybug Lingerie headquarters, stealthily watching the women who walked inside. So far, none had given him a second glance. Or pointed at him and shouted, "Impostor!"

That was a good sign.

From his observation, the Ladybug Lingerie sales force came in all shapes and sizes. There were young women, older women, slender women and, in Marco's words, hippy women. Even a couple who stood six feet tall, the same height as Sam.

Pushing himself off the wall, he tightened his grasp on his new leather handbag and tried to glide into the room. Instead, he tripped on the edge of the rug and almost landed flat on his face. But he caught himself in time, grabbing the edge of the registration table. He could just imagine the scene if he'd fallen. The weight of his body smashing his new bra against the linoleum floor, the two gel cups bursting and flooding the room.

"I know who you are," a feminine voice trilled, breaking into his doomsday reverie.

He looked at the slender African-American woman seated behind the table, the tiny hairs rising on the back of his neck. Was his cover blown already? "You do?"

"Sure. You're the new Ladybug. I can tell, 'cause you look a little nervous."

Sam cleared his throat. "I'm Philomena Gallagher. I was told to report here this morning."

"Welcome to the colony, Philomena. I'm Althea. I've been working here for ten years and I can assure you that there's nothing to be nervous about. I know you'll fit right in."

He took a deep breath. "I hope so."

"Don't worry, hon. We don't send anyone out into the field without plenty of training. You'll be assigned a mentor today. She'll teach you everything you need to know. Probably become best friends along the way, too, since you'll be her shadow for the next seven weeks."

Sam nodded, then realized Althea was staring at him. Had he applied his makeup incorrectly? Put his wig on crooked? "Is anything wrong?"

Althea leaned forward, her brow furrowed as she looked up at him. "No holes."

"Excuse me?" Panic shot through his gut. Had Amy and Marco forgotten something vital in his transformation?

"Your ears," she explained. "They aren't pierced." She reached into a basket and pulled out a pair of ladybug earrings. "Fortunately, I have a few clip-on pairs left. This is a little welcome gift from the company."

"Thank you." He took the earrings from her, noticing she wore an identical pair on her ears. "Should I put them on?"

"Might as well," Althea replied, then hitched her thumb behind her. "There's a mirror over there."

He walked over to the mirror, taking extra care to take shorter steps as Amy had instructed. The earrings were small, but he managed to clip one onto each earlobe without any problem. Then he stared into the mirror, admitting to himself that they didn't look half bad. Even if they pinched almost as badly as his shoes.

The lights dimmed and a voice came over the loudspeaker. "Please take your seats, Ladybugs. It's almost time for the show."

He looked around, then noticed Althea waving to him from a row of chairs lined up in front of a small platform.

"I saved a seat for you," she said, taking the chair next to him.

"What's going on?" he whispered. Music now emanated over the speaker, a soft, sultry jazz tune.

"A Ladybug Lingerie fashion show. We have one of these the first Monday of every month to kick off the business meeting. It's a great way for the sales gang to see all of the newest products."

New products. Would the Seductress Bra be among them? His mission might not turn out to be so hard after all. Sam leaned back in his chair, grateful for the respite. As long as the room was dark, he could let down his guard and forget about playing a woman.

The first model walked down the runway of the makeshift stage, dressed in a long, white nightgown. The moderator described the specifics of the style and fabric. "Kathleen is wearing a white silk peignoir called the Wedding Nighter. Notice the fine lace detailing on the cuffs and hem. This gown is made of one hundred percent raw silk, with tiny sequins adorning the sweetheart bodice.''

Althea leaned over to him and whispered, ''Kathleen's had four wedding nights and is on the hunt for number five, so that's the perfect gown for her.''

Sam nodded, then tried to fold his arms across his chest. Only to find his breasts were in the way. Scowling, he settled for folding his hands on his lap. He felt like an idiot.

Three more models walked across the runway, all in various stages of undress, but none of them wearing the Seductress. Althea shared a morsel of gossip about each one of them.

Then the fourth model appeared on the runway. She was a tall, slender woman in sassy pink baby doll pajamas. Her long legs seemed to go on forever.

He sat up in his chair and watched as she walked across the stage, gliding perfectly, the sexy sway of her hips mesmerizing him. Despite all the extra padding and makeup he wore to make him a woman, his body was reminding him that he was definitely a man.

''That's Lauren McBride,'' Althea whispered. ''She's the hottest new star at Ladybug Lingerie.''

Hot was certainly the word to describe her. ''I'd love to meet her.''

Althea smiled. ''I think I can arrange that. Lauren's your new mentor.''

Twenty minutes later, Sam learned the true meaning of the word torture. Lauren stood before him, still wearing those delectable baby doll pajamas that revealed so much tantalizing creamy skin that he couldn't take his eyes off of her. Here was the most beautiful, desirable woman he'd ever met and he couldn't do a damn thing about it. His blood pounded in his veins as Althea made the introductions.

"Lauren, this is our newest Ladybug, Philomena Gallagher. She'll be your protégée for the next seven weeks."

Lauren smiled at him and held out one slender hand. "It's a pleasure to meet you."

He swallowed hard, wishing he could say the same. Pleasure would be peeling off that skimpy pink silk confection and discovering the woman underneath. Kissing those succulent lips would go beyond pleasure into the realms of pure ecstasy. A fantasy that, considering the circumstances, would have to remain a fantasy.

Sam reached out to shake her hand, remembering just in time to temper his grip. "I'm looking forward to working with you."

"I've never been a mentor before," Lauren informed him, withdrawing her hand much too soon. "So you'll have to be patient with me. And please ask questions. I'll do my best to answer them."

He'd love to ask her a few questions. Was she involved with anyone? Did she always wear that subtle, tantalizing perfume that was teasing his nostrils? Were her eyes really that blue?

But those question were much too personal. This was business. Strictly business. Sam needed to remember that. He also needed to keep in mind that for the next four weeks, women were off limits. Even a woman as incredible as Lauren McBride.

Another Ladybug tapped Lauren on the shoulder, turning her attention away from him for a moment. It gave Sam a little time to collect himself. And to consider that perhaps his attraction to her was simply a matter of forbidden fruit. Did knowing he couldn't act on his desires make them that much stronger? Such a possibility eased his anxiety a little. Especially since he was usually drawn to women who were only interested in good time and nothing more, like the three who had picked him up off the road yesterday.

It only took one glance at Lauren to tell she wasn't that kind of girl. Even if she was dressed for the part. No doubt if he'd met her under different circumstances, she wouldn't have this kind of effect on him.

But when she turned to face him once again, flashing a dazzling smile, his body quickly countermanded that argument. His job was going to be even more difficult than he'd imagined.

A bell chimed, indicating the meeting was about to begin. Lauren motioned for him to follow her, then headed for one of the tables set up in a U-shaped formation.

Sam wobbled for a moment on his heels, his mind more on the pleasurable rear view of his new mentor then his task of walking and acting like a woman. Forcing himself to look away, he took small, gliding steps toward the empty chair beside her and sat down.

A woman with a towering beehive of grey and black hair stood at a podium at the front. He knew from the huge portrait hanging in the foyer of the building that this was the founder of the company, Tina Chavez.

"Good morning, Ladybugs." Mrs. Chavez wore the ladybug earrings, as well as a huge ladybug brooch on the lapel of her jacket. "We've got a lot to do today, so let's get started. Our first order of business is to introduce the newest Ladybug to our colony. Everyone please give a warm welcome to Mrs. Philomena Gallagher."

Mrs. Chavez led the applause, then motioned for Sam to stand up. "Please tell us a little about yourself, Mrs. Gallagher."

They all turned to look at Sam. He stood up, hoping his wig was on straight and his breasts were even. Then he cleared his throat. "Thank you, Mrs. Chavez. And please call me Philomena. All my friends do."

This brought smiles to all the faces in the room. Sam took a deep breath and forged ahead with the phony background Cooper had written up on his job application. "I'm recently divorced and back in the job force for the first time in twenty years, so I'm a little rusty."

"Aren't we all?" Althea chimed, to the amusement of the group.

Sam smiled. "I'm looking forward to learning more about the company and to selling the products. I've always been a big admirer of Ladybug Lingerie."

"Do you have a favorite design?" Mrs. Chavez asked.

Almost against his will, Sam's gaze turned to Lauren, still clad in the baby doll pajamas. From his vantage point, he could see the curve of her right breast and the cleft of her generous cleavage. A sweat broke out on his brow. "I really like what Lauren is wearing."

Tina nodded approvingly. "One of our most popular designs. Now in a new array of lovely pastel colors. Thank you, Philomena. We're very happy to have you here."

Sam sat down, his knees wobbly.

"Good job," Lauren whispered. "Mrs. Chavez designed these baby dolls herself, so you just scored a few points."

He pushed his glasses up on his nose, trying not look at her again. "Thanks. Are you going to…change?"

"As soon as the meeting is over." She glanced at her watch. "Then it will be time for lunch. Are you free? I know a great deli just around the corner. If we talk Ladybug business, I can put it on my expense account."

"Sounds great." Sam was certain he could handle being around Lauren once she was decently covered. A man could only take so much temptation.

Even a man wearing lipstick and a bra.

"HOW'S YOUR SANDWICH, Philomena?" Lauren asked, seated across from her at a corner table in the delicatessen. Her new protégée had been strangely quiet.

"Just fine," she replied. "How's yours?"

"Good." So much for conversation. Lauren picked up a potato chip, wondering how to break through the older woman's shell. She knew how tough a divorce could be. How difficult it was to start your entire life over again. Probably even more so for Philomena, who had been a housewife for the last twenty years. Was it any wonder that she acted so stiff and self-conscious?

"I enjoyed the fashion show today," Philomena said, breaking her silence at last. "Although I was hoping I might see the Seductress bra. I've heard so much about it."

Lauren nodded. "It's the company's best-kept secret. I haven't even seen one myself yet, although Mrs. Chavez promised to have the manufacturer ship one of the prototypes to me now that I'm a mentor."

"Interesting," Philomena said, taking another bite of her sandwich.

"So tell me about yourself." Lauren reached for her soda. "Do you have any children?"

Philomena shook her head. "No. I can't, I mean...we were never able to have children."

"I'm sorry."

"No problem." Philomena gave a hapless shrug, then turned back to her king-size sandwich. She certainly had a healthy appetite.

"I ate a lot after my divorce, too," Lauren blurted, then realized a second too late how rude it sounded. "I'm sorry...I didn't mean..."

"No, that's all right," Philomena assured her. "You're divorced?"

Lauren nodded. "Almost two years now. Funny, it seems longer."

"So, are you…seeing anyone now?"

"No. I've dated a few times, but I guess I have a case of cold feet." She broke a potato chip in half. "In fact, I have a confession to make. I had an ulterior motive when I invited you to lunch."

"Really?"

She nodded. "Chuck, my ex-husband, asked me to meet him here today. He wants to talk about reconciling. As a lawyer, his arguments are pretty persuasive."

Philomena stilled, then slowly lowered her sandwich to her plate. "So you're considering it?"

Lauren shook her head, wondering why she felt so at ease confiding in a person she just met. Perhaps it was the age difference—seeking the wisdom of an older woman. Or maybe it was their common bonds—both divorced, both employees at Ladybug Lingerie. Whatever the reason she felt an odd connection to Philomena. She sensed a quiet strength in the woman that she found comforting.

"Not really," she admitted at last. "Although, I have to admit Chuck's arguments can be convincing. Especially since I've been striking out where men are considered. And I suppose it would be one way to fulfill my New Year's resolution."

"New Year's resolution?" Philomena picked up her soda and took a sip.

She blushed. "It's nothing. I shouldn't have even brought it up."

"Now you've really piqued my curiosity."

A blush warmed her cheeks. "It's just a silly vow I made to find a man to sleep with before the year is out."

Philomena spit soda halfway across the table, then began to cough. Lauren reached over and began patting her on the back. "Are you all right?"

The woman nodded, taking a deep gulp of air. "Fine. The soda just went down the wrong way."

"I hope you weren't offended by what I said. I mean, I know it sounds a little...odd, but..." Her voice trailed off. How could she explain the reasoning behind such an unusual resolution. The near panic that had assailed her every time she went on a date. The fear that she might never know the thrill of falling in love again.

And she wanted to fall in love. Wanted to marry again someday and have a family, as well as a career in teaching. Despite everything she'd been through, Lauren still truly believed in happily-ever-after.

Philomena cleared her throat. "Please don't apologize. I'm glad you told me. So...any eligible candidates yet? Besides your ex-husband?"

Lauren smiled. "Not really."

"That surprises me."

"I just haven't found the right one, if you know what I mean."

"I think I do."

"How about you, Philomena? Any men on your romantic horizon?"

"Absolutely not."

Lauren blinked at the intensity in her tone. "Oh. Is it still too soon?"

She nodded vehemently. "Absolutely. Much too soon. I don't even want to think about it."

"I was the same way," Lauren confided. "Too worried about finding a place of my own and making ends meet to have time to think about men."

"That's it, exactly. I'm still trying to adjust to this new...lifestyle."

Lauren remembered her own confusion and chronic indecision during the first weeks after her divorce. She never wanted to go through anything like that again. Which was just one more reason to keep Chuck in the past.

As if on cue, he walked through the door of the deli, looking around until he spotted her. Then he waved and started walking to the table. She could feel herself tense up. Despite her determination to maintain control, Chuck always seemed able to keep her off balance. Make her doubt herself.

"Here he comes," Lauren whispered to Philomena. "I'm sorry to put you in the middle of all of this."

"No problem," Philomena replied, pushing her empty paper plate away.

"Hello, Lauren," Chuck said with a smile. "You look gorgeous, as usual."

Lauren forced a smile. "Hi, Chuck. I'd like you to meet a friend of mine, Philomena Gallagher. Philomena, this is Chuck McBride."

They shook hands, Chuck wincing slightly.

"Wow, that's some grip you have there, Mrs. Gallagher. You must pump iron?"

"As a matter of fact, I do. Although sometimes I use lawyers instead of barbells."

Chuck blinked, then looked at Lauren and burst out laughing. "She's a hoot. Where did you find her?"

Lauren took a deep breath, hoping her new protégée wouldn't think she was nuts. "Philomena's my new roommate."

5

SAM FOLLOWED LAUREN OUT of the deli, wishing she'd slow down a little. He still wasn't used to walking in heels.

"I'm sorry, Philomena," Lauren said, obviously still agitated by the meeting with her ex-husband. "I had no right to involve you in my problems. It's just that Chuck is so…"

"Pushy?" Sam interjected. "Annoying? Obtuse?"

She laughed. "I suppose some people might see him like that."

"But not you?"

She shrugged. "He's always been a little insecure. I think he tries to compensate and that can give people the wrong impression about him."

"I think you're too kind."

"And as for that part about being my new roommate," she slowed and turn to face him, "I just said it because Chuck's been showing up at my place uninvited recently. I was hoping it might make him back off a little."

"No problem." Sam looked down to make certain his breasts were even. So far, so good.

"But now that I think about it," Lauren said slowly, "maybe it's not such a bad idea."

He looked up at her. "What?"

"Becoming roommates. We could both save on rent that way. As well as utilities. It's always cheaper for two to live together instead of one. And my apartment has an extra bedroom. If you're interested, that is."

He froze. "You want me to move in with you?"

"It was just an idea. If you're uncomfortable with it…"

"No. It's just that I…never considered the possibility." Against his better judgment, Sam found himself considering it now. Living with Lauren McBride would be twenty-four hours of pure bliss— if he was living with her as a man. But posing as a woman presented all kinds of problems. He'd have to play the role of Philomena both day and night. Take extra care to keep her from discovering his secret. Both of his secrets. Still…

"I think we could have a lot of fun together."

He closed his eyes, trying not to get sucked into the myriad fantasies clamoring at his brain. Maybe moving in with Lauren wasn't such a bad idea. It would give him complete access to one of the top saleswomen of Ladybug Lingerie. Cooper's words reverberated in his brain: *Find a way to get close to your mentor and you'll find the Seductress bra.*

Living with Lauren would certainly give him an advantage in his mission. He might even be able to intercept the Seductress package when it arrived at her apartment. He could let the boys at Midnight Lace have a look, then return it to her without anyone being the wiser. And if his moving in with Lauren could keep that creep Chuck McBride away from her, so much the better.

"Just think about it, Philomena," Lauren said.

"I'll do it."

Her eyes lit up. "Really?"

Sam nodded, ignoring the warning bells going off in his head. "When do you want me to move in?"

"As soon as possible. Where are you living now?"

"I have a small apartment just west of here," he replied honestly. "On Cambridge Street."

"Will you have trouble getting out of your lease?"

He shook his head, knowing he wouldn't even try. It might help to have a refuge to take a break from his Philomena role once in a while. "It won't be a problem."

"Then why not move in today? We don't have any parties scheduled. I've got an afternoon class, but we can go have a copy of the apartment key made right now. This will be great." Then she reached out and hugged him.

Sam's whole body tightened at the contact. The rational side of his brain worried that she might be able to tell a few parts of him were artificial. The other side of his brain relished the feel of her soft body against him. The tantalizing scent of her hair and skin. The caress of her warm breath on his neck.

The impulsive hug was over in an instant. But it felt like an eternity to Sam. And somehow he knew the next few weeks wouldn't go any faster. She'd opened the door to purgatory and he'd rushed right in.

He just had to make sure he could get back out in one piece.

SAM STEPPED OUT OF THE shower in his apartment, ruffling the towel through his short hair. His head still itched from wearing that wig and it felt good to clean all that makeup off his skin.

Of course, he'd have to put it all back on in a few hours. Lauren's class ended at six o'clock. But he intended to enjoy the respite by spending the afternoon as a man. He threw on some jeans and an old gray T-shirt, then dragged his suitcases out of the hall closet and tossed them onto the sofa.

The clothes Amy and Marco had sent home with him were still hanging in the plastic suit bag, so packing wouldn't take long. The only question was what to take with him to Lauren's place.

He was trying to decide whether to throw in his barbells when a knock sounded on the front door. Grateful for the interruption, and even more grateful that he wasn't in his Philomena getup, he opened it to see eleven-year-old Travis Hastings standing on the other side.

Sam was involved with the Big Brother program in Pittsburgh and Travis had been assigned as his little brother last year. He lived only a couple of blocks away and spent a lot of his time at Sam's place. With his father in state prison and his mother working two jobs, the kid didn't have a lot of supervision.

Travis looked at the open suitcases. "Are you going somewhere?"

Sam wanted to kick himself for not considering

Travis when he'd made his decision to move in with Lauren. Four weeks was a long time when you were eleven years old. "Yeah, I got a new job. But it's only temporary. I'll be gone for about a month."

"Oh." Travis tossed his backpack on the floor, then headed for the kitchen. "What kind of job?"

"Actually, it's kind of like detective work. I'm going undercover."

"Cool." Travis returned to the living room with a soda in his hand. "So I won't see you for a while?"

"Afraid not, buddy. But you've got my pager number, right? So you can reach me anytime you need to talk. Day or night, okay?"

"Okay." Travis took a gulp of his soda, then wiped his hand across the back of his mouth. "Do you want to read my report on Guatemala? I got an A plus on it."

"Why don't you read it to me while I pack?"

Sam smiled to himself as Travis dug his report out of his backpack. A year ago the kid wouldn't have even known how to pronounce Guatemala. But ever since Sam had hired a tutor for him, Travis's grades had risen as steadily as his self-confidence.

"Ready?" Travis asked, perching himself on the arm of the recliner.

"Fire away." Sam sat down to listen, giving the boy his full attention. Travis didn't get enough attention at home, although his mother did her best. He'd have to find a way to make some time for the kid this month, despite the challenges of his new job.

Travis finished reading the report, then beamed. "Whadda you think?"

"Sounds like an A-plus report to me. Good job." He gave him a high five, then turned back to his suitcases, wondering how much more he could fit in. Amy and Marco had given him an extra gel bra, five pairs of nylons and a plethora of cosmetics in the handy economy-size bottles.

"Can I check your messages?" Travis asked, walking over to the telephone.

"Sure. Do you remember the secret code?"

"Duh." Travis rolled his eyes. "It's 1111. How hard is that to remember?"

Sam grinned. "Just checking." Then he snapped one of the suitcases shut while Travis dialed the number to access the automated answering machine. A moment later, he grabbed a pencil and notepad off the end table and started scribbling down messages.

"Anything important?" Sam asked, after Travis hung up the receiver.

He tore off the top page of the pad. "You have seven messages. Three are from some girl named Mariah, who said she wants you to call her back. One is from a stupid salesman, who said he'll call you back. One is from a girl named Zoe, who wants to show you her new black negligee."

Travis crinkled his brow. "What the heck is a negligee?"

"I'll tell you in a few years."

Travis rolled his eyes again, then turned back to the notepaper. "The last two are from girls, too. One named Jessica something and the other one is Rachel. Both of them giggled a lot.''

"Some girls tend to do that."

Travis shook his head in disgust. "Don't you get tired of girls calling you all the time, Sam?"

"Are you kidding? I like girls. You will, too, Travis. Probably sooner than you think."

The boy looked skeptical. "I don't know. There's this one girl in my class that I can't stand. She won't leave me alone, but she's too chicken to fight me."

Sam turned, his tone firm. "Hey, I don't want you hitting any girls. Understand?"

"Okay." Travis shrugged, stuffing the notepaper in his pocket. "If you say so. But she *really* bugs me."

Sam walked into the kitchen to grab a soda. He popped the tab, then took a long drink as he moved back into the living room. "Maybe this girl likes you, Travis. Did you ever think of that possibility?"

"I sure hope not. She's one of those gigglers." Travis wandered over to the open suitcase. Then he pulled out the size 40D gel bra, holding it by one strap. "Hey, Sam, what's this thing doing in your suitcase?"

"Uh...it belongs to a friend." Sam took the bra from him, tossed it back into the suitcase, then snapped it shut.

"Is this a new girlfriend or an old girlfriend?"

"Neither," Sam replied, wishing Travis wasn't quite so inquisitive today. Now seemed like a good time to change the subject. "Although I did meet someone new today."

Travis took a swig of his soda. "What's her name?"

Sam's brow furrowed. "What makes you think it's a girl?"

Travis rolled his eyes. "Duh."

"Well, her name is Lauren. And she's very nice."

"Do you like her?"

"Yes. I like her a lot." It surprised him how much he liked her. And bothered him more than little that he had to deceive her to do his job.

"So is she pretty?" Travis asked.

"Beautiful. And smart, too. She's even taking some college classes." He glanced at his watch. "And speaking of classes, don't you have appointment with your tutor in less than fifteen minutes?"

"I'm on my way." Travis heaved a pained sigh. He grabbed his backpack and slung it over his shoulder. "But just answer me one more question."

"Okay. Just one."

"Are you going to marry this Lauren girl?"

An ache formed deep inside his chest. Travis had asked this question before. It had taken Sam awhile to figure out that the boy feared he would move away and forget all about him. "Naw." He reached out and ruffled Travis's hair. "You know I'm not the marrying type."

"Yeah." Travis grinned. "You like to play the field."

"That's right." Sam showed him out the door, not admitting the real reason for his perennial bachelorhood. He was a playboy more out of necessity than choice. He knew if he allowed a woman to grow close to him, sooner or later she'd find him lacking. His own mother, the only person in his family who knew his secret, hadn't even been able to hide her disgust. So marriage and a family simply weren't an option for Sam T. Kane. It was a dream that could never come true.

No matter how much he might want it to.

6

SAM CARRIED THE LAST suitcase into the spare bed-room of Lauren's apartment. He dropped it in the corner, then stepped back to review his progress. Hauling the bed up here had taken awhile. It was tough to maneuver a mattress and bedsprings up three flights of stairs by yourself. Especially when the Indian summer they were enjoying made it uncomfortably warm both inside and out.

But the rest of the move had gone smoothly and fairly quickly. Since he only planned to stay for a month, he'd left most of his belongings at home. The other half fit fairly well into her apartment. He had to give Lauren credit, she certainly knew how to make her place feel cozy. The walls were painted a warm beige, the same color as the carpet. The worn, secondhand furniture in the living room was concealed with stylish throw covers and adorned with an array of bright throw pillows. One look told him she lived on a shoestring budget. But she'd certainly made the most of it.

He wiped the sweat off his brow, then checked his watch. He still had time left to go back to his apartment, transform himself into Philomena, then get back here before Lauren returned from her class.

Sam headed for the front door, pulling off his

damp T-shirt and wiping the perspiration from his neck and chest. Maybe he'd even have time for a beer before he tackled that gel bra again. He opened the door, then heard a stifled scream. He blinked, then found himself staring straight at Lauren.

She took a step back, her eyes blazing. "Who are you? And what are you doing in my apartment?"

He opened his mouth, then closed it again. Why the hell had he chanced coming over here without a dress on? At least she didn't seem to notice his resemblance to Philomena. By the look on her face, she thought he was an intruder.

"I'm Sam," he said at last. "Sam Kane. My cousin asked me to help her move in today."

Lauren's gaze flicked down to his bare chest, then back up again. "Cousin? You mean Philomena?"

He nodded. "That's right. She's back at her apartment, making sure she didn't miss anything."

"Oh." A bright pink blush stained her cheeks. "I'm sorry I screamed like that. I didn't know what to think when I saw a strange man inside my apartment."

"I don't blame you. A girl can't be too careful. Especially a girl as pretty as you."

"Well...thank you." She walked inside, brushing by him, and carefully placed her purse and books on a bench by the door.

"Philomena told me you had a class this afternoon," Sam said, not quite ready to leave. Lauren acted differently around him as a man than she did when he was playing a woman. But he couldn't quite put his finger on her behavior. Irritated? Guarded? Apprehensive?

"The professor had a family emergency," she replied, her back to him, "so the class was cut short."

He folded his arms and leaned against the door frame. "So now you get some time to play."

"Time to work, anyway." She turned and looked toward the clock. "Do you think Philomena will get here soon?"

"It will probably be awhile yet." He nodded toward the sofa. "Do you mind if I sit down? Hauling all her stuff up here wore me out."

Lauren hesitated. "Sure. Go ahead."

He could tell she wanted to tell him no, but was too polite to do so. Was it because she didn't like him? Or just the opposite? Sam sensed she'd been burned by her jerk of an ex-husband. Was that the reason she was acting so skittish around him?

They sat in silence for several moments until Lauren finally asked him a question. "May I get you something to drink?"

"A beer would be great if you have one."

"I'm not sure," she said, turning toward the kitchen. "I'll check."

Sam watched her leave the room, definitely feeling a chill in the air. He wondered what would it take to produce a thaw.

She walked back into the living room, carrying a bottle in her hand. "I didn't have any beer. But one of my friends left some wine coolers here. It's strawberry-banana."

His stomach lurched, but he smiled and took it from her. "This will be fine. Thanks."

She sat down in the chair across from him,

clenching her hands in her lap. "So are you and Philomena close?"

"Closer than you can imagine," Sam said, twisting off the bottle cap.

"That's nice."

Another uncomfortable silence descended between them. Lauren looked at the floor, the ceiling, and her watch, but rarely at him.

He took a long drink of the wine cooler, wishing he could think of some way to put her at ease. He normally didn't have this problem with women. But Lauren was different. He'd known that from the moment he'd met her.

She stood up. "Will you please excuse me? I have a few phone calls to make. Do you mind showing yourself out when you're ready to leave?"

So much for hospitality. "Sure. Go ahead."

She escaped down the hallway, leaving Sam alone in the living room to wonder what had just happened. He usually didn't have this kind of affect on women. But Lauren McBride had taken one look at him and practically run screaming out of the room.

He drained the wine cooler, then stood up to leave. Somehow, some way he was going to find out the reason.

And he knew just the person to do it.

LAUREN SAT AT THE DESK IN her bedroom, feeling like the world's biggest fool. She'd heard the front door open and close more than an hour ago, so she knew Philomena's cousin had left. Why wouldn't he? After all, she'd acted like an escapee from a lunatic asylum.

She pushed the order book out of the way and buried her face in her hands. Why did she always freeze up like that around a good-looking man? Good-looking? That didn't even begin to describe Sam Kane. He was handsome. Charming. Incredibly sexy.

A sound emanating from outside her room told her someone was in the apartment. Philomena.

She lifted her head as she heard the woman call out. "Anybody home?"

Taking a deep breath, Lauren rose out of her chair, then walked out into the hallway. Philomena stood in the kitchen, two bulging grocery sacks filling her arms. Now that Lauren had met Sam Kane, she found the resemblance between the two cousins striking.

"Hello, there," Philomena said, setting the grocery sacks onto the counter. "I picked up a few things at the store on my way over. How does paella sound for supper?"

"Wonderful." Lauren stood in the doorway to the kitchen. "But I'd better warn you—my talent in the kitchen doesn't go further than boiling water."

"No problem," Philomena replied, neatly folding the empty grocery sack. "I love to cook."

Lauren smiled. "Then this arrangement may work out even better than I thought. You can cook, I'll handle the dishes."

"Deal." Philomena must have noticed the way Lauren was staring at her, because she put a hand up to her teased blond hair, patting it into place. "Is something wrong?"

"No," Lauren assured her, slipping into a kitchen chair. "I just can't get over how much you look like your cousin."

"Oh. Sam." Philomena turned back to finish unloading the groceries. "He told me you two had met."

Lauren sighed.

"Did he mention that I was a blubbering idiot?"

"No. I think he felt badly for giving you a scare. I should have mentioned that he might be helping me move."

"It's not your fault. Or his. I…it's just that…"

"What?" Philomena prodded.

Lauren swallowed. "Sam wasn't wearing a shirt when I met him. And I…" She shook her head. "I can't tell you. It's too embarrassing."

"Did he offend you? Insult you in some way?"

"No, nothing like that."

"Then what did he do?"

"He didn't do anything. Sam was a perfect gentleman. It was me." She swallowed hard. "The poor man was simply trying to carry on a polite conversation and I…kept picturing him naked."

Philomena stared at Lauren, and it was obvious she had shocked the poor woman. "That…surprises me."

Lauren smiled. "It surprised me, too. I don't usually have that kind of reaction to men. Maybe that's a good sign. So tell me about him."

"Who?" Philomena asked, still looking a little flustered.

"Your cousin. Sam." Lauren leaned back in her chair. "How old is he?"

"Twenty-seven."

"What does he do?"

"He works for the Kane Corporation. In the creative development department."

Lauren heard the note of pride in her voice. "That sounds fascinating."

"His latest project was as the creative director of the millennium version of Chameleon."

"Wow. That's impressive. I love that game."

"I'm starting to grow rather fond of it myself."

Lauren looked down at the table, tracing the cracks in the veneer with one finger. "So do you think he might be interested?"

"Interested?" Philomena echoed, pulling a bag of chips out of the sack.

"In me," she clarified. "I mean, unless he's already involved with someone."

"No," Philomena replied abruptly, then cleared her throat. "He's not involved at all."

Lauren looked up at her new roommate, wondering if it bothered her to discuss romance so soon after her divorce. Philomena seemed a little ill at ease. "So he is available?"

The older woman slowly turned to face her. "There's something you should know about Sam," she began slowly. "He's a nice guy, but he dates a lot of women. The word commitment isn't in his vocabulary."

"You mean he's a playboy?"

"Well, let me put it this way. The T in Sam's

middle name stands for Tenacious. And he's done a very good job of tenaciously holding on to his bachelorhood.''

''I see.''

Philomena cleared her throat, then turned back to the counter, picking up a box of rice and slitting open the top. ''Time to make dinner. I'm starving.''

But Lauren wasn't ready to change the subject. She'd waited two long years to meet a man who could stir the feelings inside of her that she'd feared were dead. And she wasn't about to let him go so easily.

Sam clenched his jaw, as he searched the cupboards for a bowl for the rice, wondering how he'd ever let himself get into this mess. He hated to disappoint Lauren. Hell, he hated to disappoint himself. It would be sheer torture to live with her every day for the next four weeks and not act on his attraction to her. Especially when he knew it was mutual. That she might be picturing him naked right at this moment.

''Philomena?''

He turned. ''Yes?''

Lauren took a deep breath. ''Would you call your cousin for me?''

He frowned. ''What for?''

''To fix us up on a date. I think he might be the one.''

''The one?'' he echoed, still a little confused. Hadn't he just told her Sam was a playboy?

She nodded. ''The perfect man to help me fulfill my New Year's resolution.''

Sam dropped the box of rice on the floor sending the little brown kernels flying out in all directions over the green linoleum. "You mean…"

She gave a resolute nod.

"That's right. He's the first man I've been attracted to in a very long time. And I'm determined to get over this ridiculous fear of mine. Maybe a playboy is the perfect man to help me do that."

All his previous arguments withered under the heat of his desire for her. Lauren McBride wanted him—no strings attached. Could a man ask for anything more?

The telephone rang, breaking through the fantasy filling his mind. A fantasy that now had every chance of coming true. He reached out to the wall phone next to him and picked up the receiver, grateful for a chance to think. "Hello?"

"Hey, is this Philomena?"

Sam recognized the grating male voice on the other end of the line. "Chuck?"

"That's right. Is my girl there?"

He looked over toward Lauren, who vehemently shook her head. "Sorry, Chuck, she's unavailable at the moment."

"Darn. Could you give her a message for me?"

"Sure."

"Tell her that I've got reservations at the best steakhouse in town for next Saturday night. I'll pick her up at seven."

Sam didn't give himself time for second thoughts. Fate had obviously opened the door and he wasn't about to slam it closed. "Sorry, Chuck, I'm afraid she already has a date."

When he hung up the phone, he saw Lauren staring at him, her eyes wide. "Philomena, does that mean what I think it means?"

He nodded, anticipation awakening every nerve in his body. "I'll call Sam and set it up."

She smiled, then got up to grab a broom and sweep up the rice. "I hope he's free."

"I have a feeling he will be."

Later that night, Sam stood in his tiny bedroom and stared at himself in the mirror. Philomena stared back at him, looking faintly disapproving.

"I'll make it work," he told his reflection, then snatched off the wig. He glanced at the doorknob to make sure it was locked. But he didn't have to worry. Lauren had made it clear that she'd respect her new roommate's privacy. Besides, she'd gone to bed over an hour ago. She was so nervous and giddy about her upcoming date with him that he didn't have the heart to back out of it.

So he'd faked a phone call to himself, then told Lauren that date was on for Saturday night. Dinner at seven at Lucia's, one of the best Italian restaurants in town.

He shed his clothes down to his boxer shorts, refusing to wear the silk panties Ladybug Lingerie had provided. He did have some pride. Of course, he still had to wear the stupid gel bra. But he'd found an easier way to take it on and off. He tugged on the elastic strap and pulled it down his chest and over his hips. It dropped to his feet. He stepped out of it, then hung it by one strap on his doorknob.

He set his alarm clock for 5:00 a.m. Plenty of time to assume his Philomena costume and makeup before Lauren awoke. Checking his watch, he saw that it was almost 2:00 a.m.

Which left his conscience exactly three hours to remind him of all the reasons he shouldn't sleep with Lauren McBride.

7

"HOW MUCH ARE THESE crotchless panties?"

Lauren turned to see Becky dangling a scrap of black silk in front of Philomena's face. The poor woman sat on a love seat, her face turning three shades of red as she fumbled through the Ladybug Lingerie catalog.

"Well, let's see," Philomena said, her brow furrowed. "I know they're in here somewhere."

"The panties are ten dollars," Lauren said, sorting through a box of garter belts. "And they come in both black and red, with matching bras."

"Cool!" Becky exclaimed. "I'll take one of each. Don will die when he sees me in these."

"Just don't kill him off before the wedding," Lauren quipped.

Becky tossed the panties in Lauren's direction. "Maybe you should wear a pair for tonight."

"What happens tonight?" Mary Ann Simms asked. Mary Ann had attended St. Bartholomew's parochial school with Becky, Lauren and most of the other guests present at Becky's bridal shower.

"Lauren's got a hot date with a hunk," Becky replied before Lauren could even open her mouth.

Philomena cleared her throat, then held up the catalog. "There are some lovely silk nightgowns and matching robes in here if anyone is interested."

"Not until we hear about this hunk," Mary Ann said, taking a seat on the arm of the sofa. "What's his name? Where did you meet him? And exactly how hot is he?"

Lauren swallowed a sigh, knowing very well her friends wouldn't let her leave the party without revealing every detail. "His name is Sam. I met him at my apartment. In fact, he's Philomena's cousin. She fixed us up."

Every eye turned to her protégée. Philomena cleared her throat. "That's right. We're...I mean, they're going to Lucia's for dinner."

"Not bad," said Teresa, a former tomboy who now ran a modeling agency. "But what about after dinner. Anything special planned for dessert?"

The living filled with the sound of laughter and woof whistles. Lauren could feel a blush crawl up her cheeks. "That's enough, guys. You're embarrassing Philomena."

"She's not the one turning red," Becky said with a wide grin. "You don't mind, do you, Philomena?"

"No," Philomena relied, her voice sounding a little strained. "Not at all. Just pretend I'm not here."

Mary held her hands up in the air. "Wait a minute. First things first. What does he look like?"

Lauren slid onto the floral love seat next to Philomena. "Well, he's got short, dark hair and the most incredible blue eyes."

"Yummy," Teresa said. "What about his butt? You know I'm very particular about that part of the male anatomy."

"His butt? Well..." Lauren hesitated, letting the moment build. "Do you remember that toilet paper commercial with Mr. Whipple, where he had this irresistible urge to squeeze it? I can definitely empathize with him."

The women dissolved into laughter. Philomena shifted slightly on the love seat.

"So were you able to resist temptation?" Becky asked.

"Barely." Then Lauren stood up, not wanting to admit her erotic fantasies in front of Sam's cousin. "Okay, that's all I'm telling. We're here to make sure Becky has everything a bride needs to make her groom happy. So please fill out your order form and hand it to Philomena."

"Sure," Mary Ann teased. "Tell us about his magnificent butt, then leave us hanging."

A mischievous gleam twinkled in Teresa's eye. "Well, there's no reason we can't eat dinner at Lucia's tonight, girls, and see this hunk for ourselves."

"Absolutely not," Philomena interjected, her voice firm. Every woman in the room turned to look at her. "I think Sam and Lauren deserve some privacy so they can get to know each other better."

"Philomena's right," Becky concurred. "Besides, if it works out, maybe she can bring him as her date to my wedding. Then we can all get a gander at his gluteus maximus."

"I'll see what I can do," Lauren promised, her stomach fluttering when she looked at the clock. The bridal shower had lasted later than she had expected, which left her less time to prepare for her date.

Mary Ann handed her order form to Philomena.

"Let's get moving, girls, or Lauren won't have time to obsess over what she's going to wear tonight. You know a date isn't official unless a girl spends at least two hours panicking in front of her closet."

"And half an hour on the shoes," Teresa said. "They have to make just the right impression. I can never find the right shoes to wear."

Mary Ann shook her head. "Clothes are never a problem for me. It's my hair." She picked up a handful of her thick black curls. I go through at least half a can of hairspray for each date. Fortunately, I only average two dates a year, so I'm not exactly breaking the budget on hairspray."

"Are you going to wear your hair up or down?" Becky asked Lauren.

"Up," she replied, growing more nervous by the moment. It had been a very long time since she'd been this excited about a date. Or wanted to impress someone so much. Especially after the way she'd acted the first time Sam saw her. "Unless you think it looks better down?"

"I vote for down," Becky replied, then surveyed the room. "What does everybody else think?"

A show of hands resulted in a split decision, with half of her friends voting for her to wear it up, the other half down. She turned to Philomena for the deciding vote. "Well, what do you think?"

Philomena looked at her for a long moment. "Down. I definitely like it down."

"Then down it is." Lauren took a deep breath. "Any other advice? I need all the help I can get."

"Just be yourself," Mary Ann told her. "He won't be able to resist you."

Lauren wished she could agree, but experience had taught her otherwise. Between Chuck and her blind dates she'd come to the depressing conclusion that the men in her life had always been the ones to leave first.

The bridal shower started to break up, several of her friends giving her a hug and wishing her good luck as they left.

Philomena stood up and handed Lauren the stack of order forms she'd collected. "Looks like the party was a big success."

"What do the sales add up to?" Lauren asked, taping the forms together, then sticking them into her briefcase.

"I left my calculator at the apartment," Philomena said. "But I can figure it out once we get back."

"Don't worry about it," Lauren replied. "I'll take care of it this time. So how did you like your first Ladybug Lingerie party?"

"Very enlightening."

She smiled. "My friends tend to get carried away sometimes."

"I like them."

"Me too." She gathered all her Ladybug Lingerie samples together, gave Becky a hug goodbye, then followed Philomena out the door. The older woman seemed a little quieter than usual. Was she nervous about the upcoming date as well? Perhaps Philomena sensed that Sam was less than enthusiastic about it?

Lauren mentally kicked herself for letting her insecurities overtake her once again. From now on she was going to think positive. She planned to knock the socks off of Sam Kane. As well as the rest of his clothes.

A few hours later, Lauren stood in front of her closet, wondering if she had enough time to run out and buy a new outfit. She had nothing decent to wear for this date. The red dress she'd planned to dazzle Sam with had a small grease spot on the front that she hadn't noticed before. The blue pantsuit made her look hippy.

"Philomena!" she called out to her new roommate. "Help."

Philomena stuck her head in Lauren's bedroom. "Is something wrong?"

"I've got less than an hour before I'm supposed to meet Sam at the restaurant and at this rate, I'll be showing up naked. I don't have anything to wear."

Philomena gave her a sympathetic smile. "You've got great clothes. I love that pink thing."

"What pink thing?" she asked, sorting through the hangers in her closet for the fourth time.

"That sweater you wore the day we went out for lunch."

"I can't wear a sweater to Lucia's. It's not dressy enough."

"Couldn't you wear a skirt or something with it?"

"I don't look good in skirts."

Philomena folded her arms across her chest and leaned against the door frame. "I find that hard to believe. Besides, any man in his right mind isn't going to be looking at your clothes. He's going to be looking at you."

"I think that makes me even more nervous."

Philomena smiled, the resemblance to Sam so striking that it made Lauren blink. "You'll be fine. Really."

Lauren stepped back from the closet. "Why don't you pick something you think Sam would like. And I'll wear it. No matter what it looks like."

Philomena moved purposefully toward the closet. "Now that's an offer I can't refuse."

LAUREN SAT AT A CORNER table in Lucia's wondering why she had ever allowed Philomena to select her clothes for this date. She truly liked the older woman, but her taste in fashion left a lot to be desired. And how could she ever hope to seduce Sam Kane wearing a white, button-up-to-the-collar long-sleeve blouse, a gray wool jacket and a calf-length gray wool skirt?

Of course, it wouldn't matter what she wore if Sam stood her up. He was late. Twenty minutes late, to be exact.

The waiter approached her table, a small, sympathetic smile on his face. "Would you like to use the courtesy phone to see if your date is delayed?"

"No, thank you," she said, laying her napkin on her plate. It was obvious he wasn't coming. No doubt Philomena had twisted his arm to agree to this date in the first place. She had no reason to believe a man as gorgeous as Sam Kane would be interested in her.

She pushed back her chair, her throat tight. How she wished she hadn't mentioned it to Becky or any of her other friends. Now she'd have to see the pity in their eyes when she told them he'd stood her up. And she couldn't even get a refund on the crotchless panties, thanks to Ladybug Lingerie's no-returns policy.

Lauren walked blindly toward the front entrance, willing herself not to cry until she was alone in her car. It was stupid to be this upset anyway. She didn't even know the man. What did it matter if he was a no-show for their date? Obviously, he wasn't attracted to her. Or perhaps her behavior at their first meeting had put him off. Who knew how much arm-twisting Philomena had to do to even get him to agree to this date in the first place. Maybe he'd decided she simply wasn't worth the effort.

She was so intent on thinking of all the reasons he wouldn't show up that she ran right into the man at the front door.

"Whoa," he said, grasping her shoulders to keep her steady. "You're not leaving already, are you?"

She sucked in her breath at his touch. It felt as if a bolt of lightning had shot through her. His blue eyes twinkled and a half smile creased his handsome face.

"I...didn't think you were coming."

"I'm sorry I'm late. I was held up at the last minute. Will you let me make it up to you?"

She swallowed, wondering why it felt as if her knees were melting. "How?"

"By treating you to the best dinner in town. The chef here is a friend of mine and I've already put in a special order for us. And I have a surprise for you."

"What kind of surprise?"

He grinned. "If I tell you, it won't be a surprise. Will you stay?"

All her insecurities dissolved under the warmth of his smile. "How can I resist now?"

"Good." Then his gaze slowly skimmed over her body. "You look wonderful tonight."

"Thank you," she replied, worried that if she didn't move soon, she'd melt right into a puddle on the floor. It was disconcerting that a man could have this kind of effect on her. Maybe she was just hungry. Low blood sugar caused all kinds of physical symptoms.

When the burly maître d' approached them, Sam leaned over to whisper something to him. The big man nodded, then disappeared into the kitchen.

"I've already got a table for us," Lauren said, suspicious of the twinkle in Sam's eye.

"We won't need a table."

"We won't?"

He shook his head. "That's part of the surprise."

A moment later, the maître d' returned carrying a huge picnic basket. "Will there be anything else, sir?"

"No, thank you, Carter. This looks perfect." Then he turned and held out his arm to Lauren. "Shall we go?"

She wrapped her hand around his forearm, curious to see exactly what he had in mind. But instead of heading out the front door, he moved toward the back of the restaurant, through a door marked Emergency Exit Only, and up a steep, narrow flight of metal stairs.

They walked through another door, then Lauren

stopped to look around in disbelief. Above them was a canopy of stars shining in the night sky, the full moon bathing the rooftop with its magical glow. A large, red-and-white checked tablecloth was laid out in the center of the roof, bordered on each side by a reflecting pool. A dozen candles floated in the pools, their light bouncing off the water.

"I'm glad the weather decided to cooperate tonight," he said, walking toward the tablecloth and setting down the picnic basket. The tablecloth was set with the restaurant's finest china and silver, a bottle of wine chilling in a silver ice bucket.

"Everything is perfect," she said, a note of awe in her voice. She sat down as Sam began pulling fragrant dishes from the basket. Had he really arranged all this just for her? A cool breeze rippled above them but they were protected from it by the half brick wall bracketing the rooftop.

"How did you know about this place?" she asked, then wanted to kick herself. Philomena had told her Sam was something of a playboy. Sweeping women off their feet was his specialty.

"I didn't until this afternoon," Sam admitted, filling her glass with the rich, red wine. "I just told Carter that I had a very special date tonight and that I wanted his most private table." Sam grinned. "This is it."

She picked up her wineglass, inordinately pleased that she wasn't just one in a long line of women who had followed Sam onto the rooftop.

If he was telling the truth.

She pushed the thought away, refusing to let her old insecurities plague her. She was about to have a wonderful time and she wouldn't let anything put a damper on their evening together.

Sam held up his glass. "Shall we drink a toast?"

"To what?"

He smiled. "To Philomena. Without her, we might never have met."

She nodded, clinking her glass against his. "To Philomena."

Lauren studied Sam over the rim of the fine crystal. He wore a blue shirt with a matching silk tie and a black jacket that revealed the broadness of his shoulders and made him look almost as good as he had with his shirt off. Almost.

His dark hair was short, his jaw lean and strong. Her gaze fell to his hands, cradling his wineglass. They were broad, blunt-tipped fingers that were gently caressing the stem of the glass. She couldn't help but wonder how they would feel against her bare skin. How deftly they could peel away each tiny pearl button of this infernal blouse.

"Lauren?"

She blinked and looked up at him, realizing she'd been caught up in the fantasy and lost track of the conversation. "What?"

"Do you like the wine?"

"Yes. It's wonderful." She took another sip, savoring the rich bouquet. "Carter must be a good friend of yours to have arranged all this."

"Actually, we've beaten each other up on several occasions."

"Are you serious?"

He nodded. "Absolutely. We're both into kick-boxing and get together at the gym about once a week. We've competed against each other in several tournaments, too.''

She took another sip of her wine. ''That sounds…dangerous.''

He laughed as he dished out Caesar salad onto her plate. ''Not really. Not if you know what you're doing.''

''And you do?''

''I've won a few tournaments in my time.''

The finely honed muscles in his powerful chest and shoulders didn't dispute that fact. Maybe that's why she'd been so tongue-tied around him when she'd seen him with his shirt off. Seeing him totally naked would probably render her completely mute.

''A penny for your thoughts,'' he said, forking up a man-size bite of salad.

Her cheeks burned and Lauren knew it would take much more than a penny to reveal the erotic thoughts dancing in her head. She scrambled for something to say. ''I was just thinking about how much you and Philomena look alike.''

He choked on his salad, picking up his wineglass and taking a long swallow before he replied. ''I suppose there's some resemblance.''

''You both have blue eyes. And you're both about the same height.''

''Philomena's mother was very tall.'' Sam explained, his hand bumping against his wineglass and almost knocking it over. He caught it just in time. ''But enough about me. I want to know about you.''

''What about me?''

''Philomena tells me you're taking college classes.''

"That's right. In elementary education."

"So you want to be a teacher."

"Ever since third grade. My poor dog had to sit through endless lessons on reading and arithmetic. It's no wonder he ran away for three days when I was ten."

"But you found him?"

She nodded. "Seems he found a female dog who kept his interest longer than my math lessons. So we had him fixed. He was a much better student after that."

"Maybe that's the secret," he murmured.

"What?"

He shook his head, then reached over to refill her wine glass. "Nothing."

They ate in a silence for a few moments, then Sam brought out the entrée. The delicious aromas of garlic and oregano filled the air. "Would you like some lasagna."

"It's my favorite," she replied, her mouth already watering. "Did Philomena tell you?"

"As a matter of fact, she did." He dished a generous portion onto her dinner plate. Then handed her a basket of warm breadsticks.

"You two must be close," she said, digging her fork into the gooey pasta.

"About as close as two cousins could be."

She nodded, her thoughts drifting toward her challenging protégée. "I like Philomena a lot, but..."

"But what?" he prodded.

"I'm just curious as to why she wants to be a

Ladybug. She doesn't seem to be a big fan of lingerie.''

"On the contrary," Sam countered. "Philomena's always enjoyed fine lingerie."

Lauren took another bite of the succulent lasagna, wondering how much of her concern she should share with Sam. But her job promotion did depend on Philomena's success in the training program. "We had a Ladybug Lingerie party this afternoon and your cousin was obviously uncomfortable. She wasn't willing to help the guests try on the lingerie or model any of it herself."

Sam didn't say anything for two long beats. "There's something you should know about Philomena."

"What?"

"She has…a deformity."

"What do you mean?"

He hesitated. "I really shouldn't even be telling you this, since she's very sensitive about it. But Philomena has something on her body that your party guests might find disconcerting if she started parading around in revealing lingerie."

"Oh." Lauren was now sorry she'd even brought the subject up. Especially since it seemed to have put a damper on their date. "I'm glad you told me, Sam. I won't put her on the spot again like I did this afternoon."

"Don't worry about it," Sam said. "In fact, just forget I ever mentioned it."

They made small talk for the rest of the meal, capped off with a decadent chocolate torte. Then

Sam stood up and held out his hand. "Would you care to dance?"

"But there's no music."

He reached down by the reflecting pool and turned a small dial she now saw half-hidden behind a ceramic planter. The soft strains of violin music filled the air followed by seductive Italian lyrics.

She laughed as he helped her to her feet. "Carter thinks of everything."

"Hey, give me some credit," Sam said, as he pulled her into his arms. "I picked the song."

Her breath caught in her throat at the sensation of his hard body against her own. She forced herself to focus on the music and their conversation. "It's a beautiful piece. What is it?"

"An aria from *La Traviata*," he said huskily, his warm breath caressing her ear. "By Verdi."

"I wish I knew Italian," she said, closing her eyes and letting the music and the thrill of being this close to Sam carry her to another dimension.

"I don't know Italian either," Sam whispered, then pulled back far enough to look into her eyes. "But I think I know what it means."

"What?" The desire reflected in his eyes made her swallow hard.

"It means...I want to kiss you."

8

SAM DIDN'T STOP TO THINK about the consequences. He just gave into the desire that had been burning inside of him ever since he'd seen Lauren in those baby doll pajamas. His hands slid to her waist and he drew her closer to him, a small gasp escaping her throat.

Her eyes widened as he bent his head, capturing her lips with his own. The taste of her was even better than he had imagined. He closed his eyes, reveling in her sweetness. Then he pulled her even closer, deepening the kiss. After a moment, her arms curled around his neck.

Blood pounded in his veins as he explored her delectable mouth, all silk and softness. He heard a small moan bubble in her throat and satisfaction burned deep within him. Kissing Lauren McBride surpassed all his expectations. All his fantasies.

And when she molded her body against his own, he forgot everything except the heat that smoldered between them. Yesterday and tomorrow didn't matter anymore. Only now. This moment. The exquisite sensation of two people coming together and finding passion in each other's arms. He slid one hand over her hip, the movement causing her to arch against him.

He groaned as blood pooled low in his groin. Lauren McBride was all woman. His woman. Her reaction to his kiss left no doubt of that in his mind.

When Sam finally lifted his head, he wasn't sure if an eternity or only a moment had passed. He looked into her eyes, endless depths of cobalt-blue, and barely resisted the urge to kiss her again.

"Wow," she whispered, capturing the moment for both of them with a single word.

He stepped back, disconcerted with the effect she had on him. He'd kissed women before. Scores and scores of women, as a matter of fact. But no kiss had ever blindsided him like this one. Or made him quite so confused.

Sam had let himself believe he could control the situation. That he could successfully play Philomena Gallagher and Sam Kane at the same time. Now he wasn't so sure. Because when he'd held Lauren in his arms just now, nothing else in the world had mattered to him. Not his masquerade. Not the game. Not even the Kane Corporation.

It was a dangerous feeling. One he wasn't certain he wanted to experience again, no matter how irresistible he found her. For the first time he understood the lure of the sirens in *The Odyssey*, one of his favorite books on tape. More than one man had met his demise by following the siren's song.

And Lauren's kiss was a siren song. He had to be strong enough to resist it. There was too much at risk. Besides, there could be no future for them. Sam couldn't commit himself to any woman. He'd realized that a long time ago. No matter how tempting the idea might be. Or how tempting the woman.

He took another step back, seeing the confusion reflected in her beautiful eyes.

"Is something wrong?" she asked, still a little breathless from their kiss.

"No," he said briskly. "Everything is fine." The breeze had a definite chill in it now. So did the blood in his veins. "Are you ready to go?"

She hesitated for a moment and he could see the question forming on her lips. But instead of asking it, she just smiled and turned to pick up her handbag.

Sam's resolve faltered when she turned to him again. Her lips were full and red, still slightly swollen from their kiss. They could stay up here together on the rooftop. Find warmth and desire and so much more in each other's arms.

But then what?

Lauren wasn't like the other women in his life. She'd want more than a good time. She was a forever kind of girl—whether she knew it or not. She was the kind that he'd carefully avoided throughout his adult life.

"Thank you very much for dinner, Sam. I had a wonderful time."

Her words made him remember that they'd driven separately to the restaurant. So this was goodbye.

"Me, too," he replied, not trusting himself to say anything more. His jaw hurt from clenching it so tightly. A gust of wind blew over the rooftop, extinguishing the flames of several candles floating in the reflecting pools.

Lauren walked toward the rooftop door, then glanced over her shoulder to give him a goodbye wave. He knew she'd gotten the message and was relieved she didn't seem upset about it.

A message he wished like hell he could take back.

It was long after midnight when Sam, dressed now as Philomena, walked through the door of Lauren's apartment. He'd made the switch at his place, then driven around a while, trying to regain his equilibrium. And to remind himself why he'd taken on this charade in the first place.

To his surprise, Lauren was still awake. She sat cross-legged on the sofa, a photo album open on her lap, and was clad in a pair of flannel pajamas. For some inexplicable reason, he found them just as provocative as the pink baby doll pajamas she'd worn the day they'd met.

"You're still up," he said, closing the door and locking it behind him.

"I couldn't sleep," she replied, flipping a page of the photo album.

Sam wanted to make a beeline to his bedroom, but he knew that might make Lauren suspicious. Philomena would naturally be curious about their date. "How was your evening?"

"Fine." Lauren pointed to the coffee table. "There's some popcorn left if you'd like some."

"No thanks. I filled up on popcorn at the movie." Philomena replied, moving behind the sofa so she could see the photographs. It was Lauren and Chuck's wedding album. Then he noticed a small pile of other photo albums stacked up on the coffee table.

"Reminiscing?"

Lauren flipped another page of the album. "Actually, I'm doing a little detective work."

"That sounds intriguing."

"I'm trying to figure out what it is about me that seems to repel men." She finally looked up at him and he could see her eyes were slightly puffy and red-rimmed.

That she'd been crying hit him like a kick in the gut. Especially since he suspected she'd been crying over him. So much for thinking his rejection hadn't upset her.

She tossed the wedding album on the coffee table, then picked up another. "I've got seven years of pictures to go through. Maybe I'll be able to see when Chuck started feeling differently about me."

"Chuck is an asshole," Philomena said tightly. He should know since he felt like one himself.

She shook her head. "It's not just him. Something about me seems to drive men away. Chuck lasted seven years. Harold one date. And Brian not even that long. I've got to figure it out or I'll be destined to spend the rest of my life alone."

"That's ridiculous," Philomena said hotly.

"No, I'm serious." She sat up on the sofa. "Men go out with me, then just disappear into thin air. I never hear from them again. So either I'm driving them away or they're being abducted by aliens."

"Maybe they're the ones with the problem," Philomena countered. "Did you ever think of that?"

"I've thought about every possible reason under the sun. Analyzed every date endlessly, but I still haven't come up with any answers." She shook her head. "Why do men have to make relationships so difficult?"

Sam had heard more than one man ask the same question about women. "You just haven't found the right one yet."

"I thought I had," she murmured, then smiled up at Philomena. "Don't worry about me. I'm just feeling a little sorry for myself. The combination of a bad date and too many glasses of wine tends to bring on these little pity parties. I'll be over it by tomorrow."

He hoped like hell that was true. "I'm sorry it didn't work out with you and Sam."

"Me too." Then she stood up. "Good night, Philomena."

"Good night, Lauren." He stood and watched her walk out of the living room, hearing her bedroom door close a moment later.

Sam had told Travis that hitting a woman was against the rules. But what about the emotional punch he'd dealt Lauren? Had that hurt her just as badly? He rubbed one hand over his jaw, feeling the stubble of whiskers underneath the layer of cosmetics.

The sight of her tears had provoked questions that Sam had never asked himself before. How many other women had he made cry in his lifetime, even unwittingly? He sat down on the sofa, feeling numb inside. At age fifteen, he'd gone on his first date and had enjoyed a steady stream of women in his life ever since. There had been a few bumpy relationships along the way, but he'd soon learned the right way to romance a woman. How to say just the right thing. Make just the right move. Break it off before it got too serious.

He'd become even more polished over the years. Choosing his dates carefully, making certain they didn't have any unrealistic expectations about the future. Or at least, he thought he had.

But what man can truly know a woman's mind? Or her heart? How many tears had fallen because of him? And how the hell could he ever make this night up to Lauren?

His head began to itch under the wig, but he resisted the urge to tear it off until he was safely locked in his bedroom. All too aware that Lauren lay in bed only a few feet away. He could go to her now, tell her how very much he wanted her. That she was the most desirable woman he'd ever met.

But at what cost?

"Great thinking, Kane," he muttered to himself, closing the bedroom door behind him. He tossed the blond wig onto the plastic foam head on his closet shelf. "She'd kick your butt out of here so fast, you wouldn't know what hit you. And you'd lose the damn game in the process."

It simply wasn't worth it, no matter how tempted he was to kiss her tears away. He never should have agreed to the date in the first place. But it was better to break it off now than later. Lauren wouldn't want him if she knew the truth anyway.

Not that he was about to tell her. He'd never told anyone. And she already had a low enough opinion of him. He could just imagine the expression on her face if she discovered his best-kept secret.

Sam Kane didn't know how to read.

9

THE NEXT MORNING, Lauren was just putting the coffee on when Philomena walked into the kitchen. The older woman looked tired, with dark shadows under her blue eyes. Eyes that reminded Lauren of Sam.

"Good morning," she said cheerfully, determined to put that man out of her mind. "It looks like it's going to be another beautiful day."

Philomena blinked at her. "It sounds like you're feeling better this morning."

"Much." Lauren opened a cupboard door and replaced the coffee can on the shelf. Then she picked up the newspaper off the counter and pulled off the rubber band. "Do you want a section?"

"Maybe later." Philomena sat down at the kitchen table. "What happened to bring about this good mood? You seemed pretty down last night."

Lauren's cheeks grew warm when she remembered how pathetic she'd acted in front of her new roommate. "Nothing happened. I just decided I wasn't going to waste any more time going over every moment of my date last night. Or trying to figure out what was wrong with me."

"Maybe it wasn't you," Philomena interjected.

"Did you ever stop to think that Sam might be the one with the problem?"

"Well…no." Lauren took a seat at the table, laying the newspaper in front of her. "And that's exactly my point. Every time something like this happens, I spend days, or even weeks, endlessly analyzing the relationship. Going over every moment in my mind and looking for the slightest nuance that might explain his behavior. But not anymore."

"So you're over Sam?"

"Completely," Lauren exclaimed, wishing she felt as confident as she sounded. "Besides, it's not like he's ever going to call me again."

Philomena cocked her head to one side, her gaze a little too assessing for Lauren's comfort. "And how can you be so sure about that?"

"If you'd seen the way he acted last night, you'd be sure too," she replied, unable to keep the note of dejection out of her voice. Then she forced a smile. "So I've decided to forget about romance and take on a new project."

"Great idea. What is it?"

"You."

Philomena stared blankly at her. "I'm not sure I understand."

"It hit me last night how selfish I've been. Here I was, feeling sorry for myself, when you're the one going though such a tough transition. I remember how difficult it was in the first months after my divorce. I should be the one comforting you, not the other way around."

Philomena shook her head. "I don't need comforting. I'm fine. Really. I *wanted* the divorce. I've decided marriage isn't for me.''

"That's just your pain talking,'' Lauren said gently. "I was the same way. I just wanted to curl up in a ball and make the world go away.''

"No, it's really me talking,'' Philomena insisted. "I'm perfectly content with my life just the way it is.''

"You think that now, but once you get out and start experiencing life again, you'll feel differently.''

Philomena looked wary. "What exactly do you mean by 'experiencing life.'''

"Well, I have a few surprises planned. My first one is a trip to my friend Becky's clinic for some therapy.''

"I don't need a shrink,'' Philomena replied, growing more agitated by the moment. "I'll admit I've had a few…identity conflicts recently, but that's perfectly normal for a person in my situation.''

"Becky's not a shrink, she's a yoga instructor. She works at the Healing Arts clinic downtown.

"Oh.'' Philomena's brow furrowed. "Is yoga the exercise where you do a lot of humming?''

She smiled at the skepticism she saw on her protégée's face. "It's a combination of stretching exercises and meditation. Humming is optional.''

"I think I can probably handle that,'' Philomena said grudgingly. "But you don't need to worry about me, Lauren. I'll be just fine.''

"I know you will,'' she said, rising out of the chair to pour each of them a cup of coffee. "And keep up that positive attitude. That's the best way to start building your brand-new life.''

"What about you?"

She turned and walked back to the table, two cups of steaming coffee in her hands. "What about me?"

"What do you want out of your life?"

She set down the coffee cups.

"Well, you know I'd like to be a teacher."

"Is that all?"

She sat down. "That's seems like enough of a challenge at the moment. I've got three years of college still ahead of me, and that's only if I can keep going full-time. I'll be almost thirty when I finally get my degree."

"What made you decide to go back to school?"

"I never wanted to leave," she admitted, picking up her cup and blowing on the steaming brew. "But after Chuck and I got married, finances were tight. Really tight. So he suggested that one of us quit college and go to work full time."

Philomena's mouth thinned. "Did he also suggest you be the one to do it?"

"It made sense at the time. A lawyer makes quite a bit more money than a teacher. The plan was that I would work until he graduated from law school, then he would support us until I got my teaching degree."

"But it didn't work out that way."

"No." Lauren's gaze dropped to her coffee cup, waiting for the old, familiar pain. But she felt fine. Normal. Was she truly over him? "Chuck found a new study partner. A blonde with big brown eyes and plenty of free time."

"He cheated on you?"

She nodded, then took a sip of her coffee. "At least our marriage ended before we had children."

"I don't think that makes him any less of a jerk."

"That seems to be the type of man I attract." She saw Philomena wince and instantly regretted her words. "I'm sorry, I didn't mean to imply that your cousin is an asshole."

"I suppose I couldn't blame you if you did."

"Let's not talk about men," Lauren said, more than ready to change the subject.

"Good idea." Philomena stood up and rubbed her hands together. "I'm going to make you the best breakfast ever. How does a Spanish omelette with crispy hash browns sound?"

"Fattening, but delicious."

"Good. We've got to have some incentive to do that yoga thing." Then Philomena turned to the refrigerator and began pulling out an armful of ingredients.

Lauren's eyes widened. "Where did all that food come from?"

"I picked up a few more things at the grocery store yesterday afternoon while you were at class."

"I can't let you buy me food." She got up to retrieve her checkbook, hoping she had enough in her account to cover her share. "I'll pay for half."

"Absolutely not." Philomena's firm tone brooked no argument. "It's the least I can do after...all you've done for me."

"But you're already paying half the rent and utilities."

Philomena turned to look at her. "Let me do this, Lauren. Please."

Lauren's pride battled with her stomach. Then her stomach growled, making the decision for her. "All right," she conceded, "you win. This time, anyway."

"You won't regret it," Philomena promised, as she pulled a skillet out of the cupboard.

Lauren smiled. "Hey, maybe that's why Sam lost interest in me so fast last night. I ate so much, it probably scared him."

Philomena turned. "I thought you weren't going to analyze your date."

"You're right. Thanks for reminding me."

Philomena looked around the kitchen. "Spatula?"

"In the drawer by the sink," Lauren replied as the doorbell rang. She got up and walked out of the kitchen, humming softly under her breath as she walked to the door. There was something about Philomena that made her feel good about herself.

But that feeling faded when she opened the door and saw her ex-husband standing on the other side. He didn't look happy.

"Chuck." Lauren ran a hand through her disheveled hair. "What are you doing here so early?"

"We need to talk," Chuck replied briskly, then walked inside without waiting for an invitation.

Lauren opened her mouth to call him on it, then closed it again. She didn't want to start her day off with an argument. Especially since Chuck was always so good at getting in the last word.

He sat down on the sofa, his mouth set in a firm line.

She closed the door, then took a seat opposite him in the rocking chair. "Well?"

"Is that coffee I smell?"

"Yes, it is. But I only made enough for me and Philomena."

"So I take it she's moved in here already?"

Lauren nodded. "Over a week ago."

Chuck leaned back against the sofa. "Isn't that a little sudden? I mean, you two are practically strangers. What do you even know about the woman?"

"She's very nice."

Chuck snorted. "I'm sure a lot of people thought Lizzie Borden was nice, too."

"Philomena doesn't own an ax, if that makes you feel any better."

"It doesn't." Chuck sat up again, clearly agitated. "I want to know about this mysterious date of yours."

Lauren stared at him, wondering if he'd been this overbearing when they were married. Had she been too blinded by love to see it? Or too young to chafe at his high-handed manner like she did now? "That's really none of your business, Chuck."

His nostrils flared. "Just because we're divorced doesn't mean I don't care about you anymore."

"Actually, that's exactly what it means."

He shook his head. "What happened to you, Lauren? You used to be so..."

"Meek?" She guessed with a wry smile. "Gullible? Trusting?"

"Yes. You still are," he waved his hand around her Spartan apartment, "no matter how many changes you make in your life. That's why I want to know something about this man you're dating. I don't want anyone to take advantage of you.''

"His name is Sam Kane," she said, hoping the information would hasten his exit. "We had dinner at Lucia's. The maître d's name is Carter if you want to check out my story."

"Sam Kane," Chuck mused, a scowl forming on his brow. "Can't say the name sounds familiar."

"Hardly surprising in a city of almost four hundred thousand people."

"So how did you meet him?"

"He's Philomena's cousin."

Chuck smiled. "So she set you up. This was just a blind date."

"Yes, it was a setup." Lauren said, wondering why she was bothering to explain. "I'd met Sam the day Philomena moved in and I liked him. I liked him a lot. So I asked her to arrange a date between us."

His smile faded. "That doesn't sound like you."

"I know," she said proudly. "That's another change I'm making in my life. A change for the better." Then she stood up to prove it to him. "Thanks for stopping by. I'm sure you have to get going."

He hesitated clearly surprised by her none-too-subtle suggestion that he leave. She opened the door just to make certain he got the message.

But before he left, he turned and put his hand over the one she had braced on the door frame. "Have dinner with me tomorrow night."

Lauren pulled her hand away, then saw a movement out of the corner of her eye. Philomena stood poised just inside the living room, a spatula in her hand.

"Good morning, Philomena," Chuck called, giving her a polite nod. "I just stopped by to see my favorite girl."

"Lauren's breakfast is getting cold," Philomena said bluntly.

"I'll be there in a minute," Lauren promised, then turned back to Chuck. "As for dinner…"

"Don't give me an answer yet," he said quickly, obviously seeing her refusal in her eyes. "Just promise me you'll think about it. I'll call you later tonight."

"I'm not sure I'll be here."

"Why?" Chuck asked, narrowing his eyes. "Don't tell me you have another date with that Kane fellow."

"Okay, I won't," she said, then smiled. "In fact, I'm not telling you anything anymore. Bye."

She closed the door, but not before seeing the astonished expression on his face. Then she took a deep breath, a little astonished herself.

She'd finally gotten the last word.

10

SAM LAY ON HIS BACK WITH his legs sticking straight up in the air. Becky's yoga class was the biggest challenge he'd faced yet as a woman. But Lauren had been so enthusiastic about helping Philomena experience life again that he just didn't have the heart to say no. They'd been shopping together, attended a seminar on self-defense for women, and been reading passages out of a new book called *How To Jump-Start Your Love Life,* among other things.

Sam might not be crazy about all of his new activities, but he was definitely becoming crazy about Lauren. He couldn't remember when he'd spent so much time with a woman he wasn't romantically involved with. Maybe he never had. It was an enlightening experience.

"Now take a deep breath," Becky instructed. "Close your eyes and think of a place that makes you feel special. That's it...now exhale...inhale... relax."

His wig had shifted slightly, the synthetic hair tickling his nose. Sam turned his head far enough to look at the clock on the wall. Forty-five minutes down, fifteen more to go. He wore a baggy gray sweatshirt and matching pants, having turned down the skintight leotard that Lauren had dug out of her closet. He had a hard enough time keeping his breasts on straight without a revealing every nook and cranny of his fake figure.

His gaze strayed to the right, where Lauren lay stretched out beside him, and he found himself wishing she'd chosen sweats as well. The black leotard she wore hugged her body in a way that made sweat break out on his forehead. Her long, slender legs were encased in black tights and pointed gracefully toward the ceiling. He closed his eyes, imagining those legs wrapped around him.

"It's your turn, Philomena," Becky called out.

His eyes flew open. "What?"

"Share your special place with us. I could tell by the expression on your face that it was a place that brings you pleasure."

That would be an understatement. He scrambled for something to say. "A Steelers game. The old Three Rivers Stadium. Hot dogs. Beer. Ecstasy."

The women in the room laughed, then a lively discussion began about which teams had the sexiest men.

Lauren turned toward him. "So you like football, Philomena?"

"I love it. In fact I used to play...tapes of my favorite teams over and over again," he said, catching himself just in time.

"How about Sam? Is he a big fan of the Steelers, too?"

It was the first time she'd mentioned his name all week. "The biggest."

"Ladies." Becky held up her hands to silence the chatter filling the room. "Let's remember we're here to generate peace and harmony in our lives. To celebrate what it means to be a woman.''

"My feet are numb," Sam said, tired of celebrating.

Lauren sat up. "Mine, too."

Becky clapped her hands together. "All right, ladies, let's move to the lotus position. Legs crossed, back straight, hands open to receive the energy emanating all around us."

Sam felt his pager vibrate in the pocket of his sweatpants. He stood up, surreptitiously adjusting his wig at the same time. "Will you please excuse me for a moment?"

Becky nodded toward him, placing a finger to her lips to indicate he should leave quietly.

Lauren looked up. "Are you all right?"

"I'm fine," he whispered. "I'll be right back."

He maneuvered his way around the three rows of women in the room, then walked out into the foyer. Pulling his pager out of his pocket, he saw a familiar number blinking at him. Travis.

Moving toward the pay phone, he patted the pockets of his sweatpants, relieved to find a stray quarter. He dropped it in the coin slot, then dialed Travis's number.

Travis answered the telephone on the second ring. "Hello?"

"Hi, Travis. You called?"

Silence carried over the line. "Who is this?"

Too late Sam realized he was still speaking in his Philomena voice. He glanced toward the open door, then turned and spoke softly into the phone using his normal voice. "It's me. Sam. I was just fooling around."

"Hey, Sam. You got my page?"

"Sure did. What's up?"

"Nothin'." But the boy's tone told a different story.

"Aren't you supposed to be in school today?"

"Nope."

The one-word answers were another indication that something wasn't right. "Is it some kind of school holiday?"

"Not exactly," Travis hedged.

"Then what exactly?" Sam asked, casting another glance toward the door. "Come on, Trav. You know you can tell me anything."

"I just decided not to go today. School is boring."

Sam's heart lurched. He could tell from the dejection he heard in the boy's voice that there was more to the story.

Movement from inside the classroom caught his attention. He heard the sound of laughter and sensed the yoga session was coming to an end. "Listen, Trav, since you took the day off, why don't you meet me at the hot-dog stand on your corner for lunch. My treat."

"Cool."

Sam tensed as a shadow spilled over the doorway. He didn't have much time left. "I'll be there in twenty minutes."

"Okay. Bye, Sam."

He hung up the receiver a moment before as Lauren walked out of the classroom, a gym bag slung over her shoulder.

"Ready for lunch?" she asked, giving him a smile that warmed him from the inside out.

He cleared his throat, slipping back into his Philomena persona again. "I'm going to have to take a rain check. I already have a date."

Lauren's face brightened. "That's wonderful! What's his name?"

"Travis. But it's not that kind of date. He's only eleven years old."

"Shouldn't he be in school?" she asked, echoing the same question Sam had asked.

"Yes. It seems he got into some trouble. That's why I want to talk to him about. See if I can help out."

"How do you know him?"

"He lived in my old neighborhood. Sort of, in my neighborhood, and we got to be pals."

Lauren smiled up at him. "And shared a few hot dogs at a Steelers game?"

Sam stopped walking, dazzled by her smile. "More than a few."

Lauren looked thoughtful. "I haven't been to a game in a long time. It sounds like fun."

"I'd better go," Sam said, knowing he didn't have much time to change out of his Philomena costume.

"Okay. I'll see you later."

Sam watched her walk away and wondered if his life could possibly get anymore complicated. He spent his days with Lauren pretending to be a woman and his nights in her apartment trying to forget he was a man. And he'd neglected Travis and now the kid was in some kind of trouble.

To top it off, he was no closer to getting his hands on the Seductress bra. When he'd mentioned it again to Lauren, she'd called Mrs. Chavez, who had assured her it was on its way. At least Lauren seemed to have put their disastrous date completely out of her mind. She hadn't mentioned Sam's name once in the last week.

But she'd certainly been on his mind. The more he got to know Lauren McBride, the more he liked her. And the worse he felt about deceiving her. Sam headed for the door, not wanting to be late meeting Travis at the hot-dog stand.

Maybe the kid could give him some advice about girls.

"I CAN'T BELIEVE YOU ATE three hot dogs," Sam said, as he and Travis sat on a park bench near the hot-dog stand.

"You had four," Travis countered, unconcerned of the ring of ketchup smeared around his mouth.

Sam handed him some paper napkins. "Time to come clean, kid. Why aren't you in school?"

Travis stared down at the sidewalk, the napkins crumpled in his hand. "'Cause."

"'Cause why?"

"'Cause school is stupid."

"Is there anything in particular about school that's stupid or just all of it."

His mouth tightened. "All of it."

"Even recess?"

Travis shrugged. "Okay, mainly my math teacher is stupid. Mr. Hansen."

Now they were getting somewhere. "And what kind of thing do stupid math teachers do?"

Travis looked up, his cheeks red. "Embarrass you in front of the whole class. Just 'cause I told a secret to Ashley."

"Who's Ashley?"

"That girl who used to bug me all the time," Travis replied. "But she doesn't really bug me as much anymore. Anyway, I told her a secret and Mr. Hansen saw me and made me stand up and tell it to the whole class. Only I wouldn't."

"How come?"

Travis looked at him like the answer was obvious. "Because the secret I told her was that I liked her. Everybody would have made fun of me. And made fun of her, too. She would have hated me forever."

Sam's heart ached for the kid, who was riding the roller coaster of his first romance. "So you didn't tell the secret?"

Travis shook his head and tears gleamed in his clear green eyes. "But Mr. Hansen just kept looking at me, making me stand there in front of the whole class forever."

Sam could remember a time when he'd been the center of attention, standing up in front of his fifth-grade class, a book of poetry in his hands. He was supposed to read "A Brook in the City," and was ready to do it, having memorized the passage after checking out an audiotape of Robert Frost poems from the public library. But at the very last minute, his teacher changed her mind and wanted him to read "The Cow in Apple Time." So he stood up there like an idiot, unable to read the poem. Too damn proud to tell anyone the reason why.

Not only had Sam received an F for the assignment, but his teacher had called his mother to the school to discuss her concerns about his reading ability. He could still remember the hot flush of embarrassment on his mother's face. The way she had looked at him. It wasn't long after that meeting that he and Dexter had been sent to live with their grandfather. He'd never admitted to his brother that their exile had been his fault.

"I'm never going back there," Travis proclaimed, tilting his chin up.

"Okay."

Travis blinked. "Okay?"

Sam shrugged. "You've got to do what you think is right." He let that sink in for a moment. "Although, I bet Ashley will sure miss you. Especially now that she knows you're a boy she can trust."

"But I looked stupid."

"Not to her," Sam assured him. "Do you think she wanted you to tell everybody in the class the secret?"

He slowly shook his head. "No."

"Do you think your teacher was right to embarrass you like that?"

"No."

"So are you going to let him chase you out of school? And keep you away from Ashley?"

Travis scowled. "No, cause I didn't do anything wrong."

"Sometimes, it's hard to do the right thing," Sam

said, ruffling the boy's hair. "But I'm real proud of you, Travis. I think you did the right thing."

His face brightened. "You do?"

Sam nodded, determined to have a private conference with Mr. Hansen. "And I'll be even prouder when you're brave enough to walk back into that school."

Travis took a deep breath. "I think maybe I could go back this afternoon. But can we stop for ice cream on the way? That always helps me feel brave."

Sam grinned, then gave him a high five. "Deal."

After he dropped Travis off, he drove back to his apartment to transform himself into Philomena once again. It was becoming more routine each time he did it, although he still chafed at all the makeup he had to wear. Sam stopped to check his telephone messages before heading out the door. He was shocked to hear Lauren's voice.

"Hi, Sam, this is Lauren McBride. I wanted to thank you once again for our date the other night. I had a lovely time."

So lovely she'd cried her eyes out, Sam thought to himself, feeling like a heel once more.

"And just in case you're interested, I have a couple of tickets to a Steelers game next Sunday afternoon. It's not a big deal," she said hastily, *"but I thought it might be fun to get together again."*

She hesitated, and he could almost see her working up her courage in his mind. *"Give me a call if you want to go. My number is 555-6740."*

Then he heard the dial tone and just stood there, letting the sound fill the air until he finally hung up the phone. He knew how much courage it had taken her to call him again. How much she feared rejection. Was that the reason she hadn't told Philomena about her plan to call him for another date?

Despite Sam's better judgment, he knew he couldn't let her down. He'd already made her cry once. He'd be damned if he'd do it again. And if he was honest with himself, he wanted to see her again—as a man. To kiss her again. No matter what the risk.

Sam picked up the phone.

11

LAUREN AND SAM CHEERED AS the final seconds ticked off in the football game. The Pittsburgh Steelers had pulled off an exciting win with an interception in the last two minutes. She shivered as a brisk north wind blew through the stands.

"Cold?" he asked, as they headed toward the exit.

"A little."

He unzipped his coat, then took it off and wrapped it around her shoulders, enveloping her in his warmth. "Is that better?"

"Much," she murmured, smiling up at him. Their date had been magical from the moment Sam had picked her up at her apartment. They'd exchanged funny stories of past football games on the way to the stadium. Then discovered they both shared a passion for Polish dogs and beer. She couldn't remember the last time she'd had so much fun.

Or been so attracted to a man.

She just wished he felt the same. Sam had been a perfect gentleman. Too perfect in her opinion. He hadn't held her hand, or put his arm around her or tried to kiss her once. Even when she'd dropped a hint about the Texas A&M tradition of couples kissing after the home team scored. The Steelers had racked up thirty points, but Lauren hadn't received one kiss.

"You must be freezing," she said, as they reached the parking lot. "Here, take your coat back."

He shook his head. "Believe me, freezing is not my problem at the moment."

Her own cheeks warmed at the implication, which gave her hope. Maybe he simply didn't like public displays of affection. They dined on burgers and fries at a local sports bar, playing a game of pool and three games of darts. She was surprised at how comfortable she felt with him. It was almost as if they'd been friends forever.

They arrived back at her apartment close to midnight and Lauren was as apprehensive as a teenager on her first date wondering if she'd get a good-night kiss.

But although Sam walked her to her door, he kept his distance. "I had a great time, Lauren."

"Me, too."

"Maybe we can get together again sometime."

She'd heard that line before. Why did he even agree to go out with her if he wasn't interested? Of course, a free football ticket might be hard to refuse. She gave him a polite smile. "That would be nice."

"How about tomorrow?"

Lauren looked up, surprised. "Tomorrow?"

Sam took a step closer to her. "I meant what I said. I'd really like to get together again. Soon. Can we meet for lunch?"

"I have class all day."

"Okay, then how about tomorrow night? What time do you get out of class?"

"Five o'clock. I should be home by five thirty."

He grinned. "I'll pick you up a five thirty-five."

"I'll be ready," she said, still feeling a little confused. She said good-night, then walked into the apartment, hoping Philomena could give her some insights on her cousin's unusual behavior. But the spare bedroom door was closed, her roommate obviously asleep already.

Tomorrow would have to be soon enough to find out if she could risk falling in love with Sam.

SAM PACED BACK AND FORTH outside the door to Lauren's apartment, telling himself he was crazy for even showing up here again. He should have gone straight back to his apartment, transformed himself into Philomena and put Lauren out of his mind until their date tomorrow night.

Right. He might as well tell himself to stop breathing. Setting his jaw, he rapped sharply on Lauren's door.

A few moments later, she opened it a crack, the chain still attached. "Sam?"

"Hi." He was surprised to see her already in her robe. How long had he been driving around? "I couldn't sleep. I hope I didn't get you out of bed."

"No, I was just working on a crossword puzzle. I couldn't sleep either." She unhooked the chain, then opened the door wider. "Come on in."

He hesitated. "It's late…."

"Please," she entreated, giving him the beautiful

smile he found so entrancing. ''I need help with ten down.''

He walked inside, his pulse beating a rapid warning signal that he chose to ignore. What could it hurt to stay for a few minutes? She closed the door behind him and locked it again. Then she turned to face him.

Sam swallowed hard, aware that only one lamp burned in the living room, casting cozy shadows around the small room. From the damp curls on Lauren's shoulders and the provocative scent of honeysuckle in the air, he knew she'd just emerged from a bubble bath. The honeysuckle bath beads were her favorite. Funny how living with a woman gave a man intimate knowledge of her world. Taught him so many of her secrets.

But there was so much more about Lauren that he longed to know.

She walked over to the sofa and sat down, picking up the folded newspaper and pen setting on the coffee table. ''Okay, the clue for ten down is arboreal primate. And it's five letters long and ends with an R.''

''Lemur,'' he replied, moving closer to her.

''You're right,'' she exclaimed, neatly penciling the word in the squares. ''How did you know that?''

''I watch a lot of National Geographic on television.''

She patted the sofa cushion beside. ''Sit down. You look tired.''

He felt exhausted. Juggling two identities had proved much harder than he'd ever imagined. Especially when he had to put so much energy into resisting the charms of Lauren McBride. It had been sheer hell keeping his distance from her during their date. So what was he doing here now? "I really can't stay long."

"Just help me finish this crossword puzzle. I'm almost done."

He couldn't resist the entreaty in her deep blue eyes. He sat down next to her, sinking into a deep spot on the old sofa.

"Here," she said, scooting over to make more room for him beside her. "Move a little closer. You'll be more comfortable."

He seriously doubted it, but he moved anyway. For some inexplicable reason, he'd left all his will-power at the door. Along with his better judgment.

She studied the crossword puzzled, chewing on the end of her pencil. "I'm not sure if fifteen across is right." She turned the paper toward him. "What do you think?"

He took the newspaper out of her hand and tossed it on the coffee table. "I think you need a break." Then he drew her into his arms. He told himself it was just a defense mechanism. One he'd used a hundred times before to keep from revealing his secret.

But in his heart he knew the truth. Another secret he didn't intend to admit to anyone—including himself.

"I think you're right," she said, snuggling against him. Her lips grazed his jaw, then skimmed over his neck. "Hmm. You taste good."

He closed his eyes, relishing the softness of her body against him. The way her voice soothed his raw nerves. She felt so right in his arms. So right in his life.

Then her mouth captured his in a sweet, hot kiss and he stopped thinking at all. Her hands slid under his shirt, eliciting a groan from deep in his chest when her fingertips brushed against his flat nipples. She leaned back, drawing him down with her on the sofa.

Sam's whole body tightened at the sensation of Lauren beneath him. Blood pounded in his veins as his tongue sought entrance into her mouth. She wrapped her arms around his neck and pulled him closer, her tongue tangling with his. All of Sam's good intentions to keep their relationship platonic burned away in a fiery blaze of heat and passion.

Her robe gaped open, revealing the creamy swell of her breasts. Sam lowered his head, dropping kisses along her delicate collarbone, then lower. She arched her neck as he encountered the lacy border of the pink camisole she wore under the robe. He pushed the thin fabric aside, seeking the treasure underneath.

A moan escaped her throat as his mouth closed over her breast. Sam had never wanted to please a woman more than he wanted to please Lauren in this moment. To fulfill her every desire.

She pulled him up to her again, her kisses more demanding now. Her hands tugged at his T-shirt, and they stopped kissing just long enough for her to pull it off over his head. Then they fell together again. Kissing. Touching. Exploring.

"I want you so much," Sam breathed against her mouth.

"Me too."

He felt her fingers fumbling against the fly of his jeans and groaned aloud. The sudden blare of a radio made them both jump.

Lauren sat half up on the sofa, her cheeks flushed. "That sounds like it's coming from Philomena's room. She must still be awake."

Sam closed his eyes as the strains of classical music echoed down the hallway. He'd forgotten about that damn clock radio. He'd set it this morning so he could use Philomena's presence as an excuse to put an end to their date, if need be. Only their date hadn't turned out exactly as he'd planned. And now he didn't want it to end.

Lauren leaned toward him and kissed him again, her hands caressing his bare chest. "Maybe we should go to your place."

He looked into her lambent blue eyes, wanting to carry her off to his bed so damn bad that his body literally ached. But then she'd see the makeup that he'd left strewn on his kitchen table. Along with a thousand other clues that might lead her to the inevitable conclusion that he was Philomena.

But that wasn't the only reason. Sam pulled away from her, disgust at himself washing over him. Hell. He couldn't do this. He couldn't make love to Lauren at the same time he was deceiving her. Not if he ever wanted to look at himself in the mirror again.

"What's wrong?"

He pulled away from her, sitting up on the sofa and burying his face in his hands. He had to think of a way out of this mess. A way that wouldn't hurt

Lauren. But he needed time to come up with just the right words.

"Sam?"

He resisted the urge to hold her one last time. "I should go. I never meant for this to happen...."

She leaned toward him and gave him a kiss to stop his apology. "I know. Will I see you tomorrow night?"

He gave a jerky nod. The solution came to him in that moment. A desperate answer to his problem, but Sam didn't see any other option. And he knew it would work.

By tomorrow night, she'd never want to see him again.

12

SAM WALKED INTO THE kitchen the next morning to find Lauren singing to herself and flipping pancakes. It had taken him longer than usual to transform himself into his Philomena persona, thanks to a pounding headache and a wig that refused to cooperate.

After leaving Lauren's apartment last night, he'd sprinted up the fire escape and climbed in the bedroom window just in time to hear her knocking on Philomena's door. He'd shut off the radio, then assured her in his Philomena voice that she was just fine.

But that was just one more lie.

Sam had to end this today. Before he hurt her. Before he forgot all the reasons he couldn't let himself fall in love with Lauren.

"Good morning, sleepyhead," Lauren chimed when she saw Philomena walk into the kitchen. "Hope you're hungry."

"Actually, I have a bit of headache this morning. I think I'll just have coffee."

Lauren's brow furrowed as she walked over to her and placed her smooth hand on his forehead. "Do you feel sick?"

"No," he said, drawing away from her touch. "I'm fine."

"Sit down," she ordered," I'll get you a cup."

Five minutes later, they were both seated at the table. Sam cradled a warm mug of coffee in his hands, watching Lauren consume the towering stack of whole-wheat pancakes in front of her.

"You must be hungry this morning," he said, taking a sip of his coffee.

"I always eat when I'm nervous...or happy."

"Which is it today?"

She grinned. "Definitely happy. I have another date with Sam tonight."

His stomach clenched. "Really."

She smiled. "He's so wonderful, Philomena. Handsome. Smart. Warm. Funny."

Sam stared into his coffee mug, knowing what he had to do. And dreading it at the same time. In a few moments, he'd see the light fade from her eyes. See her beautiful smile turn to a frown.

"I've never met another man like him," Lauren said wistfully. "Sam is so..."

"Dumb," he bit out.

Lauren blinked at him. "What did you say?"

"Sam is dumb. Stupid. An idiot."

Lauren set down her fork. "Philomena, you don't mean that."

He nodded, shame pooling in the pit of his stomach. "You need to know, Lauren, before this goes too far. Sam can't read. He can barely write. He's illiterate."

She shook her head. "I don't understand."

"It's a family secret," he said, not revealing that he'd never told it to anyone before. Only his mother knew, and she certainly hadn't told anyone. It was odd talking about it in the third person, as if he wasn't really speaking about himself. ''Sam hides it pretty well.''

''It's not possible. Are you sure about this?''

He could see the denial in her eyes. ''I'm positive. Sam can't read more than a few simple words.''

Lauren pushed her plate away, then carefully wiped her mouth with her napkin. It was hardly a surprise that she'd lost her appetite. His own stomach was twisted into a tight knot.

''But why can't he read? Sam's not dumb. He's one of the smartest men I've ever met.''

So she still didn't want to believe it. Sam had hoped this could be over quickly. But it looked as if his luck had finally run out. He needed to give her every grisly detail. ''No, he's not. He's just become an expert at fooling people. Did you ever notice that he won't read a menu when he's at a restaurant, but places the order ahead of time?''

''He did that on our first date. I thought that was romantic. He made me feel special.''

''He just didn't want to be found out,'' Sam said bluntly. ''He'll pretend he's busy if someone wants him to read something and ask them to read it aloud.''

''But he helped me with the crossword puzzle last night!''

''Did he really?''

She opened her mouth, then closed it again. ''Oh my God. I showed him the clue for fifteen across, but he just pushed the paper away. Then he kissed me.''

"Another distraction technique he's perfected over the years."

She swallowed. "So that's all it was. A distraction."

Sam wanted to deny it. To tell her that kiss they shared was much more than a distraction. But to what purpose? He had to end it now. Better she thought him a selfish, stupid jerk than pity him.

Lauren looked up, her face pale. "But how could he keep it a secret from his teachers? Surely he went to school. You have to be able to read and write to pass to the next grade."

"It really wasn't a problem at Carthage, the fancy private elementary school Sam went to in New York." Philomena shrugged. "Then he moved to Pittsburgh and made it to the eleventh grade before he couldn't carry it off any longer. His English teacher wouldn't let him slide by on his charm. She actually wanted results."

"Are you telling me he's a high school dropout?"

Philomena nodded, letting another nail slide into the coffin. Their romance had been doomed from the beginning. Why had he ever let it go on so long?

"Sam can't read," Lauren whispered, as if saying it aloud would make it more real. "I'm going to be a teacher and I never even suspected."

"Don't feel bad. He's become an expert at fooling people."

"But why didn't he ever try to get some help? Tell his parents or one of his teachers?"

"His parents weren't around much when he was growing up," he confided, not mentioning the fact that his mother would rather ignore that he had a problem than admit it.

"He told me his parents spend most of their time on a yacht off the coast of France."

"When they were teenagers, Sam and his brother, Dexter, spent most of their time with their grandfather, Amos Kane." He didn't know why he felt compelled to tell her so much of his life story. Maybe to assuage his own guilt. He'd been deceiving her for so long it felt good to share the truth. "Amos noticed Sam's lousy grades, but thought he was just a lazy student. Or maybe he assumed the teachers would take care of the problem."

Her lips thinned. "That obviously didn't happen."

"It's nobody's fault," he explained, her indignation pricking his pride. She was even more disgusted by his failings than he'd imagined she would be. "Sam tried to learn to read, but the letters never looked right to him. Like I said, it's some kind of mental defect." He smiled, trying to lighten the moment. "I'm just glad it doesn't run in the family."

Lauren stood up, grabbing the edge of the table to steady herself. "I need to get ready for class. I have a big exam today."

"I'm sorry, Lauren," Philomena said softly. "I thought you should know the truth. Before things went too far."

She gave a shaky nod, then fled from the room.

Sam stared at the half-eaten pancakes growing cold on her plate. His stomach lurched and for a moment he thought he might be sick. He'd never told anyone his secret before. Never shared his humiliation with a woman he cared so much about. Except his mother—and she'd rejected him, too.

Sam closed his eyes, remembering the shocked expression on Lauren's face. Fearing he'd never be able to forget it. Or her.

But he sure as hell was going to try.

"I CAN'T FIND THE SEDUCTRESS." Sam stood in Howard Cooper's office, his stomach still churning from his talk with Lauren this morning. He knew he'd done the right thing by breaking it off with her before he lost control. But he still didn't feel any better. He couldn't go on living as Philomena, not when he'd see the disgust in her eyes every time his name was mentioned.

Cooper leaned back in his office chair, his hands folded over his potbelly. "You've got less than week left before your gig is up."

Five more days with Lauren. And nights. His jaw clenched. "I don't think I can do this anymore."

Cooper sat up. "What's the problem, Sam?"

"It's personal."

The older man studied him for a long moment, then picked up the telephone and tapped out a number. "Let's see what your grandfather has to say about all of this. Maybe he'll extend the time."

Sam stood up. "It doesn't matter what he says. I'm old enough to make my own decisions. And I'm not giving you the Seductress." Then he walked out of the office without another word.

No doubt Cooper would be anxious to tell Amos Kane about this turn of events. Sam was out of the game. But he didn't care anymore. He'd lost Lauren.

Lost the one woman who had ever really mattered to him.

His throat tightened as he walked down the long corridor of Midnight Lace and out the door. The bright sun made him wince. He had an overwhelming urge to hit something.

Leaving his car parked in front of the building, he turned left and started jogging down the sidewalk. His gym was only six blocks away. Maybe a good bout of kickboxing would release the pent-up emotions inside of him. Or at least numb him with exhaustion so he wouldn't care anymore.

"Sam!" A deep voice called out behind him. "Sam Kane!"

He turned to see Chuck McBride striding toward him, dressed in a dark business suit and a bright-blue tie. Great. Just what he needed. His hand curled into a fist.

"I've been looking for you," Chuck said when he finally caught up with him.

"Why?"

"I'd like to talk to you about Lauren." He motioned to the Irish pub behind them. "Can I buy you a brew?"

Sam figured there was more than one way to get numb. Besides, he'd like to find a reason to rub that smug smile of McBride's face. Even if he had to use his fist to do it. "Sure. Why not?"

The pub was cool and dim compared to the bright sunshine outside. The few patrons inside the pub were gathered in a corner to watch a Pittsburgh Pirates baseball game playing on the large-screen television. Sam followed Chuck to the row of bar stools and took a seat as Lauren's ex-husband ordered two frosty mugs.

Sam wondered how long Lauren's class would last today. He wanted to clear Philomena's things out of the apartment this afternoon and leave a note telling her that Philomena was going back to her husband in Happy Valley.

Another lie, but it would be the last one. Then they could both get on with their lives. She had the whole world in front of her. He had a world of broken dreams.

"Good brewsky," Chuck said, wiping beer foam off his mouth with the back of his hand.

Sam picked up his mug and took a deep drink, barely tasting the icy beer washing down his throat. Then he set the mug down and fixed his gaze on McBride. "What exactly did you want to talk about?"

"My wife."

"Don't you mean ex-wife?"

Chuck shrugged. "Let's not argue over semantics. I want to know your intentions toward Lauren."

"Why?"

"Because I still care about her and I don't want to see her get hurt."

"Too bad you didn't worry about hurting her when you were still married to her."

"I made a few mistakes. I'll admit that." McBride picked up his beer mug. "But so have you."

Sam tensed. "What the hell does that mean?"

McBride narrowed his eyes. "I've done a little research on you, Kane. I know you're the heir to Amos Kane. That you dropped out of high school and have been drifting from job to job until your granddaddy found you a cushy spot at his company.''

One punch. That's all he wanted. One solid jab right in the center of McBride's chin.

"The question is what do you see in Lauren? She's not your usual type."

"My *type?*"

He nodded. "According to my research, you like them blond and beautiful and a little bit dumb. And we both know that doesn't describe Lauren."

It didn't make Sam feel any better that everything McBride accused him of was the truth. He tipped up his mug and drained it. Then he set it on the counter and rose off the stool. "Thanks for the beer."

"We're not quite finished here."

"Yes. We are." He turned and walked toward the door.

McBride slid hastily off his stool to follow him. "Give it up, Kane. I know your secret."

Sam froze, then slowly turned around. "My secret?"

"That's right." McBride puffed out his chest. "And I'll agree to keep it between us if…"

"I stop seeing Lauren."

McBride smiled. "You're smarter than I thought."

Sam took a step closer to him, gratified by the way McBride's eyes widened and by the sheen of sweat that broke out on his forehead. "If you're smart, you'll walk out of here right now."

McBride swallowed, but stood his ground. "I

mean it, Kane. Stop seeing Lauren or I'll tell her you're out of a job."

Sam's fists uncurled. "What?"

"She thinks you're some hotshot at the Kane Corporation. But you haven't been there in weeks. I tried to talk to a few employees, but old Amos must have issued a gag order. Although I think the reason is obvious."

Sam folded his arms across is chest. "Then why don't you enlighten me?"

"You couldn't handle the job. You're just a spoiled rich boy who would rather spend his time on a beach than in a boardroom."

His tension ebbed. Chuck McBride was blowing hot air. The man didn't know either one of his secrets. "Have you ever thought of becoming a private eye? I hear Inspector Clouseau is looking for a partner."

"When Lauren hears what I have to tell her, maybe she won't be so impressed with your so-called credentials. Especially if there's a chance old Amos might cut you off without a cent."

"In the first place," Sam said, his voice low and even, "if you call my grandfather *old Amos* one more time, you'll be missing a few teeth when you walk out of here. And in the second place, if you really think Lauren is just looking for a meal ticket, you're an even bigger moron than I thought. And that's saying a lot."

"Lauren's smart enough to know she can't keep up this pace forever. Going to school full-time and putting in so many hours at Ladybug Lingerie. She's barely making ends meet as it is. I know how much tuition and books cost, and I checked the amount of her rent with the apartment manager. It all adds up to more than the average salary for a Ladybug Lingerie saleswoman.''

"Lauren is far from average."

"That's why she deserves someone better than you."

"Like you, for instance?"

"At least I can afford to help her out. And I'm certainly a safer bet than counting on your cousin Philomena to come through for her."

Sam scowled. "What does Philomena have to do with this?"

"Good old Philomena has to successfully complete the Ladybug Lingerie training program before Lauren's new promotion becomes official. I checked it out with an old law school buddy of mine who's in the legal department at Ladybug Lingerie."

Complete the training program? That wasn't possible—Philomena still had three weeks to go. But if he quit now, Lauren would lose her promotion. Why hadn't she told him about that possibility? Or Philomena? The answer was obvious. Lauren wouldn't have wanted to add any pressure to her new roommate, so she'd kept a secret of her own. A secret that could have a drastic impact on her life if she lost that promotion.

Sam raked his hand through his hair, wondering what the hell to do now.

"Maybe if you were out of the picture," Chuck continued, "Lauren wouldn't be so damn stubborn. She refuses to take a dime from me. I think she'd rather starve than admit she needs help."

Sam knew from looking inside her refrigerator how close that came to the truth. Then it hit him. He finally realized what was sticking in McBride's craw. Chuck couldn't stand the fact that he was indebted to a woman. Lauren had paid his way through college and law school, but wouldn't let Chuck return the favor. For a man with his propensity to feel superior, that must chafe like hell.

Maybe she had found a little revenge after all.

"So I want you to stay away from her. Have I made myself clear?" McBride tried to sound threatening. Which was a little hard to do for a man wearing a Looney Tunes necktie.

"That's up to Lauren." But judging by her reaction this morning, she'd never want to see Sam again. He'd intended to make it easy on himself by walking out of her life for good. But now everything had changed. She needed him. Or rather, she needed Philomena.

And Sam was determined not to let her down.

13

IT WAS EARLY AFTERNOON when Lauren walked through the front door of Callahan's Gym, the scent of stale perspiration and chlorine hitting her as soon as she was inside. She looked around the exercise machines and barbell stations scattered around the gym until she saw the makeshift ring in the far corner.

Her heart skipped a beat when she saw Sam standing inside the ring. Shirtless, he wore only a pair of trunks and some boxing gloves. She sucked in her breath at the sight of his powerful, lean body poised to strike his opponent.

A man wearing a black muscle shirt approached her. "Can I help you, lady?"

She pointed to the ring. "I'm here to see Sam."

The man turned and shouted, "Hey, Sam! You got a visitor."

Sam glanced her way, then froze. At the same time, the foot of his kickboxing opponent lashed out and caught him square in the jaw. He went down like a rock.

Lauren rushed over to the boxing ring, her heart beating wildly in her chest. By the time she got there, Sam was sitting up, gingerly moving his jaw back and forth with his fingers.

"Are you all right?"

"Hell, no." Sam replied, not quite meeting her gaze. "I think I just lost."

"You owe me ten bucks," Carter said with a grin, his boxing gloves at his side. "That's our standard bet for a knockdown, isn't it?"

"Yep." He rose to his feet, then reached for the towel slung over the corner post. "I'll just deduct it from the eighty dollars you already owe me."

Lauren backed up a step as he straddled the ropes, then jumped to the floor beside her. "I didn't mean to interrupt your match."

He wiped a light sheen of perspiration of his forehead and neck, then tossed the towel into a corner. "I'm surprised to see you here."

And from his tone, not entirely pleased. Sam seemed different from the last time she'd seen him. Distant. Wary.

"I was going to call you," she explained, "then realized that I actually wanted to see you face-to-face. When you weren't at home I took a chance that you might be here."

He fingered his jaw again. "Why did you want to find me?"

She looked around the crowded gym. "Can we go somewhere a little more private?"

His brow furrowed. "Is something wrong?"

"I just need...to talk to you."

A light of understanding dawned in his eyes. "Listen, Lauren, I appreciate the fact that you want to let me down easy. But it's not necessary. Philomena already told me you don't want to see me anymore."

Lauren arched a brow. "Did she?"

He nodded, his jaw tight. "And I understand. Really. No hard feelings. But I hope we can still be friends. Okay?"

"No," she said bluntly. "It's not okay." Then she did something she wouldn't have done a week ago. Not even a day ago. She walked right up to Sam and kissed him. Not a friendly kiss. Not an affectionate peck. A hot, wet, this-is-my-man kiss intended to make everyone in the gym stop and stare.

And they did.

She wrapped her arms around Sam's neck, pulling herself closer as she ravaged his mouth. He stood there frozen for a moment, then she felt his body relax against hers and a low moan emanate from deep inside his throat.

"Somebody get the fire hose!" a deep voice called behind them, to the amusement of their audience.

Lauren broke the kiss and stepped away from him. "Are you ready to go?"

He swallowed, then gave her a shaky nod. "Yeah. I'm more than ready."

She turned and walked out of the gym, waving at the men and women who were still staring at them. One of the women at the rowing machine gave her a thumbs-up sign.

They stepped out into the bright sunshine. Then Sam stopped. "Wait a minute. I forgot something."

"What?"

He looked down. "My shirt. And my shoes."

"Don't worry," she said softly, taking a step closer to him. "You won't need them."

SAM UNLOCKED THE DOOR TO his apartment, all too aware of Lauren standing directly behind him. Her arrival at the gym had thrown him off balance. A condition further exacerbated by that hot kiss and the promise of more to come.

That's when he'd suggested they go to his apartment. She'd agreed, and even let him retrieve his shirt and shoes from his gym locker.

His hand shook slightly as he turned the key in the lock, then swung the door open. His head had been roaring ever since he'd taken that hit in the jaw. Or maybe it had started before that. As soon as he'd seen Lauren staring up at him with that killer smile of hers.

What he couldn't figure out was *why* was she smiling? She knew his secret. He'd seen the look on her face when Philomena had told her the whole sordid story. Had she convinced herself it wasn't true?

That thought cooled Sam's blood more than the brisk walk from the gym had done. It was bad enough to have to reveal his shortcomings when he was playing Philomena. He wasn't looking forward to repeating the experience.

"Nice place," Lauren said, following him inside. The apartment was cool and dark. Sam walked into the living room and switched on a table lamp, glad he'd picked up the place. "It's a little dusty."

"Makes me feel at home." Then she proved it to him by walking up to him and rumpling his hair with her fingers at the same time she leaned into him for a kiss.

Sam sighed into her mouth, all his good intentions of keeping his distance melting away at the taste of her. He wrapped his arms around her slender waist and pulled her closer, his pulse pounding in his veins.

Her hands slid down his chest to his waist, her fingers tugging his shirt out of his sweatpants. She slid her hands underneath to explore his bare skin.

Sam was powerless to stop her. He'd thought of a thousand reasons not to let this happen on the walk over here. But now they all jumbled together in his mind until he couldn't enunciate even one of them.

She tugged his shirt up over his head. It fell soundlessly to the floor as her hands slipped inside the waistband of his sweatpants.

He jerked slightly and she pulled away, a concerned frown crinkling her brow. "I'm sorry. Did I hurt you?"

Her fingertips lightly brushed the swollen side of his jaw, which he could tell without looking in a mirror was starting to bruise.

He captured her hand in his own. "No. You didn't hurt me."

But he might hurt her if he let this go on a moment longer. He took a step back from her to regain his equilibrium, but found himself unable to let go of her hand. "I'm not the man you think I am."

"Because you can't read?"

He winced at her bluntness. The memory of his mother's disgust rolled over him. He'd been running from it his whole life. It was time he face it. Faced who he really was. "Yes. I'm a twenty-seven-year-old man who can't read a newspaper. Or work on a crossword puzzle." His voice caught as he looked into her beautiful eyes. "Or write a love note to the woman I adore."

"So?"

He blinked at her nonchalance. Did it really not matter to her? Did she really still want him—flaws and all? The fear that she'd regret it later made him grab her shoulders and speak more harshly than he intended. "So what the hell are you doing here with me? You deserve better, Lauren. Much better."

Her eyes flashed. "Do you think this is easy for me?"

He dropped his hands. "Of course not. And I appreciate the fact that you're trying to pretend it doesn't matter."

"I'm not talking about you," she said, shoving her hand against his chest. "In case you didn't know, I'm not the kind of girl to waltz into a gym and try to seduce a man in front of perfect strangers. It took every ounce of courage I had. And do you know why I did it?"

He shook his head, too surprised by the passion in her voice to speak.

"I did it because I admired you so much."

His jaw sagged. "But…"

"Let me finish." She took a deep breath. "When Philomena told me you couldn't read, I found it hard to believe. You're one of the most intelligent, creative men I've ever met. So I got one of my college professors to pull a few strings and access your transcript at Carthage. For some reason, they never forwarded it to your new school in Pittsburgh.''

He knew the reason—his mother.

''According to the records, you were diagnosed as dyslexic when you were eleven.''

He stilled. ''What?''

''They tested you at that private elementary school and diagnosed you with a learning disability called dyslexia.''

''I've heard of it,'' he said, his head spinning. Why hadn't his mother told him his problem had a name?

Because she'd been too worried about the reflection on the Kane family name.

The school must have called her after conducting the test. That's when they'd suggested Sam take special classes to help him overcome his problem.

I can't believe any son of mine belongs in special ed. I told them it was a mistake. It just has to be! Her strident words rang in his head as clearly as if he'd heard them only yesterday instead of all those years ago.

''It's not too late, Sam,'' Lauren said softly. ''You can still learn to read. If you want to.''

He swallowed. ''If I want to? Of course, I want to! Don't you think I've tried?''

She placed one hand gently on his chest. ''They're developing new techniques for overcoming dyslexia all the time. All you need is someone to teach you how to do them. If anyone can do it, I know that you can.''

''How can you be so sure?''

She took a deep breath. "Because the man I love can do anything."

He stared at her, his heart hammering so hard in his chest he was certain she could see it. "You love me?"

"Yes," she breathed. "And just so you know, saying it out loud is the most difficult thing I've ever done. You might have a learning disability, but I think I have some sort of love disability. I've been so scared of letting myself get close to a man again. But I don't want to push myself on you, Sam. If you don't want me…"

He stopped her words with a kiss, wrapping his arms around her and pulling her close. Then he lifted his head just far enough to look into her eyes. "I want you. I want you so much, Lauren."

Her eyes widened. "Really?"

He scooped her up in to his arms. "Really."

She circled her arms around his neck as he carried her into his bedroom. He might not be able to read a book, but he could read a woman. And Lauren was apprehensive. Probably worried that she'd disappoint him. He couldn't wait to prove her wrong.

Lauren's pulse skyrocketed when Sam kicked his bedroom door shut behind them. She'd almost reached the point of no return and panic was setting in. It had been so long since she'd made love. What if she'd forgotten how to please a man? What if she'd never known in the first place?

When they reached the foot of the bed, he slid her down the length of his body and she could feel the warmth of his bare chest through her silk blouse.

"I think one of us is overdressed," he said huskily.

She glanced at the two large windows, the sun streaming through to illuminate every crease and flaw on her body. "Maybe we should close the curtains."

"We're on the tenth floor." He moved a step closer to her. "Nobody can see us."

She swallowed convulsively as his fingers reached for the buttons of her blouse. He popped them open one by one, not saying a word. His silence made her nervous. Then her blouse fell open and her cheeks flamed when she saw him looking at her lacy white bra. It was Ladybug Lingerie's top-of-the-line bra. A new model named the Seductress.

He leaned forward and kissed the top of her breast, the gentle touch of his lips sending a tingle through her body.

"You are so beautiful," he murmured, his lips skimming over her breast.

She took a shaky breath as he slid one strap of her bra off her shoulder. "You don't have to say that."

He slid off the other strap. "Yes. I do."

She closed her eyes as he kissed her again, easing her panic. Her head tipped back as his lips traveled the length of her throat. The next moment, she realized her bra was on the floor and Sam was gently palming her breast in his hand. His fingers stroked and teased, drawing a moan from deep within her.

"So beautiful," he breathed, kneeling to kiss the tip of one breast. When his tongue stroked her nipple, her knees buckled and she fell onto the bed. He followed her there, determined to satisfy his craving.

She lay on his bed as he lavished attention on her breasts with his hands and his mouth, making time stand still. Lauren had never felt so cherished. Or so loved.

Her hands ruffled through his hair, then she pulled him up to her, kissing him with all the desire and passion that had lain dormant inside of her for so long. This time he was the one who moaned, his body telling her that he wanted her as much as she wanted him.

His languid kisses became more heated, his fingers fumbling with the button at the waist of her skirt. She helped him unfasten it, then watched him slowly pull it down the length of her legs. She saw his eyes widen when he glimpsed her crotchless panties.

"Did I ever tell you how much I like your job?" he said huskily.

She smiled, then leaned up to loosen the drawstring on his sweatpants. "Did I ever tell you that I've been imagining you naked since the day we met?"

He stood up and quickly shed his sweatpants and the boxer shorts underneath. "You don't have to imagine anymore."

Her breath caught in her throat at the sight of him. One thing was perfectly clear—she had a lousy imagination. None of her fantasies had come close to the magnificence of Sam Kane in all his naked glory.

He turned to open the drawer of his nightstand,

drawing out a square, foil packet and ripping it open. The next moment he was beside her on the bed again, the length of his hard body pressed against her.

Lauren closed her eyes, relishing the sensation of skin-to-skin contact. His hand slid over her hip, branding her with its warmth. Then he leaned closer to capture her mouth with his own, his tongue slipping inside.

She fell onto her back, Sam following her, touching her everywhere. She could feel a heart pounding against her chest, but wasn't certain if it was hers or his. Then he deepened the kiss and it simply didn't matter any more.

Lauren became lost in the passion of their kisses, amazed at how perfectly they fit together. Then he was inside of her and she couldn't think about anything except the waves of desire lapping at her body. She held on to his broad shoulders as he rocked above her, his steady, insistent rhythm urging her to a place she hadn't been for far too long.

Then a tidal wave of feeling caught her unaware, breaking the tension that had been building up inside of her. A primal cry erupted from her throat, the wave carrying her into the oblivion of ecstasy. Sam called out her name above her, caught in the same dizzying whirlpool of pleasure.

When she finally came to herself again, he was in her arms, his body heavy on top of her. She wrapped her arms around him and buried her face in his neck, kissing the tender skin she found there.

Neither one of them said anything for several long moments, their heavy breathing the only sound that filled the air. Then Sam rolled over on the bed, taking her with him so that she lay on top of him.

But instead of seeing a satisfied smile on his handsome face, she was taken back by his serious expression. "Is something wrong?"

He hesitated just long enough to make her nervous. "I've never said this to a woman before...."

A latent twinge of insecurity caught her deep in the chest. Making love to Sam had been the most incredible experience of her life, but maybe he didn't feel the same way. Despite her impulse to silence him with a kiss, she took a deep breath and prepared for the worse. She wasn't going to run scared anymore. "Go ahead. You can tell me."

Sam looked into her eyes. "I think I'm falling in with love with you, Lauren McBride."

14

LAUREN FELT A LITTLE DIZZY at hearing Sam's declaration of love. She propped herself up on her elbow and trickled her fingers through the hair on his chest. "Say it again."

He gazed sleepily at her. "I love you."

"A girl could get used to hearing that."

"Good. Because I intend to say it often." He moved closer to her. "I love you, Lauren."

She leaned down to kiss him, one hand cradling his jaw. She felt the scrape of whiskers against her palm, then his body shifted against her and she knew he wanted her again. They made slow, lazy love as long shadows stretched across the bedroom floor.

"You don't know what you do to me," Sam breathed, as he lay heavily on top of her.

"Maybe it's not me," she teased. "Maybe it's this new Seductress bra I was wearing. It just arrived today."

He leaned down to kiss her. "It's you. It's definitely you."

She smiled against his mouth, sheer joy pulsing through her body.

Then he rolled to his side and brushed a tendril of hair off her brow. "I think we should stay in bed all day."

She glanced at the alarm clock on the night table. "I'd love to, but I have a class in twenty minutes."

He kissed her again and almost succeeded in changing her mind about leaving him. But she forced herself to leave his bed. He folded his arms behind his head and watched her as she reached for the Seductress bra.

"I'm not sure you should wear that to class," he teased. "It's sure to cause an unfair disadvantage to all those poor male students who won't be able to take their eyes off of you."

She tossed the bra to him. "Okay. I won't wear it."

He caught it, then half sat up in bed. "Hey, I was just kidding."

"I know, but this is a day for me to be a little daring." She pulled her blouse on, then reached for her skirt. "Besides, no one will be able to tell."

"I beg to differ," he said, his gaze trailing over her body.

She turned and searched for her shoes before he enticed her back into his bed.

He lay back against the pillows. "Can I make dinner for you tonight?"

"Depends," she said, finding her shoes tucked under the bed. "Are you as good a cook as Philomena?"

He didn't say anything for a long moment. "You could say we learned to cook together."

"Then it's a date." She leaned down to kiss him. "I'll be here at seven."

"I'll be waiting."

She headed out of the bedroom, then turned at the door. "Oh, one more thing."

"Yes?"

"Don't bother to dress for dinner."

He flashed a grin. "I won't."

SAM WOKE FROM HIS NAP SLOWLY, looking around his bedroom in confusion. Then he saw the Seductress bra laying on top of the quilt and the events of the afternoon all came back to him one delicious rush. He'd made love to Lauren. And they had been even more incredible together than he'd imagined.

He smiled, picking up the Seductress bra by one lacy strap. This was the reason he'd been sent on this odd mission in the first place. The reason he'd met the love of his life.

Made of spandex and lace, it didn't look all that special. Although when he'd seen Lauren in it, he'd been half-mad with desire for her. But he couldn't give the credit to the bra. It was the woman who wore it.

He tossed the bra aside, then breathed a long sigh as he lay back on his pillow. It could work between them. He could make it work. All he had to do was keep playing Philomena for another three weeks. Once Lauren's promotion was secured, he'd send his *cousin* away for good.

The deception still bothered him, but what choice did he have? Lauren needed Philomena to complete the Ladybug training program. If she knew the truth, Sam was certain her pride and integrity wouldn't allow her to let the charade continue. She'd lose everything—because of him.

Sam couldn't let that happen.

A knock at the door made him groan under his breath. He was tempted to pretend he wasn't home, but the thought that it might be Travis standing outside his door made him lumber out of bed and search his closet for his blue terry cloth robe. Then he remembered that he'd taken it over to Lauren's apartment for Philomena to wear.

The knock sounded louder and more insistent as Sam gathered the clothes he'd left scattered over the carpet. "I'm coming," he shouted.

A few moments later, he walked into the living room, slid the chain off the lock, then opened the door. A messenger stood on the other side.

"Sam T. Kane?" the messenger asked, holding a small white envelope in his hand.

"I'm him." Sam reached for the envelope.

The messenger handed it to him, then waited, his hand still outstretched.

Sam patted the empty pockets of his jeans. "Hang on a minute." He turned toward the end table, where he kept an ashtray full of loose change. After tipping the messenger, he closed the door and studied the plain white envelope, turning it over in his hand.

Then he sat down on the arm of the sofa and tore open the seal. He knew as soon as he pulled out the familiar game card that it was from his grandfather.

He could make out a few of the words printed on the card, but not enough for it to make sense. He'd either have to find someone to read it for him...or put an end to the game once and for all.

SAM PACED BACK AND FORTH across the floor in his grandfather's luxurious private office at the Kane Corporation. Amos was in the building, according to his secretary, but all her intercom pages had gone unanswered. Sam checked his watch, wondering how much longer he should wait. Especially since he had a special dinner to prepare for Lauren.

"Well, this is certainly a surprise." Amos stood in the doorway to the office, wearing a lime-green blazer and green plaid slacks.

Sam breathed a sigh of relief. "Didn't your secretary tell you I was in here?"

"Sally was away from her desk." Amos closed the door behind him, then folded his arms across his chest and studied his grandson. "Something's different about you, Sam. But I can't quite put my finger on it."

I'm madly in love. But Sam wasn't ready to tell his grandfather about Lauren yet. Not until he settled the unfinished business between them. "I came here to tell you I'm quitting the game."

Amos walked over to his leather office chair and sat down, folding his hands over his potbelly. "Are you sure that's a wise decision? You've only got five days left before your gig is up. You'd be throwing away your share of the company—worth well over a million dollars."

"I'm sure," Sam said without hesitation. "I can't profit from deceiving the woman I love. It isn't right."

"I see."

"I'm sorry if you're disappointed in me, Gramps. But I'm not the right man to take over the company."

Amos looked up at him. "And why is that?"

Sam reached into his pocket and pulled out the game card, placing it on the wide mahogany desk between them. "Because I can't even read this simple game card."

Amos's gray brows rose high on his forehead. "What are you saying?"

"I can't read, Gramps. That's the reason I dropped out of high school." Sam braced himself, not certain how his grandfather would react to this revelation.

But instead of expressing shock or disgust, Amos simply nodded. "I suspected as much."

Sam blinked. "You did?"

"Yes," Amos replied with a sigh. "Three weeks ago, when you and Dexter were on the plane with me. I gave you the game card that could very well determine your future, but you barely glanced at it. Instead, you flipped it around to show your brother."

"And he read it aloud," Sam finished.

Amos nodded. "It struck me as odd. Then I started to remember all the other times you avoided reading, both at home and at work. How you always had an audiobook playing on your stereo, but none of the books on your shelves even had a crack in the spine. They'd never been touched."

"I found a lot of ways to compensate."

Amos nodded. "Like intently studying the menu at a new restaurant, always making the waitress take all the other orders at the table. Then you'd inevitably order the exact same meal as someone else at the table. There were so many little signs that all added up to one big problem.''

"I'm dyslexic.''

Amos sighed. "And I'm an idiot for not noticing a lot sooner.''

Sam sat down in the armchair behind him. "It's not your fault, Gramps. Most of my teachers didn't realize it either.'' His mouth curved into a wry smile. "Until I met up with Philomena Gallagher. She wasn't so easy to fool.''

"Maybe not, but it explains a lot of things. Like why your parents weren't more upset when they learned that you dropped out of high school. They knew, didn't they?''

Sam shrugged. "I guess they couldn't handle it.''

For one of the few times in his life, Sam saw raw anger burn in his grandfather's blue eyes. "I've never approved of the life my son's led, but until now I've never actually been ashamed of him.''

"I'm not blaming Mother or Dad for my problem,'' Sam said. "I'm not certain Dad even knows about it. The truth is that I'm the one who chose to keep it a secret all these years.''

"Until now. Care to tell me what, or perhaps who, is responsible for prompting this revelation?''

"Her name is Lauren.'' Sam grinned. "And she's the most incredible woman I've ever met.''

"This certainly is a day for surprises.'' Amos picked up the remote control on his desk and switched on the television set mounted in the corner of his office. "I want to hear all about her. But first I have to watch the six o'clock news.''

"Since when do you watch the news?''

"I try to avoid it—too depressing. But your brother insisted that I watch it tonight."

"You talked to Dexter?" That was expressly forbidden in the rules of the game. He found it hard to believe that his straight-arrow big brother would purposely break a rule.

"Just a little while ago. I found him in his office. Though he certainly wasn't acting like himself."

Sam checked his watch again, knowing he didn't have much time left before Lauren was due to arrive at his apartment.

"Look, Gramps, I can't stick around much longer. I just wanted to let you know that I appreciate you letting me compete in the game. But Dexter is the one who deserves to win the Kane Corporation. He's the one with the college degree."

"And what about you, Sam?" Amos asked, tilting his head to one side as he looked up at his grandson. "What do you deserve?"

It was a difficult question to answer. He'd spent so many years telling himself that he didn't deserve much of anything. Certainly not a wife and a family. Now he had a promising future full of unlimited possibilities ahead of him—once he learned to read. Lauren believed in him. Maybe it was time for Sam to do the same.

"I deserve to be proud of who I am," he said at last. "And I need to stop being too proud to admit when I need help."

Amos smiled and picked up the game card. "Do you want to know what this says?"

"If you want to tell me."

Amos flipped the card around. *"To thine own self be true."*

Sam looked his cagey old grandfather in the eye, suddenly understanding the reason for his particular assignment. He'd been lying to himself all these years, pretending he was the only one affected by his disability. But by becoming Philomena, he'd been able to see himself from another perspective—and he didn't always like the view. For the first time, he'd learned to put someone else's needs first—and had found true happiness at last.

At least until the sound of Dexter's voice broke into his thoughts. He looked up at the television, unable to believe his ears.

"What the hell does he think he's doing?" Sam asked, his stomach twisting into a tight knot as he listened to his brother's statement.

"It sounds like he's telling the world about his game. And yours."

Sam didn't wait to hear the rest. He sprinted out of the office, hoping Lauren had been delayed in class. Hoping she didn't turn on the six o'clock news.

Hoping he hadn't just lost her forever.

15

LAUREN HAD SAILED THROUGH her literature test, surprising herself and the professor when she was the first one done. Happy to have some extra time to prepare for her dinner with Sam, she stopped at a small boutique on the way home and splurged on a new dress she found on the clearance rack. Her budget didn't have room for extras, but she couldn't resist.

It was a small black number that hugged her body as if it had been made just for her. The salesgirl tried to press a pair of three-inch black heels on her, too, but the whimpers she heard emanating from her checkbook made her reluctantly decline.

"Philomena, I'm home," Lauren called out as she walked into her apartment. Only silence met her, and quick glimpse into her roommate's bedroom told her that Philomena was out again. Lauren hummed to herself as she hung her new dress up in her closet. Maybe Philomena had enjoyed a romantic afternoon rendezvous as well. Her roommate had been acting a little mysterious lately. And definitely showing all the signs of a woman with a secret. Lauren hoped love was the reason. She wanted everyone to feel as good as she did at this moment.

The telephone rang and she skipped into the living room, certain it was Sam on the line. "Hello?"

"Where have your been all afternoon?"

Her heart sank at the sound of Chuck's voice. But she squared her shoulders, determined not to let him ruin her perfect day. "I was out."

"I know that. I tried calling three or four times. Don't you ever check your machine?"

She held one hand out and studied her fingernails, wondering if she had time to polish them. "Did you want something, Chuck?"

"I want you to turn on your television."

"I was just on my way out...."

"Sam's brother is about to hold a news conference," Chuck interjected. "And I think what he has to say might interest you."

Lauren's curiosity to see Sam's brother made her walk over to the small, portable television and flip it on. "Anything else?"

"Call me when it's over," Chuck said, then hung up.

She stared at the cordless receiver for a moment, then smiled and shook her head. Chuck had always had a flare for the dramatic. He could sit by his telephone all night waiting for her to call as far as she was concerned.

Walking over to the sofa, she picked up the remote, then clicked the button to the local news station.

"This is Darryl Starr reporting to you live from Handy Press, the small company that published How To Jump-Start Your Love Life, *authored by*

the notorious Harry Hanover. Mr. Hanover, will be giving a brief statement in just a moment.''

What did the author of *How To Jump-Start Your Love Life* have to do with Sam's brother? It didn't make sense, but since Lauren had purchased a copy of the book the day before she met Sam, her curiosity was aroused. She sat down, tucking her legs underneath her, then settled back against the sofa to watch the impending news conference.

Soon a man who looked surprisingly like Sam appeared on the television screen. He was a little taller and wore a pair of glasses, but the shape of his jaw reminded her of Sam—and Philomena.

The man nervously cleared his throat, then directed a question to someone standing off-camera. *''Am I on?''*

One of the reporters gathered around him shouted a question. *''Do you plan to turn yourself in to the police, Mr. Hanover?''*

Lauren was confused. Despite the resemblance to Sam, this man's name was apparently Hanover. No relation to Sam. But why had Chuck said he was Sam's brother?

She got her answer as soon as the man opened his mouth.

''No. Because I'm not Harry Hanover. My name is Dexter Kane and I work for the Kane Corporation. But for the last few weeks, I've been masquerading as Harry Hanover.''

All the reporters began shouting questions as Lauren sat up on the sofa, mesmerized by the scene unfolding before her eyes.

Dexter Kane held up both hands to quiet the mob

of reporters surrounding him. *"If you'll just let me make my statement, I think it will answer all of your questions."*

Some of the reporters ignored his plea for silence, but Dexter Kane forged ahead anyway, looking straight into the television camera.

"A few weeks ago, Handy Press hired me to portray Harry Hanover, author of How to Jump-Start You Love Life. *They were duped by him into believing that he was agoraphobic, but they wanted to give this book,"* he held a copy high in the air, *"the kind of promotion that would make a difference in the lives of people everywhere."*

Lauren looked at the telephone and wondered if she should call Sam. Did he know about this? But the sound of Dexter's deep voice drew her attention back to the television set.

"When Handy Press's publicist, Kylie Timberlake, approached me to impersonate Mr. Hanover, she had no idea that I was associated with the Kane Corporation. You see, Harry Hanover wasn't the only one duping Handy Press. I was playing the role of a male escort and didn't reveal my real identity for one very simple reason. My grandfather had forbidden me from telling anyone that I was playing a real-life version of Chameleon, the career-role playing game that made his company internationally famous."

She saw Dexter look around the now-silent crowd of reporters. When no new questions arose, he continued his story.

"The rules were simple. Tell no one and play the game for one month. My only competition was my

brother, who's playing a game of his own. The prize is ownership of the family business."

Lauren's entire body grew numb. Sam did know. And, according to his brother, he was playing a game of his own. So why hadn't he told her about it?

"Well, that month is up in five more days," Dexter continued. *"But I'm not going to play the game anymore. I'd rather lose that company, the one I've dreamed of owning my entire life, than lose the woman I love. I may not be the real author of* How To Jump-Start Your Love Life, *but it taught me that love is more important than business. Hell, it's more important than anything."* He smiled into the camera.

Lauren picked up the remote and flipped off the television set. Then she stood up, her knees shaking so badly that she had to reach out to the sofa to steady herself. Sam was playing a game. And she had a sinking feeling in the pit of her stomach that she knew just what that game was.

She walked to Philomena's bedroom and flipped on the light. The room was spartan, the bed neatly made and the top of dresser bare except for a fine layer of dust. No hand lotion, no perfume, no hair spray. Nothing to indicate the room belonged to a woman.

But then Philomena Gallagher wasn't your ordinary woman. In fact, she was like no woman Lauren had ever met before.

All the oddities about her roommate began to suddenly cram her fuzzy brain. Philomena always wore heavy makeup, even first thing in the morning. She talked about Sam easily enough, but rarely mentioned anything about herself or her past. And she was tall. Very tall. The same height as Sam. And her eyes were the exact same shade of blue.

The telephone began to ring, but she ignored it. She didn't want to talk to Chuck right now. And certainly not to Sam. Not when her life was falling apart. She walked over to the closet, her stomach churning. She wanted so badly to be wrong, but all her instincts told her she was right. Pulling open the closet door, she saw a row of pantsuits hanging on the rod in front of her. And on the shelf above were three wigs on plastic foam heads.

She whirled and headed for the dresser, haphazardly pulling open drawers. Inside was a vast array of cosmetics. Not over-the-counter brands you could find at the local department store, but expensive jars of theater makeup that were obviously used by professionals.

When she reached the bottom drawer, she found the three items that broke her heart. One was a stack of boxer shorts. The second was a man's razor and a can of shaving cream. Men's shaving cream. But the irrefutable evidence of his betrayal was the ticket stub to the Steelers game they'd attended last Sunday. Section B, Row 13, Seat 12.

Sam was Philomena.

She sagged onto the floor, her throat tight. He'd lied to her. Everything had been a lie. Tears burned in her eyes as she thought of the afternoon they had just shared together. She squeezed her eyes shut as every moment of the past few weeks played over again in her mind.

Lauren groaned aloud when she thought of all the intimate conversations she'd had with Philomena. All the things she'd told her roommate about Sam. When she was really telling Sam himself. He must have loved that. But one thing seemed certain—he didn't love her or he never would have deceived her this way.

Hot tears rolled over her cheeks. It didn't make any sense. Why would Sam do this to her? It was a question that wouldn't be answered.

Because Lauren never wanted to see him again.

SAM WAS COMPLETELY OUT OF breath by the time he raced up the stairs to Lauren's third-floor apartment. Every second that ticked by was just more time for someone to tell Lauren about Dexter's press conference. He wanted the chance to explain in his own words. To try and make her understand.

But the message that was waiting for him outside her apartment door told him that he was too late. A box sat on the floor, overflowing with Philomena's clothes and wigs.

Sam pushed the box out of the way, then knocked on the door. "Lauren?"

No answer. He turned the doorknob and found it locked. "Lauren, let me in!"

Silence emanated from the other side of the door, but his gut told him she was inside. He had to talk to her. He had to try and make her understand.

Reaching into his pocket for his key, he unlocked the dead bolt, but he could only open the door as far as the chain lock would allow. It was far enough for him to see Lauren sitting on the floor of the living room, her back against the sofa. A single candle burned on the coffee table.

"Lauren?"

She looked up at him, her eyes red-rimmed. He'd made her cry. Again. Bitterness rose in the back of Sam's throat and he felt more ashamed than the day his mother had discovered he couldn't read.

"Go away," Lauren said, her hoarse voice laced with despair.

"Please let me in."

"I'll call the police if you don't leave right now."

The threat didn't faze him. He was more scared of losing Lauren than losing his freedom. "You saw my brother on television."

"You lied to me."

"I can explain."

"Funny." A ghost of a smile haunted her mouth. "That's just what Chuck used to say when he'd been out half the night."

Sam's jaw clenched. "I'm not Chuck."

"I know," she replied, meeting his gaze dead on. "You're worse. You barged into my life, into my apartment, pretending to be a woman. The only question is why?"

He owed her at least that much. "It was the bra."

Her brow crinkled. "The bra?"

"The Seductress. I was working for Midnight Lace. They wanted me to obtain a prototype of the Seductress before it hit the market."

She shook her head in wonder. "And I gave it to you." Her eyes gleamed in the candlelight. "Along with my heart and my body. Congratulations. I hope you're duly compensated for a job well done."

"It wasn't like that, Lauren. I never intended to give Midnight Lace the bra. Not after I got to know you. Not after I fell in love with you."

She closed her eyes. "Please leave."

"Let me in."

"If you ever cared about me, you'll leave right now."

"But I love you. And you love me. You told me so this afternoon."

"How can I possibly love you?" Her eyes blazed with anger and hurt. "I don't even know who you are!"

Then she got up and walked out of the living room without another word. He watched her disappear down the hallway, overwhelmed by the urge to break down the door and follow her. But that was something Chuck McBride would do, and he'd been compared to that jerk enough already.

Sam closed the door to the apartment, giving Lauren her privacy. He wasn't about to let her go forever. But if he ever wanted to win her back, he'd sure as hell have to find some way to make it up to her. If that were even possible.

His grandfather should have added another lesson to his recent education: Love wasn't a game.

16

THE NEXT MORNING, Sam awoke to the sound of someone banging on his front door. He winced as he sat up in bed, his head pounding. After leaving Lauren's apartment last night, he'd dropped all his Philomena paraphernalia off at a local women's shelter, then driven around until the wee hours of the morning, trying to figure out how to win Lauren back.

And came up empty.

The beer he'd bought on his way home hadn't helped either. In fact, it had made matters worse. In addition to his throbbing head, his eyes felt dry and itchy, his mouth like it was stuffed with old cotton balls.

"Hey, Sam!" called a squeaky voice from outside his apartment. "Wake up!"

Travis. Sam swallowed a groan as he forced himself out of bed. He'd promised the kid a trip to the gym so he could practice his hoop shots. Travis had enrolled in a winter basketball league at Sam's urging and was a little nervous about his chances of making a good team.

"I'm coming," Sam called out, then grabbed his robe and walked unsteadily to the door. He opened it and the aroma of fried bacon in the hallway made his stomach flip-flop. He grasped the door and swallowed hard, willing himself not to be sick.

"Wow, you look awful," Travis said with a grin as he walked into the apartment.

"I think I'm coming down with something," Sam said, closing the door, then sagging onto the sofa.

"Looks like the vodka flu to me. Or maybe the whiskey flu. My dad used to get one of those just about every weekend."

Sam mentally kicked himself. Not only had he let Lauren down, he was setting a bad example for Travis. "I call it the stupid flu, because I brought it on myself."

"Does this mean we're not going to the gym?"

"No, we're going," Sam assured him. He'd take the kid there even if he had to crawl all the way. And judging by the condition of his head and his stomach, that was a definite possibility. "But I need to clean up first. Have you eaten breakfast?"

"Not yet."

"There should be some cereal in the cupboard. Help yourself."

While Travis poured himself a heaping bowl of cereal, Sam leaned his head back and closed his eyes. He couldn't entirely blame his hangover for the way he was feeling. A blanket of despair weighed heavily on him. He'd lost Lauren. Possibly forever. And the worst part was that he could have prevented it. He could have come clean the moment he'd realized that his attraction to her was turning into something more. Something permanent.

"You want some, Sam?" Travis asked, walking

into the living room with the cereal bowl in one hand and a spoon in the other.

"No, thanks."

Travis sat next to him on the sofa and dug into his cereal.

Sam watched him eat, noting the kid needed a haircut. "So how's the Ashley problem?"

"We're going steady," Travis said between huge, slurping mouthfuls.

Sam smiled. "When did this happen?"

"A couple of days ago. She said if I didn't go steady with her she'd punch me in the nose. So I thought I might as well. You know how easy I get nosebleeds."

"Sounds like a smart decision to me."

"So how's the Lauren problem?"

Sam's heart contracted. "There isn't a problem anymore. She dumped me."

"Why?"

Sam hesitated for a long moment, then decided that if he was going to mentor the kid, he needed to show him that even adults make mistakes. "I lied to her."

Travis's eyes widened. "*You* lied?"

The boy's astonishment made him feel even worse. "Yes. I did. When she found out, she decided she didn't want to see me anymore."

Travis set his empty bowl on the coffee table. "But why did you lie to her if you liked her?"

That was the question he'd been asking himself ever since Lauren had kicked him out of her apartment. Why had playing the game been so important to him? Especially after he'd realized that Lauren was special. "Because I was greedy. I had to lie to her to get something I wanted. Something that would make me a lot of money."

"Did you get it?"

Sam shook his head. "No. But I don't care about that anymore. I lost Lauren because she doesn't believe she can ever trust me again."

The boy's brow crinkled. "Just because of one mistake?"

"It was a whopper of a mistake."

"I think she should give you another chance."

Sam nodded. "Me too. I'd even be willing to let her give me a bloody nose if it would make her feel better."

"Really?"

"Really. Lauren is a special lady. She works a lot of hours for Ladybug Lingerie so she can afford to go to college."

"What's Ladybug Lingerie?"

"It's a company that sells…pajamas. Women's pajamas."

A light dawned in Travis's eyes. "Oh, you mean like negligees."

"I thought you didn't know what that word meant."

"I looked it up in the dictionary. My tutor helped me."

Sam took a deep breath.

"Do you think she'd help me?"

Travis wrinkled his brow. "Why do you need help?"

"Because I don't know how to read." Saying it aloud wasn't as difficult as he'd imagined. Maybe because Lauren had been so understanding. So accepting. His grandfather, too. Sam's pride had prevented him from revealing the truth for all of these years. But he wasn't going to lie anymore. About anything.

"But you're a grown-up," Travis replied. "You have to know how to read."

"I never learned how. I have a learning disability called dyslexia. It makes it harder for people like me to figure out words and letters. But Lauren said there are ways to fix it."

Travis jumped up. "Hey, maybe you could come to my tutoring lessons with me. That would be so cool!"

"I'll phone your tutor and see if she's willing to take on another student."

"I know she will. She loves telling people what to do." Travis grinned and held up his hand in the air. "Anytime you need help with your homework, Sam, just give me a call."

Sam gave him a high five. "You've got a deal."

TWO DAYS LATER, Lauren sat in the private office of Tina Chavez, head of Ladybug Lingerie. No doubt Lauren had been summoned here because of her failure to bring her protégée successfully through the training program. But how could Lauren tell Mrs. Chavez the reason without revealing every humiliating detail?

Lauren had tried to put Sam out of her mind, but she thought about him constantly. It didn't help matters that he'd been calling her and leaving messages on her answering machine. Each message made his

motives in playing Philomena a little clearer. She
knew now that ownership of his grandfather's company was at stake. That he'd quit the game after that
incredible afternoon they'd shared together in his
bed. And that he'd never intended to hurt her. Or so
he claimed. Part of Lauren wanted so badly to believe him.

But did she dare?

Tina Chavez walked into the office, her brisk
steps an indication of how she'd built a small custom sewing business into the Ladybug Lingerie em-
pire. The petite woman had more energy and optimism than anyone Lauren had ever met.

"Hello, Lauren," Mrs. Chavez said, setting a
handful of file folders on top of her antique desk.
"Nice to see you again. I appreciate your prompt-
ness."

The queen of the Ladybugs wore her salt-and-
pepper hair in its trademark beehive. Ladybug earrings sparkled in her ears and her bright smile re-
assured Lauren that she wasn't about to get fired.

Lauren sat forward in her chair. "I think I know
why you asked me here."

Mrs. Chavez took a seat behind her desk. "I want
to talk to you about the Seductress bra."

The Seductress? A wave of panic washed over
her. Sam still had the prototype. Or at least, she
hoped he did. Had he lied to her again and given it
to Midnight Lace?

She cleared her throat. "What about it?"

"As you know, I've only allowed one prototype
out among my most trusted saleswomen. Considering all the money we've put into advertising, I

wouldn't want our competition coming out with an imitation right when we're about to launch the Seductress on the market.''

''That makes sense,'' she replied, scrambling to come up with a good excuse for why she didn't have it. As soon as she left here, she'd have to go to Sam's apartment. To see him one more time. The thought made her go queasy inside. It had been hard enough to maintain her anger and indignation while he'd kept his distance. Her intuition told her the protective wall she'd built would crumble with one touch of his hand. One look into his blue eyes. One kiss.

''Lauren?''

She blinked, then realized she hadn't been paying attention. Because she'd been thinking about Sam again. She had to stop doing that. ''I'm sorry. What did you say?''

Tina smiled, ever patient with her Ladybugs. ''I said that I think your idea was a stroke of genius.''

''My idea?''

''Come now, don't be modest. We women have to take credit for our successes in this world. It's the only way we'll get ahead.''

''I'd love to take credit,'' Lauren replied. ''But I don't have the faintest idea what you're talking about.''

Her brow furrowed. ''You mean you're not the one who put the full-page advertisement in the paper?''

She shook her head. ''I don't have the kind of money to pay for a full-page ad.''

"Then can you explain this?" Tina pulled a newspaper out of her desk drawer and opened it up.

Lauren looked down at the colorful advertisement, fashioned off of the old Cinderella fairy tale. Only the text read like a kooky personal ad with a picture of a bra lying on a pink silk pillow. "A slightly tarnished Prince Charming seeks the woman who left the Seductress Bra on his doorstep. She won his heart and now he wants to win her hand."

At the bottom of the advertisement was a list of the styles and colors the bra came in, as well as the telephone number of Ladybug Lingerie.

"Pre-orders of the bra had been rather disappointing until this hit the stands." She jabbed her index finger in the center of the advertisement. "Our phones have been ringing off the hook all morning. I've already put in a second order with the supply house. Thanks to this ad, everybody wants the Seductress."

Lauren folded her arms across her chest, determined not to let her feelings soften toward Sam. Yes, the advertisement was cute and romantic. Yes, he'd given the Seductress a huge plug and at the same time curtailed any competitors, like Midnight Lace, from stealing the Seductress's thunder with a cheap knockoff.

"You must know something about this," Tina said. "How else would someone obtain a picture of the Seductress?"

"You'll have to ask Philomena that question."

Tina frowned. "I was sorry to hear that Philomena resigned as a Ladybug. Although she made it perfectly clear that personal issues, and not your mentoring abilities, were behind her decision. In fact, she couldn't say enough good things about you."

Lauren sensed another crumble in the wall. "Really?"

Tina nodded. "And I happen to agree with her. Which you'll see when you receive your next paycheck."

"You mean…"

"That's right," Tina interjected with a smile. "You're officially a Ladybug mentor. You've earned your wings."

Lauren wondered why she didn't feel happier about it. "Thank you."

"You're very welcome." Tina picked up the newspaper. "I must say I was sorry to see Philomena go. I thought she had real potential."

"I'm not sure she ever felt comfortable in lingerie," Lauren said.

"Not everyone does," Tina concurred, then pulled a file out from under the pile on her desk. "But we are getting new customers every day. In fact, one specifically requested you for his party."

Lauren tensed, instantly suspecting Sam wasn't done springing his surprises. "*His* party?"

"It's a little boy who wants to give his mother a Ladybug Lingerie party as a birthday surprise. Isn't that sweet?"

Lauren relaxed, reaching for the folder. "Yes, it is."

"He forwarded a list of all his mother's friends so we could send out the invitations and insisted the party be held this Saturday. Are you free then?"

This Saturday and every one after it. "Sure. But why did he request me?" she asked, studying the limited information in front of her. The name Travis Henry didn't sound familiar.

Tina shrugged. "Oh, I don't know. One of his mother's friends probably recommended you." Then her gaze settled on Lauren. "Is there anything bothering you? You look...different."

"I'm fine."

Tina hesitated a moment. "It's Philomena, isn't it? I noticed your sales figures have sagged a bit lately. Did her leaving upset you?"

"Yes." Lauren swallowed hard, realizing she truly did miss Philomena. But that was ridiculous, because Philomena was Sam. And Sam was Philomena. She'd lost her new best friend and her new lover all in one fell swoop. "I have a feeling I'll never see her again."

"I have a feeling you will," Tina said, tapping on the folder. "Her name is on the Travis Henry guest list."

17

BY SATURDAY, LAUREN HAD changed her mind approximately twenty times about doing the Travis Henry party. But two factors convinced to go through with it. The first was the fact that she'd have to make up some excuse to Tina Chavez for backing out. And she knew Tina didn't admire cowards. The second was her determination to show Sam that he couldn't rattle her. She could face him again without melting into a puddle on the floor.

At least, that's what she kept telling herself.

Half expecting to find Sam answer the door, she was surprised to see a young boy open it and regard her with open curiosity. "Are you Lauren?"

"Yes," she replied, taking in his freckles and the cowlick in his red hair. "You must be Travis."

"I thought you weren't coming," he said, opening the door wider. "Almost everyone is here already."

She walked inside to see the tiny apartment brimming with women. All of them young, most of them blond, and none of them resembling Philomena.

"Hey, everybody, this is Lauren," Travis announced, as more guests arrived at the door.

She smiled, more confused than ever. Her suspicion that this was some sort of romantic trap Sam had set for her didn't seem to be coming true.

She set up her displays, gave her presentation, then handed out the Ladybug Lingerie catalogs. The women poured over them as Travis, playing the perfect little host, passed out cookies and red Kool-Aid.

This was a dream party, since all the women seemed eager to try on the display samples she had brought with her. Every single one inquired about the Seductress bra, and most of them placed orders for it.

"Which one is your mother?" Lauren asked Travis, during a break in the bustle of women submitting their orders.

"Oh, she's not here yet," Travis said, not quite meeting her gaze. Then he moved to the center of the room and clapped his hands. "Okay, everybody, time to be quiet."

The women shushed each other with indulgent smiles, all obviously charmed by their little host.

"The reason I invited everybody to this party was because of Sam."

Lauren tensed, her suspicions rising to the surface once again. Was this the same Travis that Philomena had told her about? The one Sam had met through the Big Brother program. She folded her arms across her chest, not too impressed with the fact that he was using this cute little kid to get to her.

"Is Sam here?" one of the woman asked eagerly, looking around the room.

"I hope so," replied another woman with a broad smile. "I was almost ready to file a missing persons report on him."

"Me, too," chimed another. "I haven't heard from him in weeks."

"Sam is in love with Lauren," Travis announced, and Lauren felt thirty pairs of eyes rivet on her. "But he made a big mistake, so now she won't talk to him anymore. I thought since all of you used to be his girlfriends, you could tell her how cool he is."

Lauren blinked. *His girlfriends?*

The women seemed just as surprised by this revelation, looking around at each other in disbelief. *"You dated Sam?"* echoed across the room.

"Everybody here dated Sam," Travis said, visibly growing impatient. "I always take down Sam's messages and I kept all your names and phone numbers so Sam wouldn't lose track."

"A walking address book," murmured one of the guests.

"I've heard most of your messages on Sam's machine," Travis continued, "and I can tell how much you all like him, so you might as well admit it."

"Okay, I'll go first." A leggy blonde stood up and tossed her hair over her shoulder. "My name is Melissa and I am a Sam-o-holic."

The other women in the room laughed. Lauren just watched in stunned amazement. All these women were his girlfriends. Or former girlfriends, according to Travis. They were all gorgeous. A burning sensation clawed at her as she looked around the room. Something closely akin to jealousy. But she couldn't be jealous. She didn't want Sam anymore.

Did she?

"So is this sort of like an intervention?" asked a woman seated closest to the boy. "We're supposed to bombard Lauren with all the reasons that Sam is a great guy?"

Travis shrugged. "I don't know what an intervention is, but I do know Sam is a great guy. I think we should go around the room and tell Lauren why she should be in love with him." He pointed to the blonde next to him. "You can start."

The woman grinned. "Well, I'm not about to tell Lauren who she should love, but I don't know how anyone could resist Sam. We dated a couple of times three years ago, but I'd go out with him again in a New York minute. He's fun, witty, charming. And sexy as hell."

The other women laughed, nodding their heads in agreement. A tall redhead by the door stood up. "I'm Bianca and I went out with Sam for two weeks last May. He's the reason that I decided to pursue a degree in graphic arts. He even arranged for me to apply for one of the scholarships his family company provides for needy students."

"That sounds like Sam," another woman said, rising to her feet. "I'm Chloe and I only went out with Sam once. I'd just broken up with my fiancé and was definitely on the rebound. But instead of taking advantage of me, he just held me for three hours while I cried so much I ruined his shirt. A week later, my fiancé and I got back together and we'll be celebrating our second anniversary next month." She held up her hand, flashing a diamond wedding band.

The other women in the room all started talking

at once. Lauren couldn't keep track of all their stories, but one thing was clear—they all adored Sam. Even though it seemed that none of them had dated him for very long.

"Sam has the best sense of humor," said a woman named Simone. "He could always make me laugh."

"But he's shy in a way, too," said another woman. "And sensitive. He just tries to hide it."

"That's what makes him so adorable," chimed Bianca.

"I can't believe he's finally ready to settle down," another woman said, looking curiously at Lauren. "What's your secret?"

She shook her head. "I don't have a secret."

"There must be something about you that Sam couldn't resist," teased Simone. "He always made it clear that he was a permanent bachelor."

"Sam said Lauren is beautiful," Travis piped from the corner. "And smart and nice and a real hard worker."

A blush warmed her cheeks as everyone turned to stare at her again. It was easy to see that she wasn't the only one bitten by the jealousy bug. But she found herself just as curious as the women openly studying her.

What *did* Sam see in her? He'd deceived her by playing Philomena, but had he been telling the truth about his feelings for her? Had he really meant it when he'd said he loved her?

The possibility made her feel slightly giddy. There was one way to find out. "Is Sam the kind of man who…'' her voice trailed off, not certain she really wanted to know the answer.

"Who what?" Bianca prodded.

She squared her shoulders. "Who tells every woman he dates that he's falling in love with her."

For a moment, no one said anything. Then Simone smiled. "Okay, I'll be the first one to admit it. As much as I wanted Sam to fall in love with me, he never once uttered those words. Or even hinted at it."

"Same with me," Bianca said.

"Me, too," added another room. Soon a chorus of *Me, toos* filled the room.

"And you may certainly add my name to the list," said a very familiar voice from the doorway. Philomena's voice.

Lauren whirled, her heart pounding in her chest. She couldn't believe Sam would have the audacity to appear in drag again. Only one look told her the woman standing in the open doorway wasn't Sam.

"My name is Philomena Gallagher. So sorry I'm late for the party."

Lauren stood up, more confused than ever. She was tired of playing games. Tired of trying to fight her feelings for Sam. "*You're* Philomena?"

"That's right." The large woman bustled into the apartment, carrying an oversized briefcase in her hand. "I helped Travis arrange this little get-together."

Travis grinned. "Mrs. Gallagher is my tutor. And Sam's tutor now, too."

"Sam told me about his recent impersonation of me," Philomena said. "I can't say I approve of his charade, but Sam has a way about him...." She sighed. "And I know he has a good heart." She motioned around the room. "As you've heard from all the testimonials."

"Everybody here thinks Sam is terrific," Travis told his tutor. "They think Lauren should fall in love with him."

Philomena turned her shrewd green eyes on Lauren. "Nobody can tell us who to love, Travis. We have to figure that out for ourselves."

Lauren shook her head. "I don't know what to think anymore."

Philomena chuckled. "It's been my experience that Samuel T. Kane can have that affect on a young woman. The female grade point average at Jefferson High improved dramatically when he dropped out of school."

The women behind her started to laugh and the tension broke. Several women began gathering their purchases and their coats.

Lauren watched as the real Philomena Gallagher marched into the dining room and set her briefcase on the table. "Our lesson starts in ten minutes, Travis. I want your books on the table and a pencil in your hand."

"Yes, ma'am," Travis said meekly, before hastening down the hallway to his bedroom.

The party guests began to file out the door. "Be sure to send us a wedding invitation, Lauren," Bianca called out as she left the apartment.

Lauren turned back to Mrs. Gallagher, who was methodically removing textbooks and notepaper from her briefcase. "So you helped Travis arrange this party. Is there a reason you wanted me to meet all of Sam's old girlfriends?''

Philomena looked up. ''I just wanted you to have all the necessary information to make a decision that could affect the rest of your life. And Sam's.''

''How much did he tell you about us?''

''Not much.'' She leaned against the table and folded her arms across her ample chest. ''Care to fill me in?''

Lauren hesitated, wondering how she could possibly describe the ways Sam had changed her life. And the void he'd left behind. ''It's a long story.''

''You may write it out for me if you wish,'' Philomena said. ''Two pages, double-spaced. And I expect proper punctuation and correct spelling throughout.''

Despite her embarrassment, a smile tugged at her lips. ''That sounds like something a teacher would say.''

''I'm retired now, but do enjoy tutoring students in my spare time.'' Then Mrs. Gallagher glanced at the watch pinned to the lapel of her jacket. ''Where is that boy?''

''What did Travis mean,'' Lauren said, still trying to digest the events of the last few minutes, ''when he said that you were Sam's tutor?''

Travis suddenly appeared behind her, his arms full of books. ''Mrs. Gallagher is teaching Sam to read. You know, 'cause he has that dizzy stuff.''

''You mean dyslexia?'' Lauren asked.

''Yeah, that's the word.'' Travis dumped his books onto the table. ''He's been trying really hard.''

"Sam can be very tenacious when he sets his mind to something," Mrs. Gallagher added. "Of course, Tenacious is his middle name."

"I'm glad you're helping him."

Mrs. Gallagher's eyes softened. "I wanted to help him years ago, but he was too stubborn then to admit he had a problem. Sam was one of my brightest students, but somehow he fell through the cracks of the system."

Lauren looked up, surprised. "You knew he was dyslexic?"

"Not at the time. But I did notice how he avoided doing any written work or reading aloud in class. Obviously, something was wrong, but Sam refused to discuss it. Until a few days ago."

She swallowed. "What happened a few days ago?"

"You broke his heart."

Lauren sank down into a chair. "He lied to me."

Philomena nodded. "Sam's spent a lifetime deceiving people. It was the only way he could protect himself. I think he's only now realizing what it's cost him." She opened her briefcase again. "Here, I want to show you something."

"What is it?"

"I've been meeting daily with Sam for intensive tutoring lessons in reading and writing. He's making tremendous progress. In fact, I believe he's only borderline dyslexic. When reading proved too difficult for him in his early elementary school years, he just gave up."

"He thought he was dumb."

"He's very smart," Philomena countered. "And

very determined.'' She pulled a sheet of paper out of her briefcase. ''But learning to write has proved more difficult for him than reading. So I told him to think of the most important message he wanted to send someone. It proved quite motivational.''

Lauren swallowed hard as the real Philomena Gallagher handed her the sheet of paper. Several erasure marks covered the surface. But the line of carefully penciled words was clear enough to read. It said simply: *I love you, Lauren.*

Her throat tightened. ''Sam wrote this?''

''Yes. He's been working on it for a while. This is his latest draft.''

It was the most beautiful love note she'd ever read. She turned to Travis. ''Do you know where Sam is now?''

''He should be here any minute for our lesson,'' Travis said, then grinned. ''Boy, will he be surprised to see you!''

She wiped a lone tear off her cheek. ''Don't tell him I was here, okay?''

''Okay.'' Travis's smile faded. ''But does this mean you're still mad at him?''

''No, I'm not mad anymore.'' Then she impulsively leaned down and kissed Travis's cheek.

He grimaced and wiped it off. ''Yuck. Why do girls always have to kiss you?''

Lauren laughed and heard Philomena smother a snort of amusement. ''Sorry. Sometimes we can't help ourselves.''

''Well, next time, kiss Sam, okay?''

''Okay,'' Lauren promised. The she hastily packed her Ladybug Lingerie cases and flew out the door, hoping she wouldn't meet Sam on the way out. She needed time to gather her thoughts and her emotions. But one thing was certain.

She wasn't going to run scared from love anymore.

18

SAM STEPPED OUT OF THE elevator and headed toward his apartment. His tutoring lesson with Mrs. Gallagher had gone well. She was as strict and demanding as she'd been in high school, but now he was old enough to appreciate her single-minded devotion to her students.

Best of all, she'd approved the love note to Lauren. He'd labored over it and today she'd pronounced it perfect. He intended to take it to Lauren's apartment later and slip it under her door. Not that he had any reason to think she'd be ready to forgive him. She hadn't returned a single one of his many phone messages.

But Sam loved her too much to give up hope.

"It's about time you got home."

Sam stumbled, startled to see Lauren leaning against his door. She wore a trench coat, her long legs bare and a pair of sandals on her feet. "What are you doing here?"

"I came to answer the ad." She arched a brow. "Are you Prince Charming?"

His heart beat double time in his chest. "I think you can answer that better than I can."

Her tongue darted out to moisten her lips and he

felt his whole body tighten. "Well, you're definitely charming. And according to all your old girlfriends, you're a prince as well."

His brow furrowed. "My old girlfriends? When did you talk to them?"

"It's a long story," she replied, took a step towards him. "I'd rather see how our story ends first."

"I don't want it to end." Sam tried not to get his hopes up, but they were sky-high anyway. Maybe it had something to do with the glitter in her eyes. Or the playful smile on her lush lips. Or the overwhelming suspicion that she wasn't wearing anything under that trenchcoat.

"Would you like to come inside?"

Her smile widened. "How else are we going to see if the bra fits?"

Sam fumbled with the door key, swearing softly under his breath as he struggled to open it. At last the dead bolt clicked and he swung the door open.

Lauren walked inside, then turned around and slowly slid the trench coat off her shoulders. He'd been wrong. She wasn't naked underneath. She wore the same baby doll pajamas she'd had on the day he met her.

His mouth grew dry. "You really know how to welcome a man home."

"Well?" she asked, arching a brow. "Where's the bra? I want to make sure I'm the right woman for you."

"I'm already sure." He moved toward her. "You fit perfectly into my life. I want to go to bed each night with you in my arms and wake you up with a kiss every morning. I want to cook for you and laugh with you and make love to you."

Her eyes gleamed. "That sounds like a dream come true."

"It can be real," he said, pulling her into his arms. His heart pounded in his chest. "If you'll marry me."

She leaned up to kiss him. "Yes."

His heart threatened to explode in his chest. "Really? Even after everything that's happened between us?"

"I found out you're not perfect, which is a relief in a way. Because I'm not perfect either. I hate to dust and am a lousy cook."

He grinned. "I noticed."

"But the best thing is," she said wistfully, "I don't feel like I have to be perfect for you. Or worry that I'll disappoint you. Do you know how wonderful that makes me feel?"

"Show me," he said huskily.

She wrapped her arms around his neck and kissed him with more passion than he thought could possibly exist between two people. A fire burned between them. Not a few fleeting sparks, but a steady, growing flame that would be impossible to extinguish.

He fanned it with his mouth and his hands until she was moaning in his embrace. Then Sam broke the kiss, then pulled her close, still unable to believe he held a woman as incredible as Lauren in his arms.

Just like she held his heart.

"I love you, Lauren," he breathed in her ear, his body trembling with desire and awe.

"I know, Sam," she said, pure joy bubbling in her throat. "I know."

Epilogue

AMOS KANE HEARD THE grandfather clock in his office strike midnight. Twelve chimes. The game was over.

He knew his grandsons wouldn't disappoint him. He'd sent them a summons requesting their presence. Dexter and Sam both had quit the game before a winner could be declared, but Amos wasn't disappointed.

Just the opposite, in fact.

The door to his private office opened and Sam and Dexter walked in, each with a woman on his arm. His two grandsons wore besotted expressions on their faces.

"Gramps, this is Lauren McBride," Sam said, pride shining in his blue eyes. "My fiancée."

Amos reached across the desk to shake her hand. "Nice to meet you, Lauren."

"And this is Kylie," Dexter intoned, circling his arm around her waist. "*My* fiancée."

Amos bit back a smile. His grandsons still hadn't lost that competitive edge between them. "The game is over, boys. And now it is time to declare a winner."

Dexter stepped forward. He'd been working for the Kane Corporation for as long as Amos could remember. Emptying trash cans and delivering mail when he was a just a pimply teenager with more ambition than Amos had seen in grown men.

"I want Sam to have the Kane Corporation," Dexter announced.

Amos blinked. "What?"

"Sam can have it," Dexter said.

"I don't want it," Sam replied, pulling Lauren closer. "You can have it, Dex."

"Wait a minute," Amos held up both hands. "Neither one of you want my company?"

Dexter and Sam looked sheepishly at each other.

"It's nothing personal, Gramps," Dexter assured him. "It's just that running a company as big as the Kane Corporation takes time. Lots of time. I want to spend that time with Kylie." A blush mottled his cheeks as he gazed down at his fiancée. "And with our future children."

"And I want to go to college," Sam said. "Mrs. Gallagher told me I'm making great progress. I should be able to take my GED next summer. It's like a whole new world has opened up for me."

"I see." Amos clasped his hands together. "Do you know what this means?"

"We're disinherited?" Sam quipped.

"Hardly," Amos said with a wide smile. "You've each exceeded my wildest expectations. I should have made your father play this game years ago. Then maybe his life would have turned out differently."

"You're happy we quit the game?" Dexter asked, looking a little confused.

"I'm happy that you discovered that sometimes

you have to break the rules, Dexter. It took your love for Kylie to make you see it. You devoted so much of your life to the Kane Corporation. I think devoting the rest of it to the beautiful woman beside you is definitely a step in the right direction.''

Kylie smiled. ''Thank you, Mr. Kane. I definitely agree.''

''And what about me?'' Sam asked, arching a brow. ''What did I discover, other than how to put on panty hose?''

Lauren turned to him. ''You discovered me. I was lost until you walked into my life with your wig and your water bra.''

His gaze softened on her. ''I didn't have a life until I met you, Lauren. You gave me the courage to let my secret out at last.''

''Doesn't anyone care about my secret?'' Amos asked, causing all four of them to turn and look at him.

''I'm almost afraid to ask,'' Dexter said. ''What secret?''

''I've officially retired and divided my shares in the Kane Corporation equally between the two of you. So you can sell it, or hire someone to run it, or run it yourselves. It's totally up to you. In any event, you will each have a sizable asset to add to your financial portfolios. Enough to allow you to spend the rest of your lives in any way you wish.''

Sam grinned. ''Does that include chartering the company jet?''

''Absolutely,'' Amos replied. ''Why? Are you planning a trip?''

"I thought I might elope with Lauren before she changes her mind."

His fiancée laughed. "It's too late for that, Sam Kane. You're doomed to be a married man."

He swept her up in his arms. "And I couldn't be happier about it."

"What do you think, Sam?" Dexter asked, picking Kylie up in his arms. "Should we marry our brides in Paris?"

Sam nodded. "Sounds like a very wise executive decision."

"Dexter," Kylie exclaimed, laughing as she circled her arms around his neck. "What do you think you're doing?"

"Being impulsive." He kissed her, then grinned. "You should try it some time."

Amos chuckled as his two grandsons carried their fiancées out of his office, the sound of their laughter ringing down the hallway. "And they call *me* crazy!"

In October 2001
Look for this
New York Times bestselling author

BARBARA DELINSKY

in

Bronze Mystique

**The only men in Sasha's life lived between the covers
of her bestselling romances. She wrote about passionate,
loving heroes, but no such man existed…til Doug Donohue
rescued Sasha the night her motorcycle crashed.**

AND award-winning Harlequin Intrigue author

GAYLE WILSON

in

Secrets in Silence

This fantastic 2-in-1 collection will be on sale October 2001.

HARLEQUIN®
Makes any time special ®